Lime Tree Can't Bear Orange

AMANDA SMYTH

Lime Tree Can't Bear Orange

a novel

 THREE RIVERS PRESS • NEW YORK

Copyright © 2009 by Amanda Smyth

Published in the United States by Three Rivers Press, an imprint of the
Crown Publishing Group, a division of Random House, Inc., New York.
www.crownpublishing.com

Three Rivers Press and the Tugboat design are
registered trademarks of Random House, Inc.

Originally published in Great Britain by Serpent's Tail,
an imprint of Profile Books Ltd., London.

Library of Congress Cataloging-in-Publication Data is available upon request.

ISBN 978-0-307-46064-6

Printed in the United States of America

Design by Lynne Amft

10 9 8 7 6 5 4 3 2 1

First American Edition

For my grandmother, Lorna

Lime Tree Can't Bear Orange

ONE

I KNEW ABOUT MY PARENTS FROM THE THINGS I WAS
told. I had never seen a photograph of either of them because there
weren't any. But Aunt Tassi said that of course my mother was pretty
and when I asked her how pretty she pointed at a pink hibiscus flower
sticking out of a bush and said, "Pretty like that." How did she wear
her hair? She tied her hair in a knot and wrapped a cloth around her
head, she told me one cool afternoon while we were walking into
Black Rock village to look for cassava. And how tall was she? And what
color exactly were her eyes? You say black but were they woody black
or black like those African bees that once flew out of the rotten silk
cotton tree or black like pitch that comes from the lake in Trinidad?
Were they round or slanted, big or small? What did people think of
her when they saw her? Would they turn their heads or pass her by?

Mostly when I asked these sorts of questions, my aunt carried on
doing whatever she was doing as if I had not said anything at all. But
it did not stop me from asking about my mother or thinking about
my mother and wondering what she was like. I knew that she had
worked in a barbershop called Mona's in Bacolet and she met my father in this same salon. My father was passing through the islands on
his way home to England from panning gold in British Guiana. And
I knew that she probably didn't cut hair like his too often. How could
she, I told Aunt Tassi, if he was a white man. Whenever I said this was

a romantic way to meet, my aunt said I shouldn't get caught in romance; she usually said this when Roman Bartholomew, her husband, was in earshot.

She said my mother died after a long and difficult labor. Did she see me, I asked when I was five years old. I could not bear the idea of my mother never having seen me. Yes, Aunt Tassi said. Before she died she saw your tiny face and it made her laugh and cry at the same time because for the first time in her life she was happy. Then my aunt shook her head as if thinking about my mother made her sad, and I felt bad for asking. I was lying on my mother's stomach covered in her slimy juices when she took her last breath. And we were in a room without windows and it was very hot, so they moved her to another room with a window and they opened it wide so her soul could fly out into the sky. It was night and someone lit a flambeau in the yard to help her find her way.

Aunt Tassi sent a letter to my father in Southampton, England, but my father did not reply and they buried my mother in St. George's graveyard and they put a little cross of wood because they did not have money for a stone. When I asked my aunt if I had killed my mother she said of course not and how could I think so. When one soul flies in, another flies out. I was unlucky.

It just so happened that Aunt Tassi had a postcard from Southampton, sent to her by Father Carmichael. It was a photograph of a port and a lot of people waving at passengers I couldn't quite make out. I could see the bow of a large boat but not the passengers. SOUTHAMPTON was written in white capital letters along the bottom. Sometimes I took this postcard from behind Aunt Tassi's dresser where it was held in place with a hair clip and I stared at the waving English people and I wondered if my father could be one of them or at least look like one of them.

.   .   .

EVERYONE SAID I was lucky to have Aunt Tassi. My cousins, Vera and Violet, were three years younger than me. They looked the same and they spoke the same and they both laughed in the same way. Aunt Tassi often said how beautiful they were, but I never thought so. Their skin, yes. Their skin was dark and shiny and smooth like a melongen. But their faces were ordinary and identical, and their bodies were straight and thin, like stick men you draw when you don't know how to draw somebody. Like me, they didn't have a father. The moment Vera and Violet were born, their father ran away with a girl from Barbados and no one ever saw or heard from him again. I was very young so I don't remember too much about this. But I remember that Aunt Tassi was often too sad to leave the house.

Then one afternoon, she took a walk into Buccoo, and along the Buccoo road came Roman Bartholomew, a short, skinny man whom the villagers called Allah, because he thought he was God. He said, Hello, Tassi D'Abadie, and took off his hat. My aunt nodded, politely. She knew of Roman Bartholomew but had never spoken to him before. How would you like to go to a dance in Carnbee village tonight? Yes, she said, why not. I have nothing else to do. Next thing, they were an item, and Roman got a job in Campbell's Hardware Store, right there in Black Rock.

Every day on her way to Robinson Crusoe Hotel, where she cleaned rooms, Aunt Tassi would pass the blue wooden building and peer into the darkness and look for Roman. Sometimes he waved or he came out front and stepped into the bright white light. It was like that sometimes: a glaring light blasting everything as the sun climbed high above the island. And he might say, Tassi, you have anything? And she'd say, Yes, I brought you juice or a mango, or sugar cake or whatever she carried, or she might say, No, nothing you didn't get already, and then she would turn and be on her way. Sometimes Roman asked her for money. "Tassi, you have a little change?" And she would dig inside the pocket of her blue-and-white-checkered apron and

pull out a coin and give it to him. I didn't like the way Roman looked
at me—out of the corner of his slitty eyes—so I always hung back near
the old pipe stand. "Celia so shy!" he'd say. "Like a little bird," and
he'd reach out his hand and whistle, as if I really was a bird.

People said it was like going from the frying pan into the fire.
But Aunt Tassi felt so lucky to have found a man willing to put up
with another man's children and her dead sister's child (me) that she
latched on to him like a raft in the sea. He didn't have two cents to
rub together, and she didn't care. As Aunt Sula once said, you see
what you want to see and hear what you want to hear. Later that year,
Roman, realizing he was on to a good thing, made Aunt Tassi "an
honest woman."

MRS. MAINGOT USED to say that Roman Bartholomew could
crawl under a snake's belly on stilts. Even then, I knew this was true.
It was clear from the beginning that he couldn't be trusted. Like that
time we came from church and the house was close to burning down
because he had fallen asleep with a cigarette. There was an orange
line creeping along the floor at the exact moment we walked through
the door. Aunt Tassi threw up her hands and shouted his name so
loud, RO—MAN! I thought the whole village would hear. I ran for a
bucket of water and Vera and Violet both started to scream so I told
them to shut up and fetch more water but they were fixed to the
ground like two posts. After the fire was gone and there were black
streaks on the floor and on the wall, Roman made as if to cry. Suddenly Aunt Tassi was putting her arms around him and telling him
not to fret. And then she opened up her purse and gave him a dollar
and off he went to Jimmy's bar at the end of the road to quieten
down and make himself feel better, because these things happen,
Aunt Tassi said. Sometimes it's the devil who's to blame.

But Roman was the devil. Since I was eight years old, he came around me, restless and pacing like a hungry dog. If I was doing my homework, he came into my room. He flicked the ribbons in my hair or he bent down and blew on the top of my head. Once he ran his fingertip down the back of my neck. I sat still as though I was made of stone. More often than not he stood in my doorway and stared and I pretended he wasn't there. It was easier to allow him to do this than not to do this and "cause trouble," as he put it, because no one would take any notice. You are nothing, he said one day, when I threatened to tell my aunt. You have nobody but Tassi, and Tassi need me like a plant need water, so who you think she will believe? I already tell her how you lie.

Tears streamed down my face. I said, "I will go to England and find my father. You can all go to hell!" Then I ran from the house and cut through the back where sunlight could not reach and made my way through the bush to the river. There were large stones there and they were warm and gray, especially on the other side. A big log that was once the trunk of a mahogany tree stretched from one side of the river to the other and I started to cross it. The water was not deep but there was a whirlpool and I slipped and fell. My arms went up and I became stiff and straight like a pencil and the water pulled me down and spun me around and I was sure that I would die. Everything was cloudy and blurred and the bottom of the river must have been stirred up because I could see gritty bits of it. I could feel it in my eyes and up my nose. Two boys fishing saw me fall. They ran to the bank and braced themselves between the rocks and hauled me out by my hair which they said afterward was like thick seaweed. When Aunt Tassi heard what had happened, she said she would never let me go to the river by myself and what in God's name was I doing there.

OUR WOODEN HOUSE stood up on stilts. There were two bedrooms, a small kitchen, a living room, and a tiny spare room that you could just about fit a bed in. I shared one room with my cousins. Around my bed was an invisible line which, when crossed, meant something very bad would happen to them. It was the same invisible line that ran around my books, my clothes, my shampoo, and my lavender toilet water. If Vera or Violet took something without first asking permission, I frightened them with stories of jumbies and La Diablesse and the terrible Soucouyant who would come and steal their skin in the night. I told them about the douens, the spirits with no faces and small feet turned backward, who would learn their names and call them away into the forest. Any mention of douens and my cousins would shiver with fear.

From our window you could see the yard and the frangipani tree and it was white like bone, like it was dead. Fat caterpillars, thick and black with yellow stripes, crawled on the branches and ate the long leaves and when the flowers came they soon fell away. We had a lime tree, and a rotting plum tree, and when I kicked it hard, tiny bees flew out. There was a breadfruit tree at the bottom of our yard; the shiny green leaves were thick and hard like plastic and the bread-fruits were sweet and yellow. Aunt Tassi begged Roman to cut away the vine that bunched around the tree like hair, but he never did. He'd sooner cruise up the road to see his friend Ruth Mackenzie, who was pretty like a doll and married to Earl. Ruth walked around Black Rock as if she was somebody and she had her daughter, Clara Mackenzie, walking in the same way. If Aunt Tassi knew about Roman's visits to Ruth's house, she kept it to herself. But Mrs. Main-got knew, because she lived opposite.

There were plants in old paint tins growing on the Maingots' steps. One had huge spikes and Mrs. Maingot stuck eggs on the ends so that no one got cut. When you passed the house you could hear her singing her old spiritual songs in a high, sweet voice. Like me, her daughter Joan was in seventh grade. I often saw her walking to school with the Johnson boy, rising up on her tiptoes in that typical Joan way and swinging her stylish yellow bag with the Spanish lettering that her father had bought in Puerto Rico. It said *Vida Feliz* on one side, *Happy Life* on the other.

But Joan wasn't always so happy. When she was ten, her father died in a fishing boat accident on the way to Trinidad. They say sharks ate the four-man crew, but I don't know if that was true. When Mrs. Maingot heard the news she locked herself up in the house, and she bawled like an animal made half of cow and half of dog for two days. I never heard a cry like that before or since.

Everyone said how sad it was that Wilfred Maingot was dead; there was no body to bury and nowhere to lay flowers. We all went to St. John's church on Sunday as usual and Father Carmichael, whom I never liked (he had yellow teeth like fangs), delivered a special service for Wilfred. I looked at Joan standing across the aisle dressed in white with her plaits hanging like two black ropes and I thought she was nearly worse off than me. At least I could hope my father was alive and somewhere in the world.

THE BEACH NEAREST our house was Courland Bay. There were often fishermen there with nothing better to do than drink and hang around under the trees, especially in the evenings. Now and then they made a fire and cooked a manicou or a goat and if we happened to be walking by, we saw the smoke puffing out into the sky. Roman used to say these men were badjohns and good-for-nothings. It takes one to know one.

The water here was usually calm. A large black rock jutted out of it, like a little island on its own. On the sand—as fine as dust—I found shells and pieces of driftwood thrown up like old bones and I usually came across a sea pussy or two, shaped like half a moon and soft like jellyfish. If I kicked it a purple dye poured out into the sand. There were many along this beach. I never knew why they were there and if they should be in the water. I guessed that they should be in the water because the sun made them shrivel and shrink. When I felt like it, I took up a stick and tossed them back in. I imagined them saying, Thank you, Celia. There were mangrove trees, and they were dark and alive with blue crabs, and farther up by the sea grape trees, I came around the island and the water there was rough and frothy. There were usually pelicans crashing into it like they were falling out of the sky. I saw all kinds of things in the sea there—paper, pieces of cloth, bottles. (One had rum inside and when I drank it, it made my head light like a cloud.) I also found a falling-apart brown shoe and a broken harmonica on the sand, and a map of a place I did not recognize. I found an empty purse, and a biscuit tin lid with a Christmas scene, and bits of broken pottery. Whatever I found I took back home, and wrapped it in a large piece of cloth from an old curtain and hid it underneath the house in a hole where Aunt Tassi kept the Coca-Cola crates. This was my beloved treasure; Lord help Vera and Violet if they went within a yard of it.

FROM AGE SIX, I went to St. Mary's school. It was a wooden building with windows at the front like two eyes, the door was a mouth and the roof a pointed hat. On the back wall of the classroom, there was a map of the world pinned with tacks to the wall. England was a small pink shape, and it was very far away from Trinidad and Tobago. (Trinidad and Tobago were also pink because they were part of the British Commonwealth.) I often placed my thumb exactly where I was in Black Rock village and spanned my hand over the Atlantic Ocean. It took three spans to reach a place called Plymouth, and Southampton was a little bit farther than that.

Miss McCartney, my teacher, said it was from Southampton that the famous ship *Titanic* set sail on April 10, 1912. More than a thousand people died when the ship hit an iceberg. "They were on their way to America in the biggest, grandest vessel in the world and then it sank." I liked Miss McCartney. She was not a pretty woman but neither was she ugly. She swept her red hair into a shape like a wave at the back of her head; I used to wonder what it looked like when she took it down. She wore long skirts and cotton blouses with buttons right up to the top as if she was cold and not living in the tropics at all. Her lace-up shoes came from a shop called Lunns in Piccadilly, London, England. She walked quickly and took little steps, leaning her body forward as if in a hurry to get somewhere. She had an unusual way of speaking. Roman said she sounded as if someone had his hands tight around her throat. But I could not imagine anyone wanting to put his hands around Miss McCartney's throat.

Once when class was over and I was packing up my books, I decided to ask her a question that had been niggling me for some time. "Miss," I said, "how come you know so much?"

Miss McCartney smiled and I saw her crooked little teeth.

"I suppose I learned a lot at university." And then, "It's a very good place to learn things and meet interesting people. If you pick a subject you like there's a lot of fun to be had. Maybe one day you will go to university."

"Don't you have to be very clever?"

"Quite," she said. "You're a bright girl, Celia. Just because you're pretty doesn't mean you should forget about your studies." She looked straight at me then, and I knew she was telling me something important. "You can be anything you want to be. Don't let anyone tell you any different."

When I got home I told Aunt Tassi. She was sweeping the floor and humming to herself, and Roman was asleep on the chair.

"At least we have some brains in the family. Maybe you'll be a doctor or a lawyer and make plenty money. You can look after your old aunt." Then she went outside and started on the steps.

Without opening his eyes, Roman said, "You could never do anything like that. You just like your mother. Dog can't make cat."

ON THE OTHER side of the village was a patch called Stony Hill where a family from Trinidad lived and where old Edmond Diaz lived and also Mrs. Jeremiah. Children were frightened of Mrs. Jeremiah. I had seen her puttering about the village, her white picky hair pulled back from her wrinkled-up face which reminded me of an old fruit. She had little slanted eyes, like a bird. The left was smoky, yellowish, and the right fixed somewhere over your shoulder as if she was watching something or someone away in the distance. She was almost blind, they said. But for all her blindness, Mrs. Jeremiah was able to see things about your life that no one else could see or know. Not your parents or your friends or even the whisperings of your own heart. People came from all over the Caribbean to hear what Mrs. Jeremiah had to say. They came from Barbados and Grenada and St. Lucia and Venezuela and Trinidad. If you didn't like what she told you, for an extra fee she would offer a spell or a potion to change your situation. There were all kinds of stories. Some said she was a kind of doctor. Mrs. Jeremiah gave concoctions of chicken's blood and hot pepper to be drunk at dawn; prayers to be sung into the night, directions for boiling the heart of a goat and wrapping it in banana leaves and putting it under your pillow where it should stay for forty nights.

After a visit to Mrs. Jeremiah, lovers were reunited or parted, relatives and enemies died in strange circumstances, a woman who could never have a child was suddenly seen nursing a baby. I would never have had to speak to her if it hadn't been for Roman Bartholomew.

. . .

ONE AFTERNOON, DRUNK and staggering all over the road on his way home from Jimmy's bar, Roman collided with Mrs. Jeremiah as she was coming out of the grocery and sent her toppling like a bag of plums. Mrs. Maingot was walking to the post office and saw her fall. Then she saw Roman try to help her up, but then he fell too—on top of Mrs. Jeremiah. Mrs. Maingot said it was like a comedy but no one was laughing. She rushed to where they were struggling like two animals and she, Mrs. Maingot, started to shout at Roman. She helped Mrs. Jeremiah to her feet and told Roman that she would never put up with half of what Tassi D'Abadie put up with and she was glad her husband had been a decent man and why did God take away a good man like Wilfred so young and leave him to run about the place like a demon. Roman looked down at the ground as if he had lost something there but couldn't remember what it was.

Mrs. Maingot guided Mrs. Jeremiah home to her little wooden house and she settled her into a chair in the veranda. She did not go inside the house because Mrs. Jeremiah said she would rather sit in the breeze. For a few moments, Mrs. Maingot sat on a stool while the old lady kept her eyes closed. She was about to leave quietly when Mrs. Jeremiah spoke in a voice like a sudden rain.

"Wilfred is doing all right; he is at peace."

Later, Mrs. Maingot told us she turned cold and hot at the same time, and her heart began to thud.

"Jesus is with him and our Lord has granted him everlasting life. If you wish him back you keep him between this world and that."

Mrs. Jeremiah smiled but not at Mrs. Maingot. She smiled at something or someone hovering above her head. Then she closed her eyes and nodded.

"Watch for butterflies," she said. "Just now plenty butterflies will come around you. They are a sign from Wilfred. His body will never be found but that don't matter, the sea is a big place. And don't worry about Joan. She will meet a good man and they will have plenty children." Then she told Mrs. Maingot she would be taken care of in her dying years. The worst was over—joy was on its way.

Mrs. Maingot hurried home. She lay on her bed and thought about her dead husband, and wept. Then she tried not to think about him, afraid she might keep him trapped between two worlds. Then she cried some more. In the end, she fell asleep. When she woke it was dark and Joan was standing in the lamplight looking up at the ceiling and there were two huge yellow butterflies hanging upside down there. Mrs. Maingot thought she was dreaming but Joan raised the lamp and pointed at them.

That evening Mrs. Maingot came over to our house and told Aunt Tassi what had happened. Aunt Tassi was surprised; Roman hadn't mentioned anything about Mrs. Jeremiah. He was sleeping in the back room, she said. When he woke she would ask him all about it. Mrs. Maingot didn't seem too bothered. She was happy and there was brightness in her eyes as though she had been drinking rum. She kept glancing around the room and I wondered what she was looking for. There weren't any butterflies.

When she left, Aunt Tassi went to the bedroom and saw a bat sucking on Roman's toe. The bat kept moving its big black wings and fanning Roman, who was sleeping soundly. Miss McCartney said the tongue of this bat is shaped like a lancet and when it pierces a vein there is little or no pain so you can sleep right through it while it drinks your blood. My aunt feared the bat was a sign. She threw open the shutters and took up a broom and she drove the creature out into the night. After that, Aunt Tassi did not sleep for worrying.

Next morning Roman was still sleeping and we were sitting at the table eating salt fish and hot bake and the sun was filling up the kitchen. I was thinking about my history class with Miss McCartney that afternoon and about my Christopher Columbus project, the picture I had sketched of him which needed coloring in, when my aunt cleared her throat.

"The tree is full of limes. They ready to drop. After school one of you must fill a bag and carry them up to Mrs. Jeremiah."

Vera set up her face as if in horror.

"I have extra lessons," Violet said, and I knew at once she was lying.

They all looked at me.

"Celia," Aunt Tassi said.

I put down my fork and finished chewing my buttery bake. I drank some cocoa, sweet and thick. Then I wiped my mouth on my arm and said, "I'm not scared."

THE PATH TO Mrs. Jeremiah's house was narrow and thick with brown leaves from the big mahogany tree. There was a damp smell and I saw a lot of mosquitoes. They made a dark cloud over a drum of water and I climbed the steps of the house. I thought the water shouldn't be there—before you know it everyone in Black Rock would be coming down with yellow fever. I was surprised by the pots of bougainvillea on either side of the entrance to the shabby little house. They must have been a gift. Over the doorway was a cross; I couldn't tell if it was made of stone or bone. There were two chairs in the veranda with blue torn cushions and I tried to picture Mrs. Maingot sitting on one of them. There was a bowl of water on a small round table. I wondered if it was holy water. Then I heard someone inside.

"Hello," I said.

"You the orphan girl."

"I brought you some limes." I pushed the curtain where a door should be. "My aunt says sorry about Uncle Roman."

I put down the brown paper bag. It was dark inside and the

shutters were closed except for the kitchen where they were slightly open and a little bit of brassy light was slicing its way in. The old woman had her hand on a large book on the table. In that half-light, after the bright afternoon glare, it looked like a little hoof. There was a candle on the table and its flame was low. One of Mrs. Jeremiah's eyes was cast near the door where I was standing.

"She should put him out but he won't last too long anyhow. Three years or less."

"Who?"

"Roman. Before he does something. He can be dangerous. You mustn't be rude to him or he will hurt you."

"I am not rude to Roman."

"Not with your mouth." She tapped the side of her skull. "In your head."

"Marriage is not for you. But you could have it if you want it. Men will want you like they want a glass of rum. Drink you up and pee you out. One man will love you. But you won't love him. You will harm him. You will destroy his life." Now, she was looking at me as if she didn't like me. My stomach was jumping like there were frogs in it.

"I never hurt anyone." My voice sounded small.

"You don't believe me. That don't matter. Just now you start to menstruate. Tassi will let you stay home from school, but only for one day because"—and this part she said in a high voice—"you have to get accustomed to that pain like all women do in the world." Then, "You'll see."

I don't know why, but I said, "Aunt Tassi is good to me."

"They tell you things about your mother and father," she said, and nodded. Then she seemed to be listening to someone else at the back of the room.

"Forget them. Forget them or make blood spill. You will make blood spill." She gasped a little and then she nodded again. She kept nodding.

"The one you love will break your heart in two." Her voice was higher now. "You don't care what happen to get what you want. It don't matter to you." She shook her head. "You won't die in this country. You'll die in a foreign place." Mrs. Jeremiah shuddered as if she was cold. Then she tossed something into the air, and I caught it. It was a piece of black rock, the size of a big tooth. "Carry this with you always. It come from the rock, right here. It will keep bad luck at bay and save you from the hard life you will make for yourself." She got up and put her hand out. My heart was beating fast.

"Now I will exorcise you," she said. Then, in a calmer voice, "Come. I will help you."

Mrs. Jeremiah began to speak in a language I could not understand. Father Carmichael had talked about speaking in tongues, but I could not imagine this ugly speech was the language of saints and angels. I turned and ran through the veranda, almost knocking over the bowl of water, and I ran down the steps and onto the path and I kept running, all the way down Stony Hill until I reached the main road which was lined with other little houses. These had lights glowing inside and I saw shadows moving in the light. I ran past Mrs. Maingot's house and Campbell's Hardware Store and along the curved road to Jimmy's bar. For some reason I went inside and looked for Roman but he wasn't there. Someone shouted something but I didn't hear what it was. I ran past the church and wondered if I should go inside, but then I saw the door was locked, so I kept running to where the road separates along the track to the house. The lights were on and I could see Aunt Tassi's big dark shape in the kitchen. Vera and Violet were sitting in the veranda. I flew up the steps. Aunt Tassi was standing over the stove. I arrived panting and sweating and puffing.

"Why you looking so red-faced? You saw Mrs. Jeremiah?"

.   .   .

NEXT MORNING, I was thinking about Mrs. Jeremiah and all that she had said when I overheard Mrs. Maingot talking to Aunt Tassi. Apparently, Joan's friend had come. "Thirteen is early," I heard her say, "but when the curse come early, what are you to do." Looking out where the two women were speaking on the steps, I wondered who this friend was and why she was a curse. At the window I said, "I wish we could have visitors. This place is always so dead." The two women turned and looked at me, and then they looked at each other and burst out laughing. "Oh Lord," Mrs. Maingot said, and threw up her skinny arms. "Celia really is a strange child! Where she came from, Tassi?" Aunt Tassi looked at her as if to say, Yes, yes, I know just what you mean.

It was only later when I heard Angela Hernandez telling someone how the blood poured out of Joan like it came from a bucket that I realized Joan's friend was in fact her period. All that afternoon I wondered, If Mrs. Jeremiah is right, when will that happen to me?

So said so done: three days later I woke with pain in my stomach. It was a new hot ache that wrapped itself around my lower back and middle. When Aunt Tassi came in and told me to dress for school, I said I was sick and showed her my bloated stomach and the brown patch on the sheet which looked like I had spilled cocoa. I must have looked unwell because, just as Mrs. Jeremiah said she would, Aunt Tassi said I could stay home from school today, but only today because I would have to "get accustomed to that pain like all women do in the world." When she said this a chill rushed through my body; Aunt Tassi didn't seem to notice. Sitting on the edge of my bed, she said that I must now be careful because I would be able to have children and before I knew it men would be coming around and I must know to push them away.

"Just now you having a baby and you're still a baby yourself."

"Like my mother."

"Yes, just like your mother."

"And like you too."

"Yes, just like me."

Aunt Tassi got up and went into her room and came back carrying a piece of white thin cloth. She folded it once, twice, three times, until the cloth was a fat little rectangle. She told me to put this in my panties to catch the blood. When it was full, not too full, because it would start to smell bad like an old piece of iron, I must put it to soak in the outside sink and hang it up on the line under the house.

TWO

WHEN ROMAN WAS AWAY OUR HOUSE WAS BRIGHTER AND quieter. I felt almost happy when it was just Aunt Tassi and me. This did not happen often. But soon after I had started my period, we were supposed to visit his dying mother in Charlotteville. The plan was to set off at sunrise. In Scarborough, Roman would rent four mules from an estate worker who hired them out cheap; the girls would sit on one, Aunt Tassi on another, I would have my own mule, and Roman would ride out front on the largest. We would ride out to the northeastern part of the island, and then down through the hilly parts, toward Speyside, and reach the small coastal village at nightfall. It was a long journey. Aunt Tassi did not want to go because she did not like old Mrs. Bartholomew. I didn't want to go either, so when I woke in the morning, I said I had a fever. (You can fake a fever if you dampen your sheets and pillow with a little water.) I could tell that Aunt Tassi knew I wasn't ill at all, and when she used my sickness as an excuse to let Roman go alone, I was pleased. But Roman was not pleased, and I knew that he was angry with me when, standing in the passageway, his black eyes crawled like two beetles over my nightie and settled on my face.

"Tassi say you sick. How come you look so well?"

I watched his lips. They were shapeless, as if God had taken a crayon and made them any old way.

"You looking real good to me."

I wanted to go in my room but I couldn't move, as though I was glued to the spot.

"I hear you're a real woman now. Tassi say your 'friend' come."

He rubbed his hand over the front of his trousers, and for the first time I felt a little bit afraid. He had never done that before.

"Your pussy turn into a nice big cat."

WHEN THEY LEFT, the sun was climbing down the mango tree and Aunt Tassi was standing on the steps and waving. She looked sad and I guessed this was because Vera and Violet had begged her to let them go because they liked the sea down there and they liked the journey, too, and she had said yes. Through the shutters I watched Roman walk up the path toward the main road with my cousins dressed up like two dolls and I knew with every one of the thirty-three bones Miss McCartney told me we have in our spines, that I hated him.

As soon as they'd gone, Aunt Tassi slowed right down. For two days she did little but sing songs and pick guavas and make jam and stew and guava cheese. I helped her prepare them, scooping out the pink flesh, plucking out the worms. When her arms grew tired I stirred the large pots. Every now and then I wanted to tell her about the way Roman had spoken to me, but I was afraid that she wouldn't believe me.

With Roman away, Aunt Tassi did not cook large meals. Instead we ate bread and corned beef and drank water and coconut milk from the yard. On the third day, the air grew very still and by late afternoon we knew a storm was coming. While Aunt Tassi was cutting cloth to make curtains, I followed her around the table where the flowery material sent by Aunt Sula was spread, holding a little tin of pins. It was hot enough to faint and the room grew so dark I thought we might soon need a candle. Yet it was only four o'clock.

"Aunt Tassi," I said, "tell me about when you were a girl."

"Oh Lord," she said.

"Please."

She lifted her eyes and shook her big head, which was wrapped like a candy in a yellow scarf. I thought she was annoyed and felt sorry I had said anything. But then she said, "Too hot to make these curtains. I can hardly see," and she walked slowly over to the bamboo seat and stepped out of her rattan slippers and sat down. Through the window, the sky was a dark backdrop and the grass was a blackish green. I sat myself on the wooden floor by her large, dry feet.

To begin with, Aunt Tassi did not say very much, and she seemed unsure of what she wanted to say. Then she started to speak. For two hours, I sat with my back straight as a stick and listened.

When they were small, Aunt Tassi said, Grace (my mother) and Sula pretended to be bushes. They called themselves Pilil and Lala and they jumped out on her like jumbies, especially in the night when she was going outside to do her business.

"One night, when the moon was full, they wait behind the guava tree and as I pass they sprang like two cats." Aunt Tassi put up her hands like claws.

"Well, I flew screaming in the air and then collapsed. They come running. I lay in the grass completely still. They fan my face and blow on it; when they pick up my arms and lift my legs they heavy like flour bags. They were sure I was dead and they start to bawl. And then I opened my eyes."

My aunt made her eyes big like a bullfrog.

"That was the last time they tease me," she said, and she prodded the air with her thick brown finger.

"Every day we walk through the bush to the river. The sun made the rocks hot. We sit on them and throw coins in the water and dive down to find them. And when the rocks too hot, we sit under Manchanille trees. But only if it hadn't been raining." She suddenly looked serious. "Or the water might drop from the leaves and blister our skin or get inside our eyes and make them blind.

"Once there was a stupid English lady. She came right here to Tobago and found a Manchanille plum on the ground. She thought it was a West Indian apple and took a big bite. She burn up her whole mouth. Inside her stomach swell with huge blisters."

Aunt Tassi put her hand on her stomach and made a face. "Imagine you pick a fruit you never saw in your life and put it in your mouth just so.

"Imagine."

She went on to tell me about a place where the river met the sea, not the river where I nearly drowned, but another river, and one particular day there was a large shape there like a boulder. It was white and brown and they were sure it was a rock until Sula saw it sway in the water. When Grace swam toward it she saw that it wasn't a rock at all, but a carcass of a giant turtle and pieces of its rotting flesh were coming away in the current. "That carcass was something else. We prayed over the bones like they belonged to a friend. Sula said a prayer and threw grass and flowers on top."

Aunt Tassi had never talked to me in this way before. Every time she finished one story, I'd think, Whatever happens please don't stop. After hearing about the turtle, I was sure she was going to stand up and say, Enough now, but she didn't. Instead, she told me about another time. "It always stuck in my head, when this pregnant girl fall down in the road. I ran to find a doctor, and Grace and Sula delivered the tiny baby right there in St. Mary's schoolyard.

"Right there," Aunt Tassi said, again. "Like it was a hospital."

"Who cut the cord?" I asked, trying to imagine how this could be done.

"Your mother," she said.

"She was brave," I said. "She saved the baby's life."

Then I said, "Why did my mother die?"

I knew what she'd say; the same thing she always said.

"One soul flies in, another flies out."

"Did she really see me?"

"Yes, of course. She said what a beautiful child I have."

I had never heard this part before. "She said that?"

"Yes."

"That I was beautiful?"

"Yes," Aunt Tassi said.

"Did my father see me, too?" I already knew the answer, but thought she might suddenly remember some other detail about my father.

"Your father wasn't here. How could he see you?"

"Was he in Southampton?"

"I suppose so."

Aunt Tassi looked out the window where the wind was blowing so hard the coconut trees beyond the bay were bending as though they might break. She got up and pulled the shutters in tight. That day, even though the sky was black like bruises and the wind took away some of the rooftops in Scarborough and we were scared our own house might be ripped up in the tail end of the storm, behind my thoughts I was glad, as though Aunt Tassi had given me a diamond to hold.

Lying beside her that night, I stared at the mountain of her soft back, and wished it was only her and me in the world; wished that the thunderstorm would find Roman and my cousins in Charlotteville and lift them from their beds and drop them in the stormy, dark sea.

THREE

Aunt Sula visited Tobago when I was four, and then again when I was twelve. I don't remember too much about her first visit, though Aunt Tassi told me we had a good holiday because Aunt Sula rented a cute little house on the other side of the island, near to the airport. Every month she sent a large parcel from Trinidad: material for dresses, crocheted things for the house, and always a little money to help with schoolbooks or other extras. In her letters, there was usually news of Tamana, the estate, and the Carr Browns who owned it. She always asked for me and sent her fondest love.

But Aunt Sula's second visit I remember very well. Aunt Tassi spent three weeks fixing up the house. She got Roman to paint the walls inside and out, and then to paint the steps. We emptied my room and moved the three small beds into the back room. Aunt Tassi got the dressmaker to make new outfits for Vera and Violet and me. In Scarborough she bought a little expensive lamp with shells around the base that had been made in China. In the evenings it gave the living room a nice glow. We put all the white things—tablecloths, sheets, rags—out in the sun to bleach. The whole yard was covered in white cloth and I watched from the window and I imagined from the picture I had seen in the library that this was how snow must look.

Roman clipped the hedge and the grass and axed away all the

dead branches from the breadfruit tree and the orange tree and put them on a heap to burn. He took stones and pelted down the Jack Spaniard nests from under the eaves and we all ran inside and closed up the shutters. The week before Aunt Sula arrived, Aunt Tassi hardly ate. She said she wanted to feel slim. She even had her hair fixed in a new style, pulled back from her big face and puffed out in the front. She looked like a cockerel.

The night before Aunt Sula arrived, Roman started to complain about how expensive these preparations were and how he could think of other, better ways to spend that kind of money. It was obvious to us all that he had been drinking. Aunt Tassi carried on serving dinner as if he wasn't there, or as if she was deaf, and he got angrier and angrier. He said no one made any effort for him these days. Sula was nothing more than a white meat–loving nigger. "Fuss, fuss, fuss," he said, in a high voice. He was standing over the table wearing his old brown trousers held up by a piece of rope and a vest with a shirt on top. His nostrils were broad and flared.

"Who we putting on this show for?" he shouted. "Like the queen of England coming to stay! If she is a queen, then I am God."

Aunt Tassi got up from the table, walked over to the kitchen, and for the first and only time in all the years I lived with her, she answered Roman back.

"Everybody say you think so. Why you think they call you Allah?"

Roman threw his dinner plate across the room so fast I never saw it leave his hands, and hit Aunt Tassi hard in her head. Everybody was silent and still. Then, slowly, like in a dream, Aunt Tassi put her hand up to her forehead and dabbed at the bright red gash. Then she looked at her fingers as if she had never seen blood before.

"What you did, Roman?" Her voice was small and cold.

Roman yelled, "You look for that! You look for it!" and he ran from the house and down the steps into the night. Violet started to scream and pull at the bobbles in her hair. Vera began to scream, too. I got up and put my arms around the two of them, and tried to hold them steady.

After she had cleaned up Aunt Tassi came into our room and lay down with my cousins. She lay still like she was dead, but her eyes were open and staring at the ceiling as if she thought it might fall in.

In the morning no one mentioned the incident and I wondered what Roman had said to make it up to her because by that afternoon they were talking as if nothing had happened. At one point, Roman put his hands around Aunt Tassi's waist while she was stirring something on the stove and I heard her say, "Roman, leave me alone," but she didn't sound as though she meant it. When she saw me standing in the doorway she pushed his hands away. He laughed and said, "Celia like a policeman," and saluted me.

WE WENT BY bus to Scarborough; the boat was due in late afternoon. It wasn't so busy at the docks, not like in the mornings when the whole world was there. At the meeting point, there was a little seating area, and myself, Vera, and Violet sat on the green wooden seats, wearing our new dresses.

Aunt Tassi said, "You have to look out for a tall white man."

"Why?" I asked, pushing out my chin.

"He's the man she works for."

"Why is *he* coming?"

"He has business here."

"What kind of business?"

"I don't know, child. He has business in Charlotteville."

"Does Aunt Sula have to go with him? To Charlotteville?" I suddenly felt troubled by this news.

"Of course not! She is staying with us at Black Rock." Aunt Tassi said this in a way that I knew not to ask any more questions.

THE FIRST TIME I saw Aunt Sula, I thought she really did look like
a queen. Her hair was ironed and oiled so all its fuzziness was gone,
and her cream dress was stylish and perfect. When she kissed me I
smelled her powdery scent. She put down her bag and I saw the delicate lace of her slip. She stared at me for a long time and I thought
how glittery her eyes were, like night. I smiled but she did not smile.
She looked at my face as if it was a map she needed to follow to get
somewhere. Then she checked my hands and my ears; she glanced
down at my feet inside my slippers. In the end when she smiled, it was
as if something had become clear to her. All this time, Vera and Violet were holding on to their mother. Aunt Tassi told them to say hello
but they ran behind her and hid. Aunt Sula nodded and gave her sister a look as if to say, Ah yes, it's you. Then she saw the little plaster
on her forehead and said, "What happen here?"

Aunt Tassi gave her a bright smile.

"You know me," she said, "clumsy like a clown. And when it
rain it slippery like glass."

Then the white man came striding over. I hadn't seen him coming. He was tall as a tree, and his shoulders were broad. He wore a
planter's hat and it was wide and made of straw. I remember him taking it off, then putting out his big hand, and Aunt Tassi saying,
"Come, Vera and Violet, shake hands with Mr. Carr Brown, shake
hands with Mr. Carr Brown." But they wouldn't. I remember thinking they were stupid; he seemed to me to be an important man, so I
moved in front of them and stuck out my hand. Aunt Tassi gave me a
look but I didn't care. The man said, "And what is your name?" I
said my name, and he said, "Pleased to meet you, Celia."

AUNT SULA STAYED for a week. I feel if it hadn't been for Roman hanging around the house she would have stayed longer. One day we went to the river, just her and me. We sat on a stone with our backs to the sun and dipped our feet in the cool water. For a while she played with my hair; she plaited it on both sides and then folded it over the top of my head like a tiara. She asked me if I was happy, and I said sometimes yes, and sometimes no. I told her that one day I would like to leave Black Rock. I mentioned that Miss McCartney had said I should go to university, and she looked surprised.

"That's wonderful." Then, "Where would you like to study?"

"My father's in Southampton. I'm sure there's a university nearby. Or maybe in London." She didn't say anything, so I asked, "Have you ever been to England, Aunt Sula?"

"No. But I've heard a lot about it. I hear it's very cold. Cold enough to see your own breath. London is a big city, you know, a place you could get lost in."

"I wouldn't mind getting lost for a while." I smiled, and there was a dragonfly hovering just above the water, its rainbow wings glistening like jewels. Miss McCartney had said that a dragonfly's wings beat 1,600 times in a single minute, yet these didn't look like they were moving at all.

"Before you go, will you visit me?"

"On the estate?"

"Yes, at Tamana." Then, "Promise me you'll come."

"I promise," I said, and my heart felt full and warm.

Now she was smiling and I thought how beautiful she was: her high cheeks plump like two round fruits, her eyes very slightly slanted, her small full mouth.

Just before we got up to leave, Aunt Sula put her hand in the pocket of her dress and took out a thin gold chain with a small cross. She fastened the chain around my neck. "To keep you safe," she said,

and then she kissed the top of my head. For some reason, it made me
want to cry.

ON THE WAY home we found a manicou lying in the road. A baby
manicou had fallen out of its pouch and was wriggling next to it. The
baby was tiny like a spool of thread. The mother was trying to get up
but couldn't. Something or somebody must have hit it, Aunt Sula
said. When I bent down to look closer, the mother drew back her lips
and hissed. She had small teeth and they looked like they could bite
hard. Somehow we got a box and put them in it and took them home.
Roman was pleased. "Manicou!" he said, and clapped his hands. He
wanted to kill the mother at once and eat it. Aunt Sula said no, and I
thought there was going to be a fight but Aunt Tassi soon calmed
things down. She gave Roman some money and told him to go down
to Jimmy's bar.

For a while, we kept the manicous under the house. I don't
know what happened to them.

AUNT SULA'S VISIT was a big thing. Mostly, life in Black Rock did
not change from one day to the next. Every day I woke early and
washed my face outside in the pipe. I lit a fire and heated milk. I put
bread and jam and cheese on the table. If my aunt was making fried
bakes I kneaded the dough and put it on a plate to rise. I washed myself in the tiny hut where the soap and bucket lived. Then I put on my
turquoise school uniform with white trim around the sailor collar
and I combed my long hair. If they weren't up already, I shouted,
"Vera, Violet!" and my aunt told me to go quietly because if I woke up
Roman too he would have a long face for the day. She peeled oranges
and cut them in half and I sucked on one half until it felt like straw in
my mouth and I held it over my teeth so that I couldn't speak. This

irritated her and she would say, "Celia, take that orange out of your mouth." Sometimes I read at the breakfast table, but my aunt said this was bad manners and told me to put the book away. I tried to leave the house early so as not to have to walk to school with my cousins.

We sang hymns at school and I stood at the back because I was tall. In the mornings we studied geography or history or religion or arithmetic, and English. At lunchtime I ate a sandwich under the samaan tree and there were usually other girls sitting there too and sometimes they included me in their talk. In the afternoons, after class, Miss McCartney read out poetry or part of a story. Then at three o'clock I walked home; sometimes alone, and sometimes with Joan Maingot. But she often left me before the turn in the road, with some excuse or other, and I guessed that she didn't want to walk with me. At home I changed into my old clothes. There were usually chores to do around the house, some washing or preparation for dinner or darning. If I had a lot of homework I got less chores, and sometimes I lied about the homework I had to do. If my aunt wasn't home, I went under the house and I read a book or took out my trea- sure. After dinner, I cleared the table and said good night to my aunt and to Roman, if he was there, and I was glad if he was not because he would lean his cheek toward me and I would have to kiss it. I went into the room I shared with my cousins, who by now were usually asleep, and I blew out the light. This is how it was in Black Rock, day in, day out.

Then on February 12, the day after my sixteenth birthday, everything changed.

FOUR

It had been raining hard like stones on the roof and the yard smelled of damp earth. Soon it would be dry again, but not for long. At that time of year the rains came quickly and often. Vera and Violet had gone with Aunt Tassi to pick up coconut cake and sweet bread buns from the baker's in the next village. When my aunt asked if I wanted to go with them I said I had homework to do. She said, "You always have your head buried in some book. One day you will disappear inside a book and we won't know where to find you." Vera and Violet laughed as if this was funny. They were both wearing green and white shift dresses.

I said, "If only I was so lucky."

When they had gone, I didn't bother to change, I went straight downstairs with a piece of bread and a glass of milk and my schoolbooks. It was hot and sticky, in that way where you feel you can't breathe. There were a lot of mosquitoes about.

I liked sitting under the house. Hens ran around and pecked at the ground and the two goats, Antoine and Antoinette, lay under the lime tree or grazed on the thick grass. Once I thought I saw a deer enter the yard and sit with them. It was night and I could not see very clearly. But five months later when the young ones came they did not look like goats, they were pretty and had speckles on their backs. They soon died. Roman said that I was lying, that Tobago didn't have deer.

It was four o'clock and I knew they would be gone for at least an hour. I wondered where Roman was, probably up at Ruth Mackenzie's house.

I lifted the Coca-Cola crates and pulled out my secret bundle, which was full of dust. Then I unwrapped it and took out things I had collected from the beach. I began to place the objects from my collection around me as though they were in a museum and people were paying to see them. That day I had some small pieces of glass to add, soft and worn by the sea, like jewels, and an old fishhook and a piece of string. I bound the string around a chunk of glass so it became a noose. I thought it might make a necklace.

I could tell Roman was drunk by the way he climbed the steps. In a high voice he said, "Good afternoon," and peered down to where I was sitting.

"Where's Tassi?"

I said, "They went to the baker's in Buccoo."

"What for?"

"Coconut cake and sweet buns."

"Oh, for the birthday girl!"

I wondered if he was going inside to lie down, or if he would eat and then lie down, as he often did. It depended on how drunk he was. I knew there was a large pot of pelau still warm on the stove; pelau was one of his favorite meals. I waited for his footsteps above my head. But I didn't hear anything except a loud kiskadee, which sang "Qu'est-ce qu'elle dit! Qu'est-ce qu'elle dit!" So I was surprised when I looked up and saw him stretched out like an animal on the steps, watching me.

"What you have there?" he said. "You have something for Uncle Roman?"

"Some old junk from the beach." I started to put everything away.

"Celia always so secretive," he said, and he rolled back his head

as though he was talking to the sky. And then I don't know whether he
tripped or slipped or meant to come down the steps to where I was almost standing and dusting off my school dress, but he was suddenly
there in front of me leaning against the pillar and swaying as if he was
on a boat. When I tried to pass him he took hold of my arm.

"Tell me a secret, Celia. Tell me something." His breath smelled
of rum. His eyes were trying to focus. I thought he looked sick and
turned to climb the steps but he kept hold of my arm.

"You don't have any secrets?" Roman was grinning like a fool.

"Your breath stinks," I said in a whisper. "That's my secret."
And I tried to pull away.

"You're full of shit," he said, gripping harder. I felt his other
hand move under my dress.

"Get off me," I said.

His fingers crawled higher.

"You want some prick? You want some prick, Miss High and
Mighty?"

Before I knew what was happening he had thrown me down and
I was half lying in the dust. I said, "Uncle Roman," and tried to get
up. I thought, Jesus, help me, but I couldn't feel the presence of
Jesus. Roman's eyes were wild and tiny and he pushed me back. I said,
"What are you doing, what are you doing?" I said, "Please, Uncle
Roman," and I tried to get up again. He kicked me hard in my side
and I curled over. He kicked me again. I thought he has gone crazy.
Then, when I looked up, he was standing over me and fumbling with
the zip on his filthy trousers. I said, "Oh God no." And I looked
away, and saw the sun shafting through underneath the house. If I
can get up, I thought, if I can get up and run through the yard, down
the road and into the village. But I couldn't get up. When I looked
again Roman's trousers were around his knees.

"Take off your panties."

Something in his eyes told me if I did not take them off I would die. I took them off. I began to cry, not cry as I was used to crying, but whimpering like a beaten cat. He was kneeling over me and I was looking at a nest and sticking out of the nest was an upright snake. I said, "Please, Uncle Roman, please." He was trying to push it in my mouth so I turned my head away and for a moment he looked confused and took it in his hand and started to jiggle it. I thought maybe this is it, and this is all he will do, but then I knew it was not all he would do, because this was something he had wanted to do for so long, and with one hand on my chest he pressed me down into the ground and with the other he pulled my dress up, and with his legs he pressed back my knees. *Our father who art in heaven hallowed be thy name thy kingdom come thy will be done on earth as it is in heaven.* He fed his hand inside me. His hand was enormous, like the branch of a tree.

Roman must have used all his strength to wedge himself into me because when he took out his hand I tried to lock myself together. He spat onto his fingers and put this spit on himself; he rubbed it on the top. Then he positioned himself at the place where I opened, only I didn't open, I locked myself together, and he rammed and rammed and rammed until he broke inside and he rammed again and again until he climbed right up and into me. I was sure he was going to burst into my stomach and my body would split in two halves like a carcass I once saw hanging in the doorway of an abattoir. I don't know how long it went on but I could see he was trying to make something happen and his face was so twisted up that if someone had said, This man is Roman Bartholomew, I would have answered, No it is not, I do not know this man. Tears fell from the corners of my eyes. I closed them and I knew then, that if I could think of something else, if I could see something other than Roman, I could save myself from something. So I put there, the picture postcard of Southampton, and I saw the people and the gray sky and the seagulls flying above the world . . . That's when Roman smacked my face and I was suddenly back, underneath the house, again. He looked crazy, and I realized he was afraid I would pass out. Then he started again. I knew now to keep my eyes open.

I did not know what he was waiting for until it came. It spilled everywhere like thick milk. Some vomit flew up into my mouth and I coughed it out. Roman climbed off me. He used his vest to wipe himself, and then he stood up and pulled on his trousers.

"If you say one thing to Tassi, I'll make you so sorry. Tassi doesn't give one shit about you. The sooner you understand that the better."

He shuffled up the steps to the house. At the top, he rubbed his face now shiny with sweat and glared at me, as if this was something I had made him do.

FIVE

I WAITED FOR A WHILE, THEN TOOK A BUCKET OF WATER and a rag and scrubbed myself as though I was filled with feces. The clear water turned pink from my blood and the gluey slime that came from inside kept coming out. I put my fingers high inside the bowl of myself to wash out every last drop of him. Then I waited in the yard until I saw their shapes appear in the half-light. They came like a vision: my aunt, my two cousins, Vera and Violet, with their arms linked. They walked slowly, as if they had until the end of the world to reach the house. Their hips swayed out, their shoulders back, swinging their bags of buns and cakes. I thought, Yes, that's why you did not come home in time, because you walk like you are in a dream. They didn't see me crawl up the steps of the house. When they arrived I was in bed with the sheet pulled up over my head.

In the kitchen I heard Aunt Tassi singing a familiar song. The song had always made me feel sad as though it was meant for me. It went:

Brown skin girl, stay home and mind baby
Brown skin girl, stay home and mind baby
I'm goin' away, in a sailing boat

And if I don't come back
Stay home and mind baby

She's the girl with the pretty eyes
She always gettin' by
She run 'til she get away
She run at the break of day . . .

I stayed in my room and when Violet came to look for me so I could taste the coconut cake they had bought I told her to go away, and that I was sick. I listened to their voices in the kitchen. Vera was laughing because Roman was sleeping on the porch with his mouth open and a fly nearly went in it.

"Daddy catching flies," she shrieked. "Why they like Daddy's mouth so?"

I listened to the crickets in the yard; something was moving in the grass, one of the goats perhaps. I wondered if they had seen what had happened.

Later, Aunt Tassi brought in a tray with a bowl of callaloo and a piece of bake. I said I didn't want any. She put the tray on the little table beside my bed and sat down.

"Celia, you should eat something."

I pulled up the sheet.

"You are such a stubborn child sometimes. Come, eat a little something."

"Maybe your food is making me ill."

I knew this would hurt her. She got up and went back into the kitchen where I heard her say she never knew a child so rude like Celia before and how my moodiness must have come from my father's side because none of her family were like that. Then I heard Roman, "She really think she's somebody. She just like Sula."

.   .   .   .

THAT NIGHT, FOR the first time in weeks, Roman stayed at home. Aunt Tassi asked him how come he not going out when she heard tonight there is some big drink up down by Uncle C's. Roman said he was practicing for Lent and she should make the most of it.

Vera and Violet came to bed. When they spoke to me I pretended to be asleep. My aunt turned on the radio and it was playing some old-time Spanish music. I heard glasses clinking and I imagined they were drinking rum. Then I heard feet shuffling on the wooden floor and I knew she was dancing. I had seen her dance for him before. She lifted the sides of her dress and moved her bottom from left to right and it seemed separate from the rest of her, and she looked over her shoulder, dropped her eyes, and, slowly, smiled, letting her big mouth stretch and part, revealing her best asset of all, her bright, white teeth. And I knew that when she did this Roman did not take his eyes off her. If this happened when I was in the room, it made me feel ashamed for her.

Soon I could hear both of their footsteps, dancing, and when I opened my door and looked down the passageway I saw that Roman had his arm around her thick waist and his face was in her neck and he was gnawing on it.

Aunt Tassi giggled as she lay down on the old bed that arrived one day from the estate where Aunt Sula worked. I listened to the groan of the mattress and the rusty frame as Roman pressed down on her. I heard him slapping up against her like sea on the side of a boat, I heard him groan. There were some puffing sounds and I knew that they came from my aunt. She said his name. She said his name. Finally there came a loud and deep moan from Roman and at the same time a high and breathy sigh from my aunt.

In the silence that followed and in the light of the bright moon,

I gathered as many of my clothes as I could find and packed them into my school bag. I put on my blue dress with the petticoat, the one I mostly wore to church and parties, and I put on my shoes shined since yesterday.

Violet looked up from her pillow. "Celia."

"I'm going to the toilet. Go back to sleep."

I pulled back my sheet and saw that there was blood there. This was not unusual; the sight of blood on my sheet and my aunt will assume I am menstruating and that I have forgotten to use a cloth. Then I went into the kitchen where I saw a huge moth sitting on the table. Its wings were as big as my hand and its body was thick and long. I couldn't imagine why it was there. At the back of the cupboard I found a cocoa tin where I knew Aunt Tassi kept money from her tips. I quietly took out the coins, there were a lot of them, and there was also a five-dollar bill. I put it all in my purse. Then I emptied the jar of sweet biscuits into a small brown paper bag. On my way out, I picked up a mango from the windowsill left there by Violet to ripen in the sun.

THE YARD LOOKED like a different yard. The bushes were silvery from the moon and thick like hair and the grass was also silvery and it looked soft like I could lie on it. At the bottom of the steps I almost tripped on a toad and was glad of my shoes. The skin of a toad was like the skin of a dead person. Aunt Tassi always said you had to be careful when you come close to a toad because it might spray urine in your eyes and blind you, which was why when I saw them in the yard I sometimes threw salt on their backs. It burns like acid. Shuddering at this, I walked quickly onto Black Rock road, the road I would take if I was going to school. The silk cotton trees were like tall people and the moon gave them the light of ghosts. I remembered a man I had heard about who found a baby crying under one of the trees. He put it on the back of his bicycle and made his way to the hospital, but soon he realized the baby was getting bigger and heavier. Then in a man's voice the baby said, "Take me back where you found me." And when he put the baby back under the silk cotton tree it shrank to its original size. If they found me I would never go back.

I hurried along the path. It was silent as though everything in the world was dead. I thought of Joan Maingot sleeping, and her mother also asleep. I thought about the kind man she would meet and marry and have her children with. She would have a normal life in Black Rock village and her children would go to St. Mary's school and every Sunday the family would dress for mass at St. John's church where Father Carmichael would welcome them and where there was now a plaque for Wilfred, her father. She would live a long and happy life. My life was not to be like hers. My life was not to be happy. Mrs. Jeremiah had said so.

It was difficult to see the opening to the bay. I wondered about the crabs that came up onto the sand at night and I hoped there wouldn't be any. There were also turtles that dragged themselves onto the sand and laid their eggs. The sea was enormous and it was hard to know where it began and where it ended. I was glad of the moon but I did not look at it too much because I knew it could send me crazy. The moon threw light on the water and the black rock was a creature climbing out of it. I decided to sleep on the beach until the sun came up. I covered myself with fallen fronds from the coconut trees. I used my bag for a pillow. There were a lot of mosquitoes; I could hear them buzzing around my head.

When dawn came I started out for Scarborough. I was the only person in the world and the loneliest person in the world. I walked quickly past the mangrove trees and at the sea grape trees I did not stop and look for pink grapes. I passed the little houses and the green where sometimes boys played cricket and everything was asleep. In the village I looked for people sitting in their doorways but no one was

there. I waited for a bus and it wasn't long before it came, and there
wasn't anybody I knew on the bus, which I was glad about. The driver
didn't notice I was sad like somebody who is running away.

By six o clock, I was standing on the edge of the town looking at
the rooftops of the stores and houses and they were shining in the
sun. The sea was flat as if it was painted and the boat that would take
me to Trinidad was waiting in the harbor like a monster. Along the
main street people were busy unloading goods from trucks and carts
for the market. They were laying out their stalls with vegetables and
fruits.

I climbed the hill. It was hot now and the sun was rising higher
in the light blue sky. Soon it would be hotter and then I would not
want to climb any hills. Outside St. George's church a lady said hello
and looked at me as though she knew me but she did not know me
and I did not say hello. I sat down on the steps of the church and took
out the mango. I bit into its yellow flesh. I sat there for a few minutes
and ate it. Down the road a little girl was walking with her mother,
their hands joined, her immaculate school dress stiff and green. I felt
like throwing the mango seed at them. But instead I put it on the
ground, and then I noticed some red hibiscus flowers on the nearby
hedge and I got up and picked one.

The grass on my mother's grave was long and there were little
stinging Ti Maria plants in it. I pulled them out and tore away some
of the grass in clumps. I traced the letters on the piece of wood that
said, *Grace Angel D'Abadie,* and the date she died, the same day as my
birthday. I put the flower at the head of the grave. Then I lay down
on my side, and put my arm over the place where I imagined her
body to be. Once again, tears ran down my cheeks. I did not feel sad.
I felt dirty and angry at what Roman had done.

SIX

SCARBOROUGH QUAY WAS CROWDED, AND IT WAS DIFFI-
cult to see where the ticket line began and ended. Most of the people
gathered near the fence were waiting to board the boat. It was supposed to leave at 11:30 a.m.

After I had bought my ticket, I tried to find a way to get through
the crowd or around the crowd but it was impossible. "Get in line," a
guard shouted from somewhere near the front. "Where the line
start?" said someone else. Then, "Here! It start here," yelled the
guard, and he stood up on a wall and pointed. Everyone surged forward and there was pushing from behind and I had no choice but to
let myself go like a wave rushing at the shore. *If one of us falls, just one of us.*
"Wait," the guard shouted. "Wait right there." A woman in front with
an enormous back jumped up and flung her arms about as if trying to
get someone's attention. From behind, somebody shouted, "Come
on! Like we have all week to get to Port of Spain," and there was more
shouting and pushing. I had never seen the quay so full of people.
Sometimes it was busy, yes, but not crowded like this. My left side was
up against a young man and my right side was pressed against the
fence. Through it I could see the glittery sea.

Packed up like cattle on the way to market, we waited in the hot
sun and the glare. There was no breeze. Beyond the fence I watched a
patch of long grass and it stayed absolutely still—not a flicker or a

bend. At one point, a flock of parrots flew overhead making a screeching sound. Miss McCartney used to say that parrots fly out early but come back when the sun is warming up; by evening they are found in the mangrove or the palms. They are sociable and move in a crowd, she said. Like people. Right now, Miss McCartney was probably talking about geometry with the fan spinning above my empty wooden desk and my chair pushed underneath it. Angela Hernandez might say, "Celia not here," and that would be that.

MORE THAN AN hour had passed before they finally started letting people through a gate and onto the gangway. I checked the clock on the Port Authority building. I couldn't imagine how the boat would leave on time.

"Are you okay, miss?"

The young man reminded me of someone but I couldn't think who.

"Yes," I said.

I wondered how I must have looked to him. My hair was knotted in a ball on top my head, strands were glued about my neck. My dress was sticking to me. I was hot, but not in the usual way where a breeze comes and you cool down. I was hot on the inside like meat when it is cooking. Apart from the pain in my back where Roman had kicked me, I was sore as if I'd been cut with a knife. Earlier, when I had gone to the toilet, there was more blood and it had shocked me. I had a spare rag but I didn't know what to do with the bloody one so I threw it away. I hoped this one would last until I got to where I was going. Now I tried to stand with my legs apart and balance on the outer soles of my feet, but there wasn't enough room.

After a few minutes, we moved again, and were soon very nearly at the front of the line. But then we stopped about ten feet from the gangway and the guard put up his hand and told us—again—to wait. I looked at the young man and he rolled his eyes.

Here the air was thick and still; it was as if we were breathing in the same hot air we'd been breathing in for the last half hour. The idea of standing up all afternoon was suddenly unbearable. I knew that it wasn't good to be out in this sort of heat, especially when you're sick. Aunt Tassi would say, Go inside, put on a hat, cool yourself, lie down. My head felt strangely light, like a balloon. There were still a lot of people. I could feel them behind me, pushing and jostling. Somebody kept stepping on the back of my shoe. I wanted to say something and I quickly turned around and that's when my head started spinning and I saw the blue sky rolling away and I thought I was going to fall . . .

THE YOUNG MAN found me a place to sit on the second level, near to the opening of the deck. Through the round window on the opposite side I could see Bacolet Bay and the tall coconut trees there. "I feel much better," I said, turning to catch the little bit of sea breeze now coming in.

"The English lady where I work, when she feel faint the doctor tell her to put her head between her knees."

"It's just the heat," I said, "I'll be okay."

I looked down at the tiny waves lapping at the side of the boat. I realized I was thirsty and asked the young man if he knew where I could get a glass of water. He went away, and came back carrying two paper cups. I thanked him and quickly drank the cool water, hoping it might stop the pounding in my head. It was easy to dehydrate. Aunt Tassi was always telling us to drink plenty. I almost said something to him about this, only I didn't feel much like talking. So we sat there on the bench, with neither of us saying a word. I wanted to be alone, but he didn't look like he was going anywhere.

Meanwhile, passengers were pouring onto the boat, looking for seats and places to put their belongings. And before long, the boat started pulling away from the harbor and there were cheers from somewhere below. On land, a few people were standing behind the barrier, waving goodbye to loved ones. I turned to the enormous sea rolled out like a ream of crinkled blue cloth, and I wondered what Aunt Tassi would say when she knew I had gone, and if she would tell the police and they'd start searching around the place. I suddenly felt small and quite afraid.

"How long does it usually take?"

The young man looked up.

"To get to Port of Spain? It depends. This afternoon should be smooth," he said, and sliced the air with his hand. "The wind is low from the east. Seven hours or so." Then, "When I came in this morning it was calm like a pond."

"You sailed here this morning?"

"I had to collect something," he said, and patted his trouser pocket. "For my brother."

He smiled and I saw that his teeth were very white. His skin was dark, a shiny bluish black. He was probably twenty-two or twenty-three and he must have been a good bit over six feet. His hands and feet were huge. Aunt Tassi was always telling us not to talk to people we didn't know. But the thought came easily to me that this man seemed to know a few things about the boat, and the crossing, and there was something about his eyes that made me feel he was okay. And I thought, perhaps, that when we reached Port of Spain he would help me because I had no idea how to get to Tamana Estate where Aunt Sula lived. I didn't even know how to find my way into Port of Spain. I had heard it was a busy place with a lot of cars and a lot of people. What else was there to do?

WILLIAM DANIEL SHAMIEL (he told me his middle name) ordered sandwiches and sweet drinks from a snack bar on the upper level. I wasn't hungry and left most of my bread. I thought about keeping it for later but a woman cleared our plates away and I didn't want to say anything. At one point, he got up from his chair and took a blanket from his bag and spread it out on the floor. He said the blanket was as good as new and if I wanted to I could lie on it and get some rest. I almost said, And what about you. Where will you be? But then I saw a woman sitting with her back against the wall, a young child was sleeping on her. If anything happened, she was right there.

I didn't know I was so tired until I lay down and closed my eyes. The boat was moving slowly and I could smell the fumes from the engine. I turned my head toward the exit; it felt like a rock that might roll away. There wasn't any sea breeze. Children were shouting and running up and down on the deck. Somewhere nearby a man began to play the cuatro and sing a familiar calypso. I don't remember what it was. Then someone picked up a bottle and beat it with a spoon so it went *clangalangalang* and a small crowd I could not see were soon clapping. And then I slept.

In my dream, Aunt Tassi was wandering around the yard in her nightdress. There was snow on the ground and yet the sun was shining. When she went under the house, there was a huge pile of snow and it was stained with blood. She called Violet and Vera and the three of them looked at the blood and started to laugh. Roman came out and he was laughing too. The objects I had found on the beach— a purse, the map of a place I could not recognize before (only now I saw it was England), the falling-apart shoe—were tied to the branches of the frangipani tree like Christmas decorations.

WHEN THE ANNOUNCEMENT came that we were approaching Port of Spain, I was surprised to wake and find William sitting in the same position. I tried to get up and my head started spinning. I sat still for a moment and took a couple deep breaths. I tried again, and the same thing happened.

William said, "Miss, I'll help you. Where you want to go?"

So I told him that I'd like to go to the bow of the boat so I could see the Dragon's Mouth and the Gulf of Paria and the Northern Range Mountains because this is probably what my father would have seen when he came from panning gold near the Essequibo River in British Guiana, and if he could help me I would be very grateful.

"Your father lives in Trinidad?"

"No," I said, "He lives in Southampton. In England."

I took hold of William's arm like it was a rail.

THE NORTHERN RANGE Mountains were clear, like someone had cut them from cardboard and stuck them there. It might have been the early evening light, soft and pinkish, which made the peaks so dark and so green. Some say that the Northern Range Mountains in Trinidad are sad because from their feet to the top of their tips they are covered with dense forest trees, vines, wild pines, tendrils; the sort you might get tangled in. I listened for the cry of monkeys but I could only hear the wind and seawater churning. And then I remembered that the howler monkeys only cry after rain and as far as I knew it hadn't been raining.

Someone said there were dolphins following the boat; I knew that dolphins were a sign of good fortune, but I couldn't see any. The sea was shimmering there and when I looked back it was silvery. There was a light breeze and it made my hot skin cold. I could see the harbor of Port of Spain, and the Port Authority building. The water there was olive green. I just about made out a crowd of people. In the distance, there were a lot of tiny lights. The sky was like a dark blue ceiling and the moon was there but a little bit of its left side had been eaten away.

SEVEN

"My mother is good with herbs and medicines," William said, lifting my bag on to his shoulder. "Tomorrow you can get a drop to the bus station. From Arima you can catch a bus to Tamana."

We were walking slowly toward the large iron gates. It was almost dark and the last passengers were drifting out ahead of us. I thought about saying, Thank you for all you've done, and hurrying away, but instead, I said, "Where is your house?"

"Right there in Laventille." He pointed somewhere up and off to the right.

Laventille. I'd heard about *Laventille.*

He gave me the blanket and I wrapped it around my shoulders and tried to stand upright. My back was hot with pain, especially around the bottom where I imagined it was bruised. At the same time, I was shivering with cold and it was clear to me now that I had a high fever.

We were lucky to find a seat; people were struggling with boxes and large bags and they couldn't find anywhere to put them. I had never been on a tram before, but I had seen pictures of them in the newspapers. I put my head on the glass and watched the road, and it was busy with cars, more cars than I had ever seen in my life, and their bright lights were moving like they were in a hurry to get somewhere.

We soon turned in to a wide street. Here, shops were lit up like

I imagined shops to look in New York: Stephens and Todd, Glendenings, Bata! In large windows there were mannequins dressed in
bright-colored materials. I saw a window filled with only shoes; another full of hats. Two sailors were standing on the corner of the
street watching the tram pass, smoking cigarettes; they looked like
Americans. I had heard there were a lot of them in Trinidad, and
they liked to be with local girls but when they went back home the
girls would never hear from them again. *If Yankees come to Trinidad, Some
of de girls go more than mad, Young girls say they treat dem nice, Make Trinidad like a
paradise . . .*

At the top of the road, we waited while some people got off. I
saw a sign for the Queen's Park Hotel, and a little troop of people
came through the swinging doors, dressed up and laughing as if they
were having a good time. This was another world. Like a dream.

BY THE TIME his brother arrived, William and I had been waiting
at the crossroads for more than an hour. I was sitting on a piece of
broken-down wall when he pulled up in a pickup truck across the
street, his face hidden by a shadow. He waited with the radio playing
loud, the engine running and the lights on. William ran over and
said something to him, and then he called me over. Solomon said
hello as if I was no one in particular. Climbing into the back of the
cabin, I heard him say, "What happen, she sick? Only you could pick
up a sick girl. She better not bring some disease into the house." He
asked William if he had something for him, and William said yes. I
shifted onto the passenger's side, leaned against the cabin, and
closed my eyes. On the road to Laventille, while I was falling in and
out of blackness, their voices were like the tapping of faraway drums.

Solomon parked at the bottom of a hill where the road stopped.
Apparently we all got out and walked up to the wooden house. But I
don't remember this.

EIGHT

THERE WAS VERY LITTLE AIR IN THE HOUSE. WHEN I
opened my eyes to drink water from a tin cup held by a woman with
silver plaited hair and a round face like a dark moon, I had no idea
where I was. My skin was on fire. She said, "Miss, drink the water.
Come, drink the water." I drank as much as I could, and then I vom-
ited it out on the floor. "Oh Lord," she said, wiping my mouth. She
tied back my hair.

It was a relief to roll back onto the mattress there on the floor
and let her, William, and Solomon's mother, Mrs. Edna Shamiel,
undress me. By now my clothes were damp and dirty. Slowly and gently, she sponged down my body. I called out when she reached the
bruises—on my back and on my arms and on my thighs, which were
swollen now and bloody. She said, "What is this, what we have here?"
And then she put me in a big nightdress and covered me with a blanket. I fell into a deep and heavy sleep.

FOR THREE DAYS I tossed and turned and the fever soared. I became delirious. I shouted out the names of the people I had so far
lived my life with. Later when Mrs. Shamiel told me this—I was bawling for Aunt Tassi, Aunt Tassi and I called out for Violet—I said I
didn't know anyone by those names, and she said, "Strange how fever

make you lose your mind," and she gave me a knowing look. At one point William came into the room and I curled into a ball and screamed at him as if he was a demon. He thought that I was dying because my eyes were rolling back inside my head. He asked me about my aunt, he wanted to let her know that I was sick, but I said she was dead. *My mother dead, my father dead, everybody dead.* Then the fever died down and for a few hours they thought I had come through. The pains in my stomach had gone and my head no longer hurt. But that same night the fever came back like a bush fire raging and by morning my eyes were red with faint streaks of blood. My gums bled and my nose bled too and the metal taste of blood made me vomit everything I tried to swallow including water. Not knowing what else to do, William arranged for Solomon to collect Dr. Emmanuel Rodriguez, his employer, from Port of Spain, and bring him up to the house.

I do not remember much about his visit. William and his mother waited outside the room while he thoroughly examined me, lifting away the gown, gently pressing and prodding, here and there. He had smooth and manicured hands and they were cool on my skin. He peered into my eyes with a little torchlight that came from his pocket and he put something on my tongue to push it down so he could see the back of my throat. It was probably yellow fever, he said. I had most of the symptoms. It was spreading fast in Trinidad and Tobago. There was nothing he could do but give me something to bring down the fever. If the symptoms got worse, the chances are it would cause liver failure and then I would die. But he didn't think this would happen. He told Mrs. Shamiel to check my skin for yellow coloring, a sure sign of the disease. He recommended a bath in cold water. "Make sure she drinks plenty of water too. Boil it first. Watch out for mosquitoes. If they come into contact with her and spread it to you, you will soon know about it."

That night my fever dropped, and for the first time in days I woke with an appetite. Mrs. Shamiel brought in a plate of cow heel soup, which I ate. Later, she came with an oil lamp and sat with me and I propped myself up on the old pillow and sipped the sweet tea she had brewed from special healing herbs. Her kindness surprised me; she didn't have any reason to be kind. "You getting better now, child. Today you turn a corner. You'll see." In the shadows, I saw William enter the room and stand behind her like a guard. He didn't say anything, but I could tell that he was relieved. Wearily, I thanked them both for saving my life.

NEXT MORNING, AFTER William and Solomon had gone, and Edna Shamiel had left for the bakery in Woodbrook, where she'd worked for seventeen years, I got up and I wrapped my sheet around me, and slowly made my way around the little wooden house. It was very small and the floor was thin and broken in places. There were two bedrooms and both had mattresses. There was a kitchen with a coal pot and a basin, a little larder; plates and pots and cutlery were stacked here. Just off the kitchen was a table and four chairs. It was hardly big enough to call a dining room. I wandered outside onto the tiny veranda where there were two wooden chairs with cushions and a little stand and a rubber plant. I sat down. Over the door was a framed picture of the Virgin Mary; she was surrounded by a golden, hazy light.

That morning, a breeze blew until around noon and kept me cool. My fever had definitely gone. But I was exhausted. Mrs. Shamiel had left a jug of lime juice on a tray in the kitchen, and there was a plate of bread and cheese. I ate a little, and then I went back outside, laid cushions on the floor and slept. In the late afternoon, I woke in time to see her climbing up the track, her bowlegs bending under the strain of her heavy frame.

"You're up!" she said. "What did I tell you. Just now you'll be feeling exactly like yourself."

So began my slow recovery.

IT WAS COOLEST on the porch, shaded by the eaves. From there I could look out on the patched-up houses below with their galvanized rooftops, right down the hill where the road stopped and where Solomon parked his truck. And every day I watched the sun light up that hill. At times I got strangely hot, took a bucket of water, stood outside, and poured it over my head. People walked up or down the mud track. When heavy rains came, the path became slippery and treacherous and everyone used another route, which was paved and narrow. No one passed the house, because it was at the end of the road. I saw neighbors as they made their way, looking up at where I was perched on the veranda. I felt far away from anyone and everyone. There were little brick steps leading up to the porch and a cluster of banana trees grew at the bottom of them. I watched them flower and their figs grow big enough to eat.

At the back, there was a breadfruit tree. It wasn't as big as Aunt Tassi's tree but it had the same shape and the same thick leaves. They say the best breadfruit comes from Tobago, but when Mrs. Shamiel baked one in her coal pot, I thought it as sweet as any I'd ever tasted.

"I could eat mine all over again," I said, when I put down my fork.

"Nothing like Tobago breadfruit, though," she said. "When you go again, bring one for me and we can test it out."

MRS. SHAMIEL DIDN'T seem to mind that I was there in her house all day doing nothing. She told me to take things easy, and when I was well enough we would talk about where I was going and what I was doing. She never asked me about the state I was in the night I came to her house, but I imagined that she knew more than she let on.

One day she said, "Whatever trouble you had is over now."

While sitting on the floor picking through a tray of rice, she told me that my arrival in her home was a blessing because she could see that William, her youngest son, was very fond of me.

"The minute he saw you, he knew there was something special about you. He say so that night he bring you here." She was smiling, proud. "He is a good man and he wouldn't harm anyone or anything. Not even an ant." She looked up. "He like you a lot."

"I like him too," I said. "If it wasn't for him, I don't know what would have happened to me. I might be dead."

"All the girls prefer Solomon, you see." She narrowed her eyes. "Because Solomon is good-looking. But he only live for money, like his father."

"There's a lot of people like that. Money is their god."

"Right now his father sitting in jail in Port of Spain serving life for killing a man in a brawl. And you know why? He owe the man money and the man tell him so. Just like the day does catch the moon, he get caught." She shook her head. "Solomon make plenty money with his truck, and yet William had to pay him to bring Dr. Rodriguez here. He have William running about the place. Like when he met you, William only in Tobago for Solomon. I doubt William know what business he doing. Solomon's right hand don't know what his left hand doing."

Then she turned to the window where the last rays of sunlight were trickling in. "He is my son and I love him, but if he wasn't my son I not sure I would like him."

EVERY EVENING, THREE of us, William, Mrs. Shamiel, and I, ate dinner around the small wooden table, which was covered with a plastic tablecloth patterned with apples and pears. It was strange that this pattern had found its way into a house in Laventille where, chances are, none of the people in it would ever taste apples and pears. And while we ate, Mrs. Shamiel talked about her good friend Ruby who worked on the cake counter, and she talked about her new boss, Mr. Abraham; she didn't like him one bit. Or she talked about her customers; those that never had money, those that spoke down to her, those she'd known for years. And once she had finished, she'd say, "So William, what happen in that madhouse today?" And he would always look across at me and I knew that he was shy.

William had worked for the Rodriguez family for six years. He managed the yard, looked after the flowers and plants and fruit trees, cut the lawn, and trimmed all the hedges and borders. He had a little plot where he grew pineapples. Now and then he brought them home; the family didn't seem to mind.

I heard about a small boy called Joe who bit his younger sister so hard the baby had to have a tetanus injection. Mrs. Shamiel said he was lucky that his father was a doctor; he had the needle right there. Joe took William's tools and hid them in the yard. He often played inside the toolshed, even though he wasn't allowed. She thought William should tell the boy something. "These children play you like a pipe," she said. "Nobody seems to discipline them."

William told us how this same baby, Consuella, pushed her head through the bars of the cot and got it stuck there, and how he had to bring a little saw and cut her free. "She turn purple," he said. "She nearly die. And the whole time the mother only standing with her face to the wall sobbing like the child already dead." He didn't know how long Helen Rodriguez would last in Trinidad when she was afraid of everything from flies to hot pepper. Mrs. Shamiel said, "She 'fraid of the sea, she 'fraid of frogs, she was even afraid of Brigid, the maid! You wonder how she ends up in Trinidad. Her husband is a good-looking man, he could have had anyone he liked. You remember him," she said, "the doctor."

William said that Dr. Rodriguez had asked about me more than once. "I tell him you feel much better. He say he very glad to hear it."

SOLOMON ALWAYS CAME home late and sometimes he brought a friend, and they sat on the porch and drank rum in the dark. If they made a lot of noise Mrs. Shamiel would get up and go outside and speak to them. She was not scared of Solomon and he knew it. He seemed to have a lot of friends and they had unusual names: Cricket, Long, Red Boy, Cobeaux, Tiny, Nathaniel. He hardly spoke to me, and sometimes when he did, I felt uncomfortable.

"So where exactly are you from, Celia?" he said one evening, when he came home. We were sitting at the table and had just finished eating dinner. "William say you have family in England?"

"Yes," I said.

"And your aunt live in an estate right here in Trinidad."

"Yes, at Tamana."

"I have a friend up there who work in Four Roads. Estate life is a sweet life, you know. All those fruits and provisions. Some of them pay real well."

I didn't know what to say.

"Board and food is taken care of."

Mrs. Shamiel got up from the table, and in a lighthearted way, said, "Solomon, why are you minding the girl business? Go inside and fix up yourself. You look like you need a bath."

Next day, he brought home a bucket of large white eggs which he put in the sink at the back of the house. No one mentioned them, and I forgot, until one afternoon soon after, when I heard some strange clacking, cracking noises. I ran outside to find baby alligators bursting out of the eggs. Some of them were as long as my fingers, their jaws were snapping and their legs were wriggling, trying to climb out of the broken shells. Their skin was smooth and shiny, and more like the skin of a snake. Something about the way they crawled over each other frightened me.

I quickly took a piece of wood and covered up the sink. When Solomon came home, in front of his mother, I told him what had happened. He narrowed his eyes at me, and then went outside; Mrs. Shamiel followed him.

"How could you bring these things here?" she said, her voice sharp.

"I'm going to grow them and sell them to the taxidermist. They don't have to get big to make a profit."

"If you want to breed alligators, get yourself an apartment near the zoo."

Next day, the alligators were gone.

NINE

ONCE I WAS WELL, I STARTED THINKING ABOUT WHAT I should do. It was okay to stay in Laventille for free when I was sick, but not now. Solomon made that clear when, to me and only me, he referred to the house as "Hotel Shamiel."

When I left Black Rock, I had wanted to go straight to the estate where Aunt Sula lived. I knew the estate was called Tamana, and I knew she worked for Joseph Carr Brown. William said it would take about a day to get there by bus. But when to go? I wanted to see Aunt Sula, yet at the same time, I didn't want to have to explain myself to her. Right now, William said, passing through the El Quemado road to Tamana was difficult; last week a heavy landslide had brought down half the hill. I would have to wait until the road was clear.

At night, Roman came into my dreams. We were always under the house, and the goats were sitting right there by the steps. He took off his clothes and showed himself to me. Then he told me to take off my clothes and I did. My body was made of short brown and white feathers, like chicken feathers. He grabbed handfuls of them and threw them all over the yard, and I chased after them, trying to stuff them back into my clothes. I woke in a cold sweat.

.   .   .

SOME DAYS, WHEN I thought a lot about my life, I felt as though
my head would burst. From the porch, I watched the sunlight flicker
on the rooftops below—it made sharp, bright silver flashes—and I
tried hard to understand why things happened in the way they had.
I always came back to the same place: there were no answers. And I
realized, too, that I had nothing. It was like living in a world where
there was only heat and the bright, white light that makes that kind of
heat. There was no shade, nowhere to rest, nowhere that the sun was
not. This was how it felt to have nothing. And in Laventille, standing
back from my life and looking at it as if it belonged to someone else,
someone I would pity, not someone I would envy, I imagined it could
always be this way. And one morning, when the house was empty, this
idea of having nothing made me feel terrible enough to want to die,
to take my own life. And that's when I got down on my knees before
the Virgin Mary and prayed with all my heart. I knew that it would
take a miracle.

NEXT DAY, AROUND four o'clock, I was woken from a light sleep
by the sound of a car. I got up and looked down the hill. A blue car
was parked where Solomon usually left his truck. I saw William get
out and then a white man got out, too. William waved and I waved
back. Who was with him? A visitor? For a moment, I thought he
might be a policeman, but then I realized he wasn't wearing a uniform. I ran inside and freshened my face with water; I straightened
and smoothed my thin cotton dress.

WILLIAM LED DR. Emmanuel Rodriguez onto the porch. I recognized him, now. He was not tall and he was not short. His dark
hair was pushed back from his tanned, narrow face. He wore navy
trousers and a cream shirt.

"Well," he said, "she certainly looks better than the last time I saw her."

William looked shy and proud at the same time, as if my good health was only because of him, which in some ways it was.

The doctor put down his bag. "Are you feeling like yourself again? No fever or sickness?"

"Yes, sir, thank you. I feel like myself." This was almost true.

"Excellent," he said, and rocked a little on his heels. "William said you were better, but I wanted to make sure." He looked around the place; the cushions on the floor where I had been sleeping, my sheet dropped there. "He's told me a bit about you. He said you come from Tobago. You have an aunt here in Trinidad, is that right?"

"Yes, sir."

"And now you wish to find work in Port of Spain?"

"I'm not sure yet, sir. I'm going to visit my aunt in the country." My voice sounded small, like a child speaking.

William offered Dr. Emmanuel Rodriguez a chair. He preferred to stand; he wasn't staying long.

"Actually, Celia," he said, and glanced at William, "my reason for coming here today isn't entirely selfless; I want to ask a favor of you."

I wondered what "favor" I could possibly do for *him*.

I looked over at William, who was smiling; I was sure he knew what was coming.

"Our maid left in a hurry this morning, and we're pretty desperate. My wife needs help with the children. At least until we find someone else. Is that something you might be interested in?" He added, "I'll pay you good rates."

I must have looked blank as a board, because he then said, "Don't make up your mind now. Why don't you come to the house tomorrow? I can show you around. You can meet my wife and the

children. They're a little noisy but mostly well behaved." He smiled.
"And we can arrange for you to see your aunt very soon."

I found myself nodding.

"I'm sure it's a lot to think about." Then, to William, "You can
bring her with you in the morning, William."

"Yes, sir," William said, looking pleased.

As soon as Dr. Emmanuel Rodriguez had left, I washed my blue
dress and hung it on the line at the back of the house and when it was
dry I used the iron to press it flat. Mrs. Shamiel said she never saw
anyone iron like me, with so much fingers and thumbs, and why
didn't I let her do it. I said I needed the practice because someday
very soon I might be ironing a lot! That night I wrapped up my hair
so it was smooth when I woke and unpinned it. I hardly slept. It
seemed to me, my miracle had come.

"You put on a little weight," William said, his face lit when I
walked into the kitchen early that morning. Mrs. Shamiel said, "It's a
good thing. You look well." Then, "Mind you don't look too well or
the English madam won't want you in the house."

In that pale morning light, when everything looked soft,
William and I walked together down through the lower part of Laventille, past the shabby little houses where people were moving around
inside. Some of them were washing right there in their yards with a
bucket and soap. Stray dogs were barking. I could hear a radio playing. We walked down the track to where the taxis pulled up near a
small row of huts that sold fruits and vegetables. William usually took
the bus, but today, because I was traveling with him, he decided to
take a taxi. While waiting, I looked back up the road at the Shamiel

house. It was teetering on the hillside with all the other houses that looked like they might fall down.

The Savannah seemed huge as we drove around it. There were men dressed in white uniforms riding horses across the grass. The hills behind were blue-green and the Poui trees had dropped their pink blossom so it lay like a carpet around them. I saw a young woman dressed up in a striped skirt with matching blouse and high heels. She was walking into a building I thought I recognized. The sign above the entrance read QUEEN'S PARK HOTEL, and I remembered it from the night I arrived. There was a big red building, and then there was a square white house like a palace, and a white and black house that made me think of a wedding cake, with fancy railings like icing. On the corner, I saw a castle straight out of a fairy-tale book. Then we turned away from the Savannah, and into a small street lined with short trees; their thick branches grew above us like clasped hands and made the road into a tunnel.

Soon there were tall palm trees, and there were large houses on either side of the quiet road. The houses had a lot of space around them and some of them had fences and gates so I couldn't see inside them so well. I wondered what kinds of people lived there. People with a lot of money, I thought.

Then William said, "Right here."

TEN

THE RODRIGUEZ HOME WAS A LARGE AND PALE GREEN colonial house. The fretwork and shutters and railings were a bright white. Casuarina trees lined the wide driveway that curved in front of a veranda with two sets of stairs leading up to the front door, the formal entrance of the house. On either side of the entrance there were two huge pots with white flowers, and hanging from the eaves were ferns, round and full. The front garden was very neat and tidy; I had never seen a garden like it. There were red and orange flowers shooting up like flames, and a wall of bougainvillea with purple and pink flowers. Everything looked alive. The grass was cropped short and all the edges were razor sharp. I followed William around the front of the house and to where he said there was a servants' entrance.

"You can come this way if you like." Dr. Emmanuel Rodriguez was looking over the rail of the veranda. "No need to go around." A small boy was holding on to his legs.

William said, "Yes, sir."

Dr. Emmanuel Rodriguez said something like "Welcome to our home." William looked happy, and I smiled at the doctor. Then I smiled at the boy, but he ran away into the house.

"That's Joe," Dr. Emmanuel Rodriguez said. Then, "Come," and he walked across the veranda and into the dining room, the table of which was right there: a large mahogany table with six chairs and feet like brass claws. My shoes sounded heavy on the wooden floor. I looked at the pictures on the wall: there were flowers in a glass vase, and in another, a white lady in a long dress; I wondered who she was. There was a gold light shaped like an upside-down umbrella with glittering drops like diamonds hanging down from it, and on the opposite wall from the paintings were two large brass plates, and a tall drinks cabinet. It was dark and cool in the dining room and there was no need for a ceiling fan even though the doctor switched it on. I looked behind me. William had gone.

He led me into a sitting room which had a modern sofa and a circular rug in the middle of the floor. There were shelves with ornaments and small framed photographs. "Celia, please sit down," he said, and I did. Through the shutters I could see part of a large rear garden; the sun was shining on it. Then he asked if I could read and I said, "Yes, of course, sir." From the pocket of his starched white shirt he brought out a piece of paper, and he leaned over and gave it to me and I caught the fresh smell of Bay Rum in his hair. On the piece of paper was a list of duties and tasks. There was nothing on the list I could not do. Again I said, "Yes."

"Do you like children?"

"Yes, sir, I used to care for my twin cousins."

"Good. William has said very nice things about you. Usually we would need a reference, and perhaps that's something we can do when you have settled in. You could get a reference, presumably?"

I nodded.

"Your room is downstairs. I can show you if you like." Then he laughed. "I'm hoping you will take the job? My wife is beside herself. Since Brigid left six months ago, we've been unlucky finding a replacement; the last girl was useless. You'll meet Mrs. Rodriguez in a moment; she's bathing Consuella."

THE ROOM WHERE I was to sleep and spend my free time ("You will have a fair amount of free time") was at the back of the house. It had a single bed and a wardrobe, and it also had its own bathroom. "You have running water." Dr. Emmanuel Rodriguez twisted the metal tap on the little sink and clear water gushed out. The window was next to the bed; it had jalousies and flowery curtains. There was a chest of drawers. When he opened the top drawer, I saw that there were clothes inside.

"The girl will probably be coming back for these things," he said. "For now, we can put them in a box and leave them out in the toolshed. She left in a little bit of a hurry."

The room had its own door with access to the yard, which meant that it was slightly separate from the house. I had never had my own room before, far less a bathroom and a proper entrance. It was like my own house.

"This is where Brigid often used to sit in the afternoon," he said, and showed me a wooden bench on the other side of the door. "I am sure you will be comfortable here."

There was a full view of the garden. I could see a lot of different trees: lime, orange, mango, five finger, and guava. I had never seen so many different fruit trees in one yard before. The grass went on and on, like in a field.

I DON'T KNOW how long Helen Rodriguez had been standing in the doorway of the kitchen when I eventually realized she was there but when I looked around and saw her I was taken aback. Then Dr. Emmanuel Rodriguez saw her too.

"Helen," he said, and walked quickly over to where she was leaning against the outside sink. He took the baby from her.

I don't know what I expected her to look like. Her hair was blond and pinned back from her face. She had small eyes and they fluttered a lot in the sun. Her skin was very pale and freckled. She looked as though she came from another world, as though she shouldn't live in the tropics at all. Through her white dressing gown, I could see her chest bones and her hip bones. She didn't seem to have any breasts; I wondered how she fed her baby.

"This is Celia. She is going to start at once, so there's no need to fret." His voice was clipped and yet warm.

Then to me, holding the baby up: "This is Consuella and she's only one year old, aren't you, Consuella." The baby was long, her hair was light and soft. I looked into her delicate face and smiled.

In an English accent Helen Rodriguez said, "Do you have your things, or do you need to go to Laventille to collect them from the house?"

I looked at her husband.

"I will ask William to go with her so she can move in here this afternoon."

She didn't say anything.

"You can manage until then, can't you?" Now he sounded a bit impatient.

She nodded, and stepped back into the shade of the kitchen from where there were sounds of someone handling pans or pots. I wondered who was there. I still hadn't seen inside the kitchen. Her husband gave me the baby and she started to cry at once. I said, "Consuella, I am Celia," and I rocked her in my arms in the way I had seen women in Black Rock comfort their babies and I was surprised at how quickly she stopped crying. For a moment they watched from the kitchen and I was glad they had seen this happen. They disappeared inside the dark house.

I took the baby away from the direct sunlight and into the shade that came from the eaves of my room. I sat on the bench and looked up the garden, and I turned her little body around so that she could look at the garden as well.

"Consuella," I said, "I am going to be looking after you and your brother. I hope we can be friends."

When William appeared in front of me, he looked surprised. He said, "You start the job already?"

I WAS SITTING on the bench drinking a cup of water when Helen Rodriguez came to my room that afternoon. William and I had just returned from collecting my things in Laventille and I was putting them away. When I saw her I got up at once. She was still wearing her dressing gown, and the shadows from the lime tree leaves made patterns on it. She looked brighter than before, as if she had put on makeup.

"Please make the room your own. We want you to be comfortable." She smiled in an awkward way. "Put pictures on the wall, whatever you like."

I thought how much her eyes moved around when she spoke. They were pale like the river where I nearly drowned. I said "Thank you," even though I did not have any pictures.

"I have an old radio you can use. We pick up BBC World Service and there's a rather good local channel with religious music which you might enjoy."

She offered me citronella candles and special coils to burn to keep away mosquitoes. She knew that I'd been sick.

"My husband thought you might die. He said that when someone is about to die they have a certain kind of look. Something in the eyes of the person. You didn't have it, but he thought it was coming. You were very lucky."

I was surprised when she said this. I thought a doctor's practices were supposed to be confidential, and also, I never for one moment believed that I might *die* in Laventille. Underneath the house in Black Rock, yes, but not in Laventille.

"Yes," I said.

She said it was good to light candles, even citronella candles, because it kept the demons away and reminded us of the light from which we came. Trinidad was full of ritual and obeah and sacrifice, which is why she always carried a string of rosary beads. She opened her hand and there they were.

"My sister had them blessed by the pope in Rome," she said, holding up the little beads. "She mailed them from London and they arrived a day before Consuella was born." She worried for her children and prayed for them every day, living in this place. She hoped I would take good care of them.

"To be honest," she said, "when I saw your necklace, I put away any doubts I might have had about employing you. My husband says I worry too much about these things, but I always say, better to be safe than sorry. The pendant is pretty."

I felt for Aunt Sula's gold cross. "Thank you."

"One day Brigid put a donkey's eye in the pram. I can't have that sort of superstition in this house. Apart from anything else, Consuella might have put it in her mouth and choked."

I didn't tell her that I knew about the smooth and round seed that looked like a donkey's eye, that it was sometimes placed among the blankets of a newborn to keep the baby safe from evil spirits, and that if I had been Brigid I might have done the same thing. And I didn't tell her about the piece of black rock from Mrs. Jeremiah that I kept under my pillow.

SHE TOOK ME upstairs into her large, dark, and cool bedroom where a beautiful carved mahogany bed was still unmade from her afternoon sleep and a mosquito net was hanging over it. There was a black-and-white photograph of Helen Rodriguez on the wall. Her pale shoulders were bare and her eyes seemed to say, I like you very much. "A present to my husband soon after we got engaged."

The wooden shutters were closed and the ceiling fan was spinning slowly. There were clothes scattered about on the floor. They looked like her underclothes; they were silky and light colored. "I'm not the tidiest person in the world," she said. Her dressing table was covered with bottles and brushes and a little dainty seat was pulled out. There were beads strung across the middle mirror and a scarf draped on the smaller mirror, to the right. A drawer was open; inside I saw lipsticks and rouge and powder. She picked up a large glass bottle.

"Two years ago I brought in a priest to bless the house. This is a container of holy water, should you ever need it for the children." She said this in a serious way and I wondered why the children would ever need holy water. "If anything should happen, you can sprinkle it on them. Like they do in church."

In a small attached room was Consuella's brand-new cot and a cupboard filled with her tiny clothes, perfectly ironed and folded. There was another cupboard with only toys. Some of them looked expensive and I could tell that many had come from overseas. Joe's bedroom was at the end of the passageway. It was painted his favorite color, she said, light blue. His father had built him a large airplane and hung it from the ceiling. I told Helen Rodriguez that it looked real and the blue looked like sky.

"If you traveled on a proper airplane you would never say that," she said, and I was sorry I had said anything.

Then, "My husband is good with his hands. His hands can build and they can heal. You know that for yourself."

"Yes, madam."

"He qualified as a surgeon, too; he carries out operations at the hospital."

I didn't know why she told me this, perhaps to make him sound even more important.

There were two beds. When the boy felt afraid of the dark—"he often has terrible dreams"—his mother slept in the other bed. "Joe has a strong character," she said, "just like his father. He needs a lot of understanding and attention. I hope you'll get along."

AFTER SHE HAD bathed and dressed and I had put away my things, we walked together to Cipriani Boulevard to collect Joe from school. She was wearing a shift dress with a collar, and her slip-on shoes had little heels. She looked attractive and delicate, but like a flower that might blow away in a strong wind. I was glad to walk beside her, pushing the navy pram with Consuella, and I noticed that people looked at us as we walked along the edge of the small park. There were swings and a colorful merry-go-round and children were playing there. And some of the people we saw were friendly and they said good afternoon. As we passed these grand houses, I found myself wanting to walk slowly so that I could look inside them.

It did not take long to reach the school. Joe was waiting outside the gates. At first he didn't say anything; then his mother told him to say good afternoon to Celia, and he did.

THAT NIGHT I closed the door to my room. I turned off the light and lay on my bed. I could make out the dark oblong of my cupboard, like an upright coffin. Outside, a toad was making a lot of noise. I could hear crickets, too. All over this island, I thought, there are toads and crickets making noise. And then I thought about the toads and crickets in Black Rock. And then I decided not to think about Black Rock, and went to sleep.

NEXT DAY, WHEN Helen Rodriguez suggested that I wear the last maid's uniform, I lied and said it wasn't in the drawer where she'd left her things. I didn't tell her that I had seen a dress which might have been a uniform among her old clothes but it was shabby and stained and I didn't want to wear it. I was surprised when she said she would "run one up right now," on her Singer sewing machine.

I stood in her sewing room with my arms up and out, watching her down on her bare knees on the wooden floor while measuring and pinning my hem. If one month ago someone had told me that I'd be working in a house in St. Clair, Port of Spain, Trinidad, and that the English madam of the house would be sewing me a new dress, I wouldn't have believed them. The material was a small yellow and white check and there was just enough, and because I was tall, it was a modern knee-length fit. It seemed a shame to use it only for working in the house. When Dr. Emmanuel Rodriguez came home from surgery that afternoon, he said my uniform looked "perfect," like it was made for me. I said it was.

MARVA CAME IN every day apart from Sunday. She lived in nearby St. James, so if there was an emergency, she said, as there was just the other day when Joe fell down the front steps and "crack his head like an egg" and the girl was *as usual* nowhere in sight, they could call on her. The people next door to where Marva lived had a telephone. Sometimes she wished she could move away and then no one would bother her. Or better still, she said, migrate to New York. She had always wanted to go to New York. "New York has so many people you could get lost there. You see people in a crowd. No one would remember you. Not like here where everybody know your business."

I didn't ask her for it, but all the same, Marva gave me a timetable of her chores. She started work at 6:30 a.m. She made breakfast for 7:30, and then she spent the rest of the morning cooking lunch. After lunch she washed the dishes. Most days, if she was lucky, she left the house at 2:00 p.m. Once a week she went to the market and bought vegetables and fruits. Helen Rodriguez ordered groceries on a Thursday and they were delivered to the house on Saturdays. William's brother Solomon brought them. "Sometimes Solomon brings so many bags you'd think Mrs. Rodriguez was feeding the whole of Port of Spain. But other times they deliver hardly anything at all. As if she forget everything she need when she telephone the order. That make my job difficult." Marva said this in such a miserable way, I wondered why she didn't find another job somewhere else.

"I really don't have time to get into all the things they have going on in this house," she said, on my first day. And when I said, "What things?" she said, "I have my own troubles but no one ever seem to think about that." She shuffled around the kitchen in a cotton dress and a green apron. She wore a green hat with a little peak; it made me think of a nurse's hat. But nurses were supposed to be kind, and from what I could tell there was nothing kind about her. William said Marva looked as if she was all day sucking a lime. "She not really sour. Marva just take a little time to know you."

ELEVEN

I SOON GOT INTO A ROUTINE. I WAS UP AT DAWN AND IF I hadn't laid the table the night before, then I did it first thing. I put juice, cereal, bread, jams, and cheese on the table. When breakfast was over I cleared the plates and gave them to Marva. I polished brass or dusted. I made up the beds and swept the floors. By lunchtime the floors were mopped and the table was laid once again. I served lunch. Then I cleared the table when lunch was over. There were many dishes and plates to clear. After lunch the house was quiet and still. Before returning to work, Dr. Emmanuel Rodriguez sometimes rested with his wife, or he went into his office and read. Sometimes I saw him reading or writing at his desk. When the baby was sleeping (she did not always like to sleep), and if William did not sit with me outside, I went into my room and lay down on my narrow bed. The yard was silent and it was also very hot. It felt good to close my eyes and drift away, as if the world was dripping with heat and I was melting into it.

In the afternoon, when Consuella woke, I dressed and fed her and put her in the pram. Then I took her to Cipriani Boulevard and met Joe outside the school gates. We walked up as far as the White House or up to Stollmeyer's Castle on the corner. White House and Stollmeyer's Castle. I liked the way their names sounded. And I liked the way the Savannah looked, with its large trees in the golden evening light and the people sitting on benches underneath them. On the way back we stopped off at the store and I bought Joe a Popsicle or a press (a cup of shaved ice with syrup) or a chocolate bar with the six cents his mother had given me. Supper was at seven. Then, after supper, I went upstairs and put the children to bed. It was usually late when I went into my room and listened to music on the old radio.

Every Sunday, the Rodriguez family went to the morning service at Our Lady's Church in Maraval. While they were gone, I washed my clothes and hung them out. I dusted and mopped inside my room. Then I set my hair, scrubbed my fingernails, soaked my feet in a bowl with lime, and scraped away the dead, hard skin. I rubbed cocoa butter into my hands, elbows, and knees. In the afternoons, I put on my blue dress and made my way across the Savannah to the Botanical Gardens. Here, there were all kinds of trees; some were enormous and strong with thick trunks, like the African pine, or the silk cotton tree, and the banyan with its big sad head, and if I felt like it I sat underneath one of them. But there were fine trees, too, like the star apple tree, and the weeping ficus, and one I never knew the name of that had pink flowers like powder puffs. Near the road, in front of the Governor's House, a brass band played the kind of tunes that made you feel happy and sad at the same time: "Take Me Back to Georgia" and "Under the Moonlight" and "Don't Leave, My Love."

At the end of the day, I went to the Anglican church on the west side of the Savannah. The church was always full and the people there were well dressed; a lot of them looked like me. There was a statue of Jesus in the corner, which I liked. His robe was open and inside it you could see a red, bright heart with rays of light fanning out. When the service was over, the old priest stood at the door and said goodbye, as if each one of us mattered to him a great deal.

THOSE EARLY DAYS in the Rodriguez house passed smoothly, but for one thing. Joe would not let me dress him for school. When I served juice he pushed his glass away. If I put food on his plate he wouldn't eat. He shoved his bowl or plate across the table, shook his head, and tightened up his mouth. He refused to let me walk him to school, so his father had to take him before he left for work, which meant arriving before anyone else. I collected him at the school gates (with this he had no choice) but he did not speak to me; to his baby sister, yes. I watched him leaning and cooing and whispering into Consuella's pram. Apart from this, our afternoon walk was made in silence. When we reached the store he pointed at whatever he wanted and I paid for it. No words were exchanged between us. It was uncomfortable.

He refused to let me bathe him, so his mother had to stop whatever she was doing and come upstairs. At first she made fun of him. She joked and said, "Come on, come on, my little mule." She tried to persuade him that I was a good person and that he could trust me, taking him to one side, speaking softly. "Celia is here to help. Celia wants to be your friend. Celia is from Tobago, you liked Tobago when you went there with Daddy and me." I heard her say, "Celia is not like Brigid, she's much nicer than Brigid." Dr. Emmanuel Rodriguez was surprised. More than once he told Joe to "cut out this nonsense" and for a little while he was better but it did not last long. Dr. Emmanuel Rodriguez threatened him with punishment. One day, he took off his belt to beat him and Joe ran upstairs and hid. Helen Rodriguez said a strap was not the answer. Seemed to me it didn't matter what they said or did, Joe's mind was made up.

A change in his behavior came only after a very disturbing event and it happened after only one month of my working in the house. One evening, I went into the upstairs bathroom and saw Joe there brushing his teeth and he turned around and with his blue eyes narrow like two slits spat at me—in my face—and hissed "nigger." Without thinking I grabbed his thick dark hair and held him firmly and took a mouthful of water from the glass I was carrying and spat right back at him. In shock, he opened his mouth wide and then began to scream. I tried to hush him but he ran to the other side of the room and pressed his back flat into the wall. I was sure the whole street could hear him. His mother came rushing in, wearing only her bed-clothes, and she looked almost afraid of me, and she held her son as though he was in danger. Her frightened face was white and long.

In a calm voice I did not recognize I said, "Before you say anything to me, ask your son what he did," and I ran from the room and down the steps into the yard and the darkness, and I ran up to the end of it, and I put my back against the toolshed, and slid to the ground wondering what would come of this event.

NEXT MORNING, WILLIAM arrived early. Everyone was still asleep. He sat beside me on the bench where I was watching the sun rising, lighting up the yard. I hadn't slept well. When I told him what had happened, he shook his head. "There's nothing worse in the world than a child spitting."

I said, "There are plenty worse things in this world."

AFTER BREAKFAST, DR. Emmanuel Rodriguez called me to his study. I sat down opposite him, across from his large desk. Joe had told him about the incident, he said.

"I can only apologize for this appalling behavior." He was looking straight at me and his tone was serious. "It was more than ungracious. It was rude and it will never happen again."

I wondered exactly what Joe had said to him. Perhaps, the truth. Dr. Emmanuel Rodriguez hoped that I would accept his apology, and not for one minute think of leaving. "Please give us another chance.

My wife feels very badly about it. She would like you to know that she is also very sorry."

When he'd finished, I was so relieved I could have dropped right there on the ground.

"Will you accept my apology, please, Celia?"

"Yes, sir," I said.

"You've fitted in so well. We've all grown fond of you. I'm certain these problems with Joe are left over from Brigid." Then, "So will you stay with us?"

"Yes, sir."

He got up from his chair. "Excellent."

At that moment, I decided that I liked Dr. Emmanuel Rodriguez. His eyes were a greenish brown; the color of grass in need of rain.

LATER THAT SAME day, I put a dollar from my first month's salary into the pocket of my blue dress and I set off in the hot sun, walking in the direction of town, not quite knowing where I was going but following William's instructions, the list of places that he said I should look out for.

Before long I found myself crossing a busy road. It was very hot and the sun beat down on my head, and as I walked down Frederick Street I wished that I had brought an umbrella. Marva always walked with an umbrella. Soon there was a lot going on, people were bustling in and around the shops—the little shops and the department stores with big windows. I wandered into Stephen's, and up the steps to the ladies' department where I found a pink dress with a petticoat. I went to a mirror and held it up. A shop assistant watched me like I had crawled out of a drain so I didn't try it on.

In Charlotte Street, loud calypso music was pouring out of a bar on the corner called The Black Hat. There were a lot of white people around. I saw a blond woman with pointed shoes and pointed breasts in a lime green dress. She was holding the hands of two small blond children. They were walking into a travel agency, Eastern Credit Union Travel, and above it was a billboard with an enormous white airplane: BOAC: LONDON! NEW YORK! WE'LL TAKE YOU THERE! I couldn't imagine picking somewhere and flying there just like that.

But it wasn't all like this: outside the general post office, a woman was squatting, and where her hands should have been there were strips of pale flesh like roots from a tree sprouting from her wrists, trailing on the dirty ground. She raised her arms and these thick tendrils of skin hung in the air. They made me think of the mangrove swamps near Black Rock. She was sitting on newspaper and there was a big yellow stain on one side that I knew was her urine. She wasn't old and she wasn't young. She looked at me in a strange way, and I realized she wanted money. People were going in and out of the post office as if she wasn't there.

"Miss, give me a little something. Look meh hands. I beg you. God will bless you." Her voice was small and crackly. "Everybody need a blessing."

"I don't have any money," I said.

The telegram I mailed to Aunt Tassi in Black Rock read: TO INFORM YOU THAT I'M WELL AND SAFE. I'M NOT COMING BACK. CELIA.

TWELVE

THOSE FIRST SIX MONTHS WORKING IN THE RODRIGUEZ household were the happiest I had known. Dr. Emmanuel Rodriguez said I carried out my chores and responsibilities with "efficiency and maturity." I didn't mind working hard; it stopped me from thinking about things. At the end of each day I was tired and used up and ready to sleep. When anyone asked me to do anything I said, yes sir, or yes madam, nothing was too much trouble. I worked every weekend. There was nowhere else I wanted to go, but more than that, I was glad of the extra money, every cent of which I saved in an old milk tin under my bed.

Perhaps because Joe Rodriguez was now afraid of me, perhaps because he saw that there would never be a winner in this game, that at very best, I might leave the Rodriguez household and someone else would come along in my place, yet another girl, not Brigid, because— as his mother told him—Brigid was *never* coming back, but another girl (maybe as hopeless as the last one) that he would have to get used to all over again, he decided at last to accept me.

I knew that Helen Rodriguez was pleased, because she told me so. I was more help to her than she had imagined. Like on that day when we were driving from the grocery and she was about to pull into Roberts Street, in Woodbrook, and I saw a little boy escape from his mother who was busy talking to somebody, and run out into the road. I called out, "Madam, stop!" She slammed her foot on the brakes and the child stopped right there, his eyes wide and frightened. When his mother came running, Helen Rodriguez put her hands up to her face. "Thank God you saw him, Celia." And another day, when she was buying material for a new dress in Glendenings, and she was flustered and hot, she dropped a ten-dollar note on the floor. "Madam, look," I said, and picked up the money.

"You're not just another pair of hands, you're another pair of eyes."

I liked to go with her on these short trips. I liked going out in the car. While she drove, she often talked about England. She told me that she came from a beautiful village in a county called Warwickshire. At college, she trained to be a schoolteacher. If she hadn't met Dr. Emmanuel Rodriguez, when he was studying at the nearby university, she might still be in England, teaching. But then, that's what true love is, she said that day, a kind of sacrifice.

"In the same way that God gave His Son as a testimony of His love for His children. When you love someone you give things up." Not that she would ever compare her love for her husband with the love of God!

Helen Rodriguez longed to go back to England. She missed her sister who still lived in the town where they had grown up. They were very close, she said. At the same time, they were quite different. Isobel was strong and capable, running the farm where she lived with her husband and four children. "I hardly know my nieces and nephews. And they don't know Consuella. They've never even seen her."

She talked about the changing seasons. When leaves turned yellow, red, orange, and fell from the trees. And winter, when snow made a thick white blanket and water froze so hard you could walk on lakes and ponds and, sometimes, rivers, too. "Of course it gets very cold, but the snow is so beautiful and children love it." She tried to describe her favorite spring flowers. "They're yellow and they have an orange spout that shoots out of the center. They have a powdery, sweet scent. Have you ever noticed that flowers here barely smell?"

"What about the frangipani, madam?" I said.

"Yes, I suppose so. But what good are they really, you can't put them in a vase." At the bottom of the road where Helen lived as a child there was a wood filled with bluebells. She asked me, "Have you ever seen bluebells?" I wanted to say, How could I? Summers, she said, were warm but never hot like here where you can't breathe. She often found herself yearning for strawberries. Once she said, "I hate this place." And then she was sorry, because, she said, Trinidad is my home.

"I have family in England as well."

"Where?" she asked, surprised.

"Southampton," and I said it in a quiet way, as if it was a private and personal matter. Sometimes she spoke to me as if I was her friend. But even then, I knew I could never be her friend.

I FOUND A way to get along with Marva. I asked about her life, and she was pleased that I was interested in it. I'd say, Marva, how is your daughter, and she'd say, my poor daughter, my poor daughter (her daughter was blind), and I would say, "The meek shall inherit the earth," or, "God is good and He will take care of her," and if Helen Rodriguez heard me say this, so much the better; a look of praise came over her face at once.

Marva had married young. Her first husband worked in a funeral parlor. After she caught him fooling around with one of the female cadavers he dressed and made up, she packed her bags and left him. "I decided to never trust a man again," she told me, one morning. "How you could sleep with a dead person? Only a man could sleep with a corpse." Her second husband was a thief. After her daughter was born, he took their savings and jumped on a boat to Grenada. "He's still there now," she said, "with a new woman young enough to call him pappy." Marva said it was easy to make a man fall in love; a woman only had to squat over a pot of hot rice, let her sweat drip into it, then serve the rice to the one she wants.

"Really?" I said.

"Yes," she said, and poked the air with her finger. "Men might be bad, but women can be worse than bad."

Marva was so busy with her own life she had no interest in mine; she never asked about my family or where I had come from or how I knew William and Solomon Shamiel. She had opinions about all sorts of things: about who and what she liked, and who and what she didn't like. She liked William, but she did not like his brother. She did not care for Joe because he was spoiled. Consuella was a sweet child, but they were going to spoil her too. "You only have to open her cupboard and see how many toys she has. Toys she can't even use. Some of them come from Alexander. They should give them away. It's bad luck to hold on to the things of a dead child." We were standing in the kitchen and I was about to lay the table for lunch.

"What dead child?" I put down the tray I was carrying.

Marva glanced at the door. "I'm surprised William never told you. It was a big thing." She lowered her voice. "Alexander was born before Consuella. Poor child had terrible epileptic fits. Around this same time, a Chinese lady used to come to Joe in his dreams and threaten to take away his baby brother. The lady would stand in the corner of the room, and Joe would wake, terrified. His mother would have to go and lie with him. Then one Saturday afternoon, the family was all in the living room—and for no reason, Alexander start to scream.

"Madam pick him up and for a second he was calm. But then she walk with him about the room, and every time she get near the corner, he bawl even more. She couldn't understand it. There was nothing there. Then Joe shouts, 'The Chinese lady. It's the Chinese lady!' Brigid was in the yard picking oranges and I was cleaning the stove. We rush inside and see Dr. Emmanuel Rodriguez and the mother standing over him. Next thing Alexander close his eyes and die. Just like that. Like when you put out a candle." Marva pursed her thin lips and blew. "They bury him in England. And in the yard they plant a special tree for him."

"Where in the yard? Which tree?"

Marva looked out the window and pointed somewhere I couldn't see.

"The little ficus tree. Just to the left of the toolshed. If you look at the trunk there is a tiny plaque and the plaque has the name and birth date and when he die. Sometimes madam pray right there on the ground."

Sure enough the plaque was there.

Not long after Marva had told me this, one evening, when the sun was going down, I saw Helen Rodriguez wander into the yard. She stopped and knelt by the tree, and, with her rosary beads wrapped around her fingers, put her hands together, in prayer. I don't know how long she was there, but when she passed my room it was pitch-black.

WILLIAM MADE IT easier for me to settle in quickly and I was grateful. Every morning, as soon as he arrived, he came to look for me. I was usually laying the table for breakfast. I'd say, "Morning William, how are you?" And he'd say, in a typically soft voice, "Good. Everything is good." And sometimes, if he was feeling more confident, "Better for seeing you," and he'd smile, and put on his yard boots, right there. Then he'd walk up the garden and begin his work. Often when I was cleaning the upstairs rooms, or walking back and forth along the passageway with Consuella, I would look out and

see him on the lawn. If I waved he waved back. If I didn't wave, he
went on with his work. While I ate lunch in the pantry, he hovered by
the outside sink washing his hands or cleaning his tools, scrubbing
something. Sometimes I pretended he wasn't there and carried on
eating and reading.

Throughout the day, in between chores, he hung about the
kitchen, mostly listening to Marva, and he often sat right there in the
doorway drinking water from a green tin cup. I would say, William,
can you please pick me some mangoes for Mrs. Rodriguez, and he
would get up and, before I knew it, have the mangoes there in his big
hands. Or when I had finished polishing one of the large brass plates
that hung on the wall, "William, this is heavy, could you please help
put it back up," and quick as a flash he would carry it upstairs and
mount the plate perfectly on the wall. He brought breadfruit from
Laventille, because he remembered how I liked it and how it made
me well (once I said, "Thank you, I'm not sick anymore, though"),
and he carried sweet buns or milk bread—a gift from his mother.
"Mother say you forget her now you live in St. Clair."

"I never have a minute, William. You see how much I have to do
here." Every afternoon when I told him goodbye, William said, "See
you tomorrow, please God."

MARVA SAID, "WILLIAM like you too bad."

I brushed her off. "William is my friend. There's nothing more
to it than that."

"Well, better William than Solomon."

I said, "Better *no one* than William or Solomon!"

TRUTH WAS, I knew that William was too shy to ask me out. He
would hint at something that was going on in Port of Spain, some-

thing he thought I might enjoy. Like the opening party of a new dance hall in St. James, where there was a modern band playing, and dancing, and all sorts of young people just like him and me. Or he would tell me about a movie, like *Anne of the Indies* or a film with Rita Hayworth because he knew by the picture I had put on my wall that I liked her. William went to the cinema at least once a week. On Sunday afternoons, he took a picnic and went to the beach with friends. "The water is calm like a lake," he'd say. "Like stepping into a bathtub." It wasn't that I didn't like William; I just didn't want to have to think about him in any way other than as a friend. I liked things as they were; I didn't want them to change.

WHEN THE HOUSE was quiet and I was in my room or sitting on the bench, I found myself thinking about Black Rock. If I thought about Aunt Tassi, it was with a heaviness and sadness. And if I thought about my cousins, I felt irritated. I tried not to think about Roman Bartholomew. I was sorry I never told Miss McCartney good-bye. I would close my eyes and see the school as if it was right there: the whole first row of my class, my wooden desk, the pictures on the walls, and at the back of the classroom the map of the world, the pink place that was England. I could see Joan Maingot walking on her tip-toes, and her boyfriend. I was no longer jealous of her happy life. It didn't matter; Black Rock was far away. There was nothing there for me now.

IT WAS ON one of these quiet nights, while I was putting away my memories like old belongings in a trunk, that I decided to take a trip to Tamana to see Aunt Sula.

.   .   .

AFTER I HAD spoken to Mrs. Rodriguez, in a brief note I wrote and told Aunt Sula that I would like to visit one weekend in May. She replied at once:

> *Dearest Celia,*
>
> *I can't tell you how happy I was to hear from you. I am guessing you must be working in Port of Spain for the family you mentioned. You are welcome here anytime, so tell me when you wish to come. If you can get a lift, that would be best. Otherwise you can take a bus to Arima and change there. Buses to Tamana run twice a day. Let me know. Sooner the better. I'll wait to hear from you.*
>
> *Much love,*
> *Aunt Sula*

THIRTEEN

IT WAS MY FIRST WEEKEND OFF IN MONTHS. SOLOMON arrived at 7:00 a.m. I heard the horn outside and picked up the lunch I had made for us both, in the brown paper bag on the kitchen table. I had a change of clothes, because I wasn't sure what kind of state I would be in when I got there. It was a long drive to Tamana, three hours, they said. Which was why Solomon had asked for five dollars, to cover gas and the wear and tear on his tires from the country roads. "You know how rough those roads are when you get onto the estate." If it was somebody else, he would charge more, but as it's me, and he knows how William like me, he was prepared to do a deal. Also, he was going that way to see his friend Nathaniel.

William said the price was not so bad when you think how Solomon would sell his mother if he could get a good deal.

I said, "One day your brother will end up in jail like his father."

William shook his head. "Solomon could fall in a sewer and come out smelling like a prince."

The sky was blue as usual, and everything looked clear. Sometimes, it was as if the colors of things—signposts, a wall, the flowers in the yard—were brighter than ever. When the sun was high, the light was dazzling. It was dry season and there was a lot of dust everywhere. Around the Savannah, the land was parched like old bones left out in the sun, and when a horse or a car or a sudden wind ran over it,

sheets of dust flew up in the air. The Poui trees had let their blossom
fall and it lay on the ground in sprinklings of pink and yellow. That
day, there were still a few with flowers on their pale branches.

Solomon drove through the back part of town, past the hospital
and the gas station, and along the edge of Laventille, where all the
houses looked brown and broken and patched up. And eventually, we
came out onto the main road. Most of the cars were coming in the
opposite direction, so the road was quite clear. It didn't seem like the
same truck William and I had traveled in that night I came from
Tobago. I didn't remember it being so tatty inside or so noisy. It
would be difficult to talk.

"So how are things? How's business?"

"Which one?" Solomon spoke as if it took a lot of effort.

"The delivery service you were running. You were working with
the grocery."

"I only do that now and again; I have a lot of other things going
on right now. Plenty irons in the fire."

He drove with one hand on the wheel, the other holding a cigarette. He was much better-looking than William; he had a square jaw
and slanted eyes; a wide mouth. His teeth were even and straight. Yet
there was something dead or cold about his eyes, and it frightened
me a little. They made me think of a cavalli fish Roman once caught
and brought home. It was a long, beautiful silver fish. When he slit
open its belly, a big white cockroach crawled out. The fish's eyes were
open and staring and it occurred to me then that, alive or dead, they
would look the same. This is how Solomon's eyes were.

The breeze was hot and did little to cool us down. The fields on
either side were dry, and they seemed to go on and on. Small houses
on stilts were dotted here and there. I could see the Northern Range
Mountains. They looked almost blue or purple. Little clouds of
smoke told me where there were fires. It was typical at this time of
year. The fires could soon get out of hand. I had noticed them in

St. Ann's when I went with Helen Rodriguez to the pharmacy; black ugly scars from the bush fires all over the hills. A piece of glass thrown in dry bush, or a cigarette, and, next thing, fire was burning down the place.

On a dusty bank, a flock of vultures were crowding around a white cow dead on its back. Its stomach was blown up like a big balloon. The birds had started on the cow's head; the skin was ripped away so you could see the bloody flesh; the eyes had gone. They didn't seem to be in a hurry; it was as if they had all day. Apart from wild dogs, I couldn't imagine what else could keep them away from the carcass. I rolled up my window to keep out the smell of rotting. "Someone must have hit it with a car," Solomon said. "It happens all the time. Especially at night. If you hit it, you may as well cut it up and take the meat. Why leave it there."

We stopped in Arima. I gave Solomon money to buy sweet drinks. Then we sat in the truck and I took out the bread rolls filled with corned beef. The place was busy with people, and the market on the side of the road was full of traders, noise, dust, chaos. I was hoping that we would soon leave, but then Solomon got out and wandered over to a man outside a rum shop; they slapped each other's backs and had a laugh about something.

After a while, he brought a beer to my window. "No thanks," I said, politely. I picked up a newspaper from the floor and used it to fan myself. For some reason, there were a lot of flies and I wondered if there was garbage nearby. I decided that I hated this place. By the time we left Arima it was 10:00 a.m.

Soon the land was different. It was dense and dark, with the bushes and trees high on either side of the road. Now and then I saw houses, but they were remote, hidden. The song of cicadas rattled and hissed through the forest. That meant they were mating. I knew this from Miss McCartney. She said that you could hear the song from half a mile away. It was cooler in these parts, but I felt as though we were a long way from anywhere and if I called out no one would hear me. The tall bamboo said *swish, swish, swish,* and the bright green leaves were trembling. We carried on on this road for almost an hour. We passed through Brazil and then Talparo. At a certain bend, on the El Quemado road, little children were playing. A tiny stream poured down from a rock and they were bathing underneath it. They stared as we passed, and when I waved they waved back. Solomon said I shouldn't encourage them, next thing they jump in the tray of the truck.

We stopped at a waterfall. After I had washed my face, I checked myself in the small mirror Helen Rodriguez had given me. I didn't bother to change, we were almost there and I looked okay; it didn't matter now. Solomon went to pee behind some bushes. I could hear it hitting the ground hard.

AT THE TOP of a small hill, there was a large wooden gate, big enough to drive through. The sign said TAMANA ESTATE. PRIVATE PROPERTY. I got out and opened it, and we made our way along the narrow road, which was rough and more like a track, just as Solomon said it would be. There were fields of cocoa trees; I liked their sad and colorful leaves, and the pods that hung down from their branches. Some men were walking by the trees carrying sacks and cutlasses. They watched us pass; they didn't look too friendly.

Farther down the hill were outbuildings with galvanized roofs, and below were three raised and exposed platforms. "That's where they dry the cocoa," he said. On the highest one of these platforms, I saw a tall, white man. He wore beige trousers and a white shirt, boots high to his knees, and a planter's hat. He was looking out, his hands on his hips. He was exactly as I remembered him.

"Joseph Carr Brown," Solomon said. "You could get a job here and be better off than working for Rodriguez." Then, "Carr Brown

not easy; if he like you he treat you good. But if you do him something, you soon know about it." Solomon waved, but the man didn't
wave back. Instead, he sent a young boy running down the hill,
shouting for us to stop. We pulled up at the side of the track.

"Hello," I said. "I've come to see Sula D'Abadie. Do you know
Sula?"

The boy pointed. "Yes, miss. She lives off to the right, past the
big house, near to the river. She has a yellow house with a coconut
tree in the yard. You won't miss it. Mr. Carr Brown want to know
who you are."

"Tell him I am Celia. Sula's niece, and I've come to visit her for
the afternoon."

SOLOMON SLOWED DOWN as we drove past the plantation house.
It was a large wooden house, raised off the ground and built on stilts.
It had two stories and it sprawled over the land, with a long veranda
and steps leading up to it. It was bigger than the Rodriguez house,
although it wasn't as well kept. There were baskets hanging from the
eves with huge ferns growing in them. Some people were sitting on
the porch. They watched as we passed, and one of them stood up; a tiny
woman who I imagined to be Mr. Carr Brown's wife. Some white children were running around the underneath of the house, chasing a cat.
They stopped playing and looked at us. Even the cat was looking at us.

I asked Solomon to drop me at the bottom of the track and I
would walk the rest of the way. Now he was going to look for his
friend, Nathaniel, who worked in the cristophene fields at Four
Roads. "I'll come for you before sunset," he said. "Look for me
around five-thirty."

.   .   .   .

AUNT SULA WAS in the yard picking ginger lilies when I saw her.
She turned around, and I wondered if she had heard the truck.
"Celia," she said. Then she rested the flowers on the ground, wiped
her hands on her apron, and started toward me. She looked a little
older, and she was thinner, too; though her hair was oiled and
ironed just as I remembered it.

"Welcome to Tamana," she said, and cupped my face in her
hands. "You've changed so much since I saw you last." Then, stepping back, "You're so tall. You're a tall and beautiful woman!"

"Am I?" I said, and then suddenly felt foolish.

"Of course!"

When she put her arms around me, I found myself smiling, not
in the way I was used to, but from right inside the center of myself.

HER LITTLE HOUSE was spotless and carefully decorated. While
she arranged the flowers in a shiny vase I looked around. There were
many paintings on the walls.

"That came from Venezuela," Aunt Sula said. The portrait was
of a Spanish girl with her hair draped over her shoulders. "It used to
be in the big house, and I always liked it. Mr. Carr Brown gave it to
me one year for Christmas."

Although the house was small, it didn't feel stuffy or claustro-
phobic like Aunt Tassi's where I always wanted to get outside to
breathe. On the one hand, there were old things that I could imagine
where they might have come from, like the woven mat on the floor,
the lamp like Aunt Tassi's, and on the other, there were things that
surprised me, things that cost money. Like the pretty plate with the
gold rim mounted on the wall, the polished rocking chair, and the
beautiful mahogany tea chest.

In the corner, on a side table was a gramophone player. A stack of records were next to it. I said, "This is a new model. I've seen it in Stephens."

"Music always lifts up my spirit, don't you find so?"

"Yes," I said.

"Do you like my little house?"

"Yes, very much. It's unusual." I realized I had been walking about as if I was inspecting it. I sat down at the table, covered with an immaculate white tablecloth. There were proper china cups, saucers, and napkins. She had made sandwiches cut into triangles, and there were cheese puffs, and little guava squares. In the center of the table was a perfect chocolate cake.

Aunt Sula poured tea. "Tell me, how is it in Port of Spain?"

"It's okay. I have a nice room and I look after the children. So there's not so much housework to do."

"Who's the family, Rodriguez? And he's a doctor? I think Mr. Carr Brown knows him."

OVER TEA, AS if she knew that I didn't want to talk about Black Rock, Aunt Sula spoke about the estate and how she had worked there for more than twenty years. She used to work up at the house, and look after the children. Mrs. Carr Brown had six children and they had all left home. These days she did a few chores; she swept the ground floor, polished the brass, mended clothes. Sometimes she ironed. She hadn't been feeling as well as she used to; she got tired quickly these days. When you live on a plantation, you don't need to go anywhere, really. Your food is right there on the land, and you keep company with people you work with. You have a different kind of life. She never wanted to live in the city. "Everybody there looking for something, they're restless."

We walked around her little garden. Orchids hung from the lower branches of a large mango tree in the back. "These mangoes are sweet; next time you come they should be ripe and you can taste them." There were ferns with little flowers like tiny red bells, where, she said, hummingbirds liked to come and feed. "We have the baby hummingbirds too. Did you ever see them? They look like big bees." She showed me a large bush of white flowers. "These are Lady of the Night. If you were to stay after dark, you would smell them."

A hedge with pale blue flowers gave the yard a border. She got a boy from the estate to bring water every day and she watered the plants. "Lord knows this place needs rain," she said.

"Port of Spain is just as bad," I said. "The Savannah looks like a desert."

"I like the Savannah. It always makes you feel good when you look at it."

For a while we sat on her porch. Aunt Sula had special chairs with arms that folded out so you could rest your drinks on them. And there were two little stools to put your feet on. I hadn't felt so relaxed in a long time. When I heard the clock chime, I couldn't believe how quickly the day had gone. Solomon could wait; I wasn't ready to leave. Everything was still—as if it was waiting for something. I could see the roof of the big house; the outhouse; some sheds farther up.

"Can you stay here in this house for as long as you like?"

"Yes," Aunt Sula said. "For as long as I'm alive. Which will hopefully be for a little while longer." She smiled, and I noticed her round high cheeks. She was still beautiful.

"And what about you? Do you want to stay with the family?"

"Right now I will. I can see what comes up."

"I hope they're paying you well. You could get a good position anywhere, Celia." She was looking at me closely. "Tassi said you were good at school. Remember when I came and you told me your teacher had said you should go to university."

"I don't have time for that now. I have to earn a living. No one will mind me if I don't mind myself."

"Tassi says you could go back to Black Rock and pick up in school again. It might be late, and you will be older than the other children, but you could do it."

"I will never go back there. Aunt Tassi didn't care for me like she should have. You don't know the half of it. She believes Roman's lies. I curse his soul every day. I curse him and hope he rots in hell." I didn't expect my words to come out like this; like when you taste something rotten and spit it from your mouth—spit, spit, spit—until it's gone.

Aunt Sula looked down at her hands folded in her lap. There was a long pause; neither of us said anything. I fixed my eyes on the sky; it was empty, not a cloud in sight. Now I could feel her looking at me, and I wondered what she was thinking. I wanted to cry.

"I'm sorry, Celia. I'm so sorry for whatever it is you've gone through."

I heard a yellow bird call, loud like it was right there. *Yellow bird, up high in banana tree, yellow bird, you sit all alone like me . . .*

"Come, child. Come." Aunt Sula got up, and gently put her hand on my shoulder.

IN THE LATE afternoon, when the light was pink and creamy and soft like in a dream, we walked slowly in silence along the path. Apart from a cock crowing, it was quiet as if the world was sleeping. Bushes and shrubs covered parts of the ground; some were fine with leaves delicate as lace; others had long green leaves like tongues and some of these tongues were spiked and pointed. The land spread out and the tall trees ahead looked strong and old as if they'd been there for hundreds of years. Farther up on one side, there were clusters of bamboo and a stream where, later, Aunt Sula told me, the Carr Brown children used to play when they were small.

I saw him first from the cotton tree. Joseph Carr Brown rode through the cocoa trees, slowed at the open ground, and then jumped down from the horse. He patted its neck, and took something from his pocket and gave it to the horse. I was sure that he had seen us but he carried on taking up the saddle and loosening the bridle before starting in our direction. There was a dog at his heels. "Good afternoon, Sula." His voice was friendly.

"This is Celia, my niece." Aunt Sula stood to one side.

"Hello, Celia. We're glad to have you here at Tamana. I saw you earlier in the truck."

"That's right, sir."

"I met you before. In Tobago."

"Yes, sir. I remember."

"You do? That's a good sign. It's always nice to be remembered."

His blue eyes were deeply set and his fine-boned face was long. When he took off his hat, I was surprised to see such thick white hair. He was probably older than he looked.

"This is Shadow," he said, and the dog's ears pricked up. The dog's coat was black and shiny.

"Whenever we're looking for Mr. Carr Brown, we look for Shadow first." Aunt Sula put out her hand and stroked his head. Then the dog lay down and rolled on the dusty ground. "He loves to be stroked," she said, and rubbed his belly.

"Your aunt tells me you live in Port of Spain?"

"Yes, sir."

"I'm going into town tomorrow. I'll be leaving after breakfast if you'd like to get a ride."

"Thank you, sir, but my driver's coming to collect me soon." I said "my driver" like I was an important person.

"It's up to you," he said, "You could always give your driver the evening off." He smiled, and I looked at Aunt Sula and she smiled too. "I'm sure your aunt wants you to stay. She's been looking forward to your visit for weeks." Something about the way he said this made me think I didn't have a choice.

I FOUND SOLOMON parked up at the bottom of the track, smoking a cigarette. When he saw me, he started up the engine.

"Sorry," I said," I've decided to spend the night; go on without me. I'll get a lift tomorrow with Mr. Carr Brown."

He rolled his dead eyes, and then flicked his ash in the grass. "You could've told me, Celia. I was ready to leave an hour ago." Then he revved the engine, and without another word took off back up the track.

AFTER DINNER, AUNT Sula and I listened to the record player, and then, surprisingly, I fell asleep. I slept well in her little house. This place was silent like Black Rock, only more so; there was no Roman. There was nothing to fear.

IN THE MORNING, after breakfast: grapefruit, eggs, and fried bakes, we made our way up to the yard where Joseph Carr Brown kept his motorcars. There were two large sheds, one for the truck and tractor. Leaning against the workbench, Aunt Sula asked if I would mind if she gave Aunt Tassi my address.

I turned and looked at her. "Roman was bad, and Aunt Tassi is bad for standing by him. He's done some things you won't ever know about."

She shook her head. I knew that this was very disappointing to her.

"I don't have to tell her anything but your address. I know she wants to write you." Then she said, "I am just so glad you came," and she pushed five dollars into my hand. "Please use it to come back."

I HAD THOUGHT there might be a driver, but it turned out Joseph Carr Brown liked to drive himself. The big Ford motorcar was white and quite new. It had pointed lights and large shiny wheels. There were red leather seats and the steering wheel looked like it was made of special polished wood. I liked the smell of leather, the large padded front seat was comfortable. At first I felt nervous and a little shy, but then I told myself there was no need to feel this way.

Joseph Carr Brown drove slowly through the village, whistling a tune I thought I knew. "You'll have to put up with it, I'm afraid. My wife tells me I even whistle in my sleep. It's an old habit; I'll probably be doing it in my grave." Passing the church, a large, striking woman with a basket on her head put out her hand, and he stopped the car. "Thank you, Mr. Carr Brown," the woman said, opening the back door. She climbed in, resting the basket on the seat beside her. Shadow shifted over to the window. "That sun out there hot today already." Then, "Morning, Shadow," and she patted the dog.

"This is Celia," he said. "Sula's niece from Port of Spain."

"Good day," she said, looking at me from the corners of her eyes.

Then the woman, whose name I learned was Hazra, and Joseph Carr Brown started to talk; they talked about the rains and the landslide that took away three houses. They talked about the Toco boy who hanged himself in the lighthouse. They talked about the new telephone line at the post office where the woman worked in Four Roads. "At last, people can get hold of you when they need to," she said. "That's if the telephone line's working. When the rains come we're in trouble."

Hearing their voices, and looking out at the open road and the tall bamboo on either side of it, I suddenly felt a lightness, as if a breeze had passed right under my heart. And it came to me then that there were things I might look forward to; that life was not so hard as before, as it had been in Black Rock. And I felt glad to be riding in this big car with Joseph Carr Brown, owner of the Tamana estate, all the way to Port of Spain where I had a job and a room of my own and people there who seemed to like me. And I felt glad to know that Aunt Sula was there; that I could come back and visit when I wished to.

WE DROPPED HAZRA at the market in Arima, and then carried on toward Port of Spain. Along the main stretch, the clouds were gathering over the hills and I wondered if the rain would start before we reached.

"Do you like Port of Spain, Celia?"

"Yes, sir. I like St. Clair."

"But you used to live in Tobago, right?"

"Yes, sir."

"With Tassi in Black Rock?"

"I didn't like Black Rock so much."

He looked surprised.

"Sula tells me you want to go to England?"

"Yes, one day, when I have enough money."

"England is a long way from St. Clair." Then he said, "We have friends who know the Rodriguez family well. I've met them a couple times myself. Actually, I didn't meet the wife, but I was introduced to the doctor at a house party in Bayshore. She's an English girl, I hear."

I said, "Yes," though I had never thought of Helen Rodriguez as a "girl."

"I always say this: Better to marry someone from your own town. And if not from your town, then someone from your country.

If you can't marry someone from your country, then find someone from your part of the world. I used to tell my children this, and so far so good. Both my daughters married Trinidadians."

"But just because they come from the same village doesn't mean they're right for you."

"No, that's true."

And then I don't know why, but I said, "Aunt Tassi lives with a man and he's from the same place and I wouldn't wish him on anyone."

"That's a shame." Then, "Does he drink?"

"Yes, sir. He drinks."

Before I got out of the car, Joseph Carr Brown nodded as if he had understood something.

"Well, let's hope you don't end up with someone like that. Not that we ever decide these things. I believe you follow your life, Celia. You don't lead your life. It's a mistake people make. We're not that powerful or important."

"Yes, sir."

He waited until I was inside the gate. Then he waved, and I watched him drive slowly away. By now, Shadow had jumped into the front seat; he was leaning out of the window, ears pinned back like two black flaps in the breeze.

FOURTEEN

DURING SCHOOL HOLIDAYS THE RODRIGUEZ FAMILY
stayed at Avalon, down the islands. We set off early on Saturday morning. Dr. Emmanuel Rodriguez drove the blue Hillman car along the
coast, through St. James, Bayshore, and out toward Carenage. I sat in
the back and held Consuella, and Joe sat on the other side. If her
husband drove too fast, Helen Rodriguez complained. She said we
would all end up in Port of Spain General Hospital and people only go
there to die. I always wanted him to go faster; not because I wanted to
go to the hospital or I wanted to die, but because I liked to feel the
warm wind blowing on my face as it rushed through the window.

At a certain place in the road we came to a checkpoint, and we
stopped. The American guard was always polite and immaculately
dressed. He said good morning, and then he peered through the
windows, checking the back, and made a note of the registration
number. Joe always liked this part of the trip. There was never a
problem; the guard raised the bar, we drove through, and Joe turned
and saluted. And if the guard was friendly, he would salute right
back. Dr. Emmanuel Rodriguez didn't care for the Americans; he
said they weren't to be trusted, and all that land they were using in
Chaguaramas would be someday lost forever. The only good things
the Americans brought to Trinidad, he said, were hamburgers and
Coca-Cola.

One time, a guard with a pointed face and a light tan asked everyone to step outside the car. Helen Rodriguez quickly got out, looking worried. She took Consuella from me, and held her hand like a shade over her daughter's head. The sun was very bright and the glare made it hard to see. Joe took his father's hand and we all stood alongside the shiny car. The guard looked at everyone, but he was particularly interested in me. He asked where I was from and what I did for a living. Was I a servant? The way he said "servant" made me feel uncomfortable.

I didn't know how to answer him. "Not exactly, sir."

Dr. Emmanuel Rodriguez said, "She works for us and she lives with us."

"Where would that be, sir?"

"St. Clair."

"Which street? Near the square? The college?" He fired the words like pellets.

"Mary Street."

"Yes, I know Mary Street, sir. It's a very nice street."

Then, it was as if Dr. Emmanuel Rodriguez suddenly realized something, that the guard wanted to know where I lived for other reasons, and that this interrogation had nothing to do with security.

"I think that's enough, don't you?" Dr. Emmanuel Rodriguez's tone was sharp, and it must have surprised the guard.

"Yes, sir, thank you, sir."

Next thing, we all got back in the car, the barrier lifted, and we drove off.

THE HARBOR WAS wide and full of boats. We parked in a shaded place, and while Joe looked for Vishnu, the skinny Indian boy who took care of the boat, we got everything out of the car. Dr. Emmanuel Rodriguez called Vishnu "Missing Ball" because like a missing ball no one could ever find him. He was either in the hut, or talking to someone on the jetty, or cleaning fish, or washing down the boat, which was a small, brightly painted pirogue called *Sapodilla.* The first time I saw it, I didn't know how we would all fit, but there was plenty of room.

The sea was blue at first and it was often choppy. Carrera Island stuck out of it like the back of an animal. There was a prison on the island. It looked old and broken down, and I wondered what it must be like to live there. William told me prisoners on Carrera Island were so hungry they ate rats.

"How do they kill them?" I asked.

"They jump on them and beat them with their hands."

"How do they cook them?"

"They strip them, put the meat on the iron bars, and roast it in the sun. Rat is like chicken," William said. "Rat is better than dog. You know how many restaurants cook dog and rat and call it chicken?" He said the prison was much worse than Port of Spain jail because no one went there to inspect it, it was too far away.

"No one goes there to see anybody."

I said, "Yes, why would they."

"Carrera is the worst place you could end up. A terrible place. Better they hang you than stick you in there."

We crossed the first Boca and entered Monos Bay. Beyond we could just see Huevos and Chacachacare, the island of lepers. Before we reached Monos it looked like there was nothing on our part of the island at all. It was very green. After a few minutes we saw houses scattered here and there. We often saw people in the houses, sitting on the porch, drinking and talking, and their children played in front or swam in the sea. A lot of people had second homes here. Avalon was hidden behind a piece of land that jutted out and the boat had to tilt and curve around it. The house was pink and large. It had a concrete veranda and a wall went around it, and there were steps that led down to the bay. The water here was green and calm.

We carried everything onto the small jetty and Joe ran up the steps behind his father, who opened up the doors of the house. Vishnu helped us, although sometimes Dr. Emmanuel Rodriguez told him not to bother. I watched the boat turn and disappear and leave behind a white frill in the water, and I always felt the same thing—we could die here and no one would find us for days.

I unpacked the food; usually Marva had made pilau or baked fish or stew chicken. There were vegetables and rice and she always made a cake—ginger or chocolate—and she also made biscuits that had a lot of butter in them. She made lime juice and orange juice and put the juices in large bottles. There were always some basic provisions in the house. Helen Rodriguez said it was better to prepare food and bring it. Apart from anything else, the stove was temperamental. I served lunch on the long, thin table. While everyone ate, I made up the beds, dusted the bedrooms, and washed out the shower rooms.

My bedroom was downstairs. It was a small room with a window above the bed. There was a clump of banana trees right outside and I could stand on my bed and lean out and pick a banana. But once when I was outside, at the back of the house, I saw something crawling where the figs grew. The spider was like a man's hand. I had never seen a spider like it. It was dark brown and hairy and its fat body was puffed up as if it had just eaten something. From then on, I slept with the window closed, even though it made the room hot. I left the door open to let the sea air in.

In the afternoons, we sat in the large drawing room. Joe took out a jigsaw puzzle and we put it on the table, or we played dominoes, or cards. Upstairs, Helen Rodriguez rested in her room. Dr. Emmanuel Rodriguez also went upstairs, or he stayed and read his

medical journal that came every month from America, until he fell
asleep. The sea air made me sleepy, too. If everyone was resting, I
went in my room and lay down; there wasn't much else to do.

Around four o'clock, I made tea. Then Joe and I went for a
walk, usually behind the house. The land here was overgrown. There
were stone steps and they were old and crumbling but we still climbed
right up, into the back. The bush was thick and wild and full. Joe
liked standing on the top of the hill. From there we could see the bay
and Heuvos and Chacachacare, and they were blue-gray, and beyond
them were the paler hills of Venezuela. Once when we were there, I
told him about the tiger cats that roamed in those parts.

"Their paws are enormous." I made a big shape with my hands.

"Really?" he said, and he looked around and down the craggy
hillside.

"A tiger cat has a sweet tooth and a particular fondness for
milk."

"Tigers can kill you, right?" His round face was serious.

"They won't *kill* you but they might creep into your house and
lie down in your bed and sleep, or steal into the pantry and take
food, cakes, and cream and biscuits."

"How do you know?"

"My schoolteacher Miss McCartney told me so. They arrived
with Warahoons in canoe boats from Venezuela."

Joe liked to hear about these things, but I had to be careful.
Next thing he would tell his mother and she'd say I was filling his
head with lies and superstition.

ONE LATE AFTERNOON, when we were coming back down the
hill, and the sky was deep blue with yellow and orange streaks, we
heard voices. Through the leaves, I saw Helen Rodriguez standing at
the kitchen window. She said, "Celia, Celia," as though she wasn't

sure it was me. Then, "We have guests, could you come now," and she said "now" as if I had done something wrong. I hurried down the steps. I was surprised to see her so red-faced and worried. She was pouring rum and juice in a silver flask and then shaking it up. There were little drops of sweat on her forehead. "They arrived about ten minutes ago. We couldn't find you. I'm making cocktails."

While sailing around the islands, the Smith family from San Fernando had seen the house and decided to stop by. Charles Smith had known Dr. Emmanuel Rodriguez when he was a student in medical school. Charles had gone on to become a gynecologist. He had been to Avalon once before, some years ago, and was pleased that he had remembered where it was. He was with his wife and his parents. The young woman was very attractive; her long dark hair reached her tiny waist. When I took in a tray of drinks, Charles Smith had his arm around her and he was playing with the ends of her hair. She was telling Dr. Emmanuel Rodriguez how they met and I could see that he was interested in her story. Helen Rodriguez was sitting opposite, looking at the woman as if, for some reason, she hated her.

Later, I took in shrimps and a bowl of dipping sauce. Apart from Helen Rodriguez, everyone seemed glad of them, and Dr. Emmanuel Rodriguez told me to mix more drinks and I did. His wife said she didn't want any punch, just a glass of water.

Soon there was a lot of laughter coming from the veranda. Dr. Emmanuel Rodriguez was telling a story about a professor who was terrified of snakes; how one night, he and Charles found a dead boa constrictor in the road. They took the dead snake into the lecture theater and draped it around the lectern like a scarf. When the professor saw it he passed out. At this point, Helen Rodriguez said, "You might have killed him. I suppose that would be funny too." Everybody stopped laughing and looked at her. Then she got up and went inside.

A few minutes later, Mrs. Smith came to the kitchen. I said

Mrs. Rodriguez had probably gone upstairs to put Joe to bed, which was true. They left.

Next day, it was midmorning, and we were all outside when Helen Rodriguez came out in her red nightdress and sat on the veranda wall. As usual, the sky was bright and sunny. There were a lot of leaves on the veranda, big leaves from the almond trees. They had blown down the hill. I was sweeping them into a heap and putting them in a bag. Then I started wiping down the chairs; the sea blast made them sticky. Joe was climbing down the steps into the sea. He called, "Come in, Mother. The water's lovely. Please."

But she did not want to swim. Her head was already aching from the sun. She was sitting at the edge of the water, with her feet tucked underneath her. She looked pale and out of place. To no one in particular she said, "Doesn't it seem hotter than ever today?" Dr. Emmanuel Rodriguez didn't say anything. He took off his shirt and trousers and threw them over a chair. He was wearing navy blue swimming trunks.

"I'm coming to get you," he shouted to Joe. And he dived into the sea and Joe screamed, and then started swimming away.

Helen Rodriguez said, "Please, Emmanuel, don't frighten him." But he didn't hear her.

I went to the steps and watched his shape moving quickly underwater. Joe's little legs kicked hard, his arms slapped down on the water. His father came up for air and, again, ducked underwater. He grabbed Joe's ankle and the boy screamed and wriggled like a fish on a hook and soon he was laughing and screaming and splashing.

Helen Rodriguez seemed to be watching her husband and her son, but as far as I could tell, she was staring at nothing. She was sitting in the same position without moving, as if she was made from stone. I was about to ask if she was all right. But then she fell into the sea. She fell like someone who has died. Facedown into the green water and her blond hair fanned out and her white limbs flopped down and her nightdress puffed out like a red balloon. I shouted something, I don't remember what, and Dr. Emmanuel Rodriguez heard me shout. I jumped in, right where she was sinking or drowning, and I pulled at her heavy body, and I knew it was heavy because it wanted to go down. I looked at her face under the water and it did not look like Helen Rodriguez. It was deathly white like coral and her pale eyes seemed to say, Let me be. I put my arm around her throat and pulled her up, and with my other arm, I reached out and held on to the side of the wall. By the time I lifted up her head—heavy and soft like a big fruit, and she gasped at the air, Dr. Emmanuel Rodriguez was there.

I got out of the water, and ran into the house to get towels. When I came back, he was kneeling beside his wife, and she was sitting on a chair, holding her head. Her nightdress was sticking to her and she was so thin I felt sorry for her. Joe was sitting on the ground with his hands over his face so I could only see his eyes. She said she didn't know what happened, she just felt her head spinning and lost her balance. She was feeling much better now. "Thank God for Celia," and she laughed. When she wrapped a towel around her and went inside, I thought she seemed okay.

Dr. Emmanuel Rodriguez ran his fingers through his hair. He looked concerned. Then he stood up, and for the first time I noticed his hands, neck, and face were much darker than the rest of his body. I thought, You are a white man; without your clothes you are thinner than I would have imagined. And then I wondered why I was thinking about how white or thin or fat he was.

WE WERE SUPPOSED to stay another night at Avalon, but after Helen Rodriguez went inside, and we were all drying off in the sun, we heard her call out. I looked back at the house. She was standing tall and straight on the balcony. The ledge around the bottom of the balcony made her look as if she was floating. She said, "I want to leave."

Alone, Dr. Emmanuel Rodriguez made his way around the other side of the island, first by swimming, and then climbing through the dense foliage, over the ridge, to the only other inhabited house, where—luckily—the owner was able to lend him a boat to carry us all back to the mainland.

Later Marva told me that madam didn't like having guests in her house, and that's probably why the whole thing happened.

"You never notice how empty this place is. And the doctor knows plenty people. Madam doesn't like to entertain. She doesn't like people in her home. You ask William, he knows about this."

Then Marva said, "As long as it had nothing to do with you."

"Why would it have anything to do with me?"

We never went back to Avalon.

FIFTEEN

ONE MORNING DURING BREAKFAST, DR. RODRIGUEZ brought in the mail as usual, and while sorting through it, he got up and passed me a letter. I knew at once it was from Aunt Tassi; I recognized Vera's careful and neat handwriting. The envelope had been stamped at the general post office in Scarborough.

He said, "Good news, I hope."

I said, "Yes, sir. I'm sure of it," and put it in my apron pocket. I kept the letter for a week before I opened it.

Dear Celia,

Thank you for your telegram. It was in the house for two months. Uncle Roman put it somewhere and forget to tell me.

I am happy you are okay. When Uncle Roman told me the things you said that day, that you hated me, that I had never been a mother to you, and how you hated your cousins because they were spoiled, and then I saw you took the money I'd been saving all this time, I was very sad. But I start to worry when we didn't hear anything for so long. Celia, no matter what you think I always did my best.

Love, Aunt T

That night, I took the letter, went outside, and sat on the bench outside my room. I read it again. Then I looked up through the

branches of the trees to the sky and it was black and empty as if there
was nothing there. There were no stars and no planets and no piece
of a moon. Everything was still as if it was a picture I was looking at.
And for the first time since I had left Black Rock, I started to cry.

I cried for all the bad things that had happened to me. For what
Roman did. I cried for when I had yellow fever; I cried for living with
a family I didn't know. I cried for Aunt Tassi and her ignorance. For
my dead mother and for my English father, wherever he was. I cried
for Vera and Violet, who, like me, didn't know their real father, but
worse than me, had Roman Bartholomew for a father. Aloud, I said,
"They even call him daddy." I cried for Alexander Rodriguez. I cried
for the future. I cried for all the things that Mrs. Jeremiah had
warned me about; for the hard life I would make for myself. At last,
the river that ran to and from my heart had burst its banks.

So with all this, I didn't hear Dr. Emmanuel Rodriguez come
into the yard. I didn't know he was there until he was suddenly standing in front of me. He gave me a fright and I got up at once. The
light from my room fell across his face; he looked different.

"What is it, Celia? I heard you from inside the house."

"Nothing. It's nothing." I wiped my eyes, and looked down at
the ground.

Then he said, "Celia, please sit," and I noticed that he didn't
say it in the same way as when I first came to the house and we were in
the living room and he showed me a list of chores. He didn't say it in
the way a man speaks to a girl, or in the way that a master speaks to a
servant, or an employer speaks to an employee. He said it in a way
that a man speaks to a woman. In a way I didn't recognize. I didn't
know what to do, so I sat down on the bench with my back straight
and without looking at him.

"Is it something in the letter? Is it something someone said to you? Are you unhappy here?" I could feel his eyes all over me, searching like two police lights.

He pulled a strand of hair from my cheek where it was stuck and tucked it behind my ear. My back stiffened. And then he turned my face toward him. I must have looked at him as if he was mad but it didn't seem to make any difference to what happened next.

"You are quite lovely when you are sad," he said, and put his face against my neck and his thick hair fell against it. I could smell Bay Rum. This was his smell; the woody, spicy smell I knew to be his; I caught it first thing in the morning at breakfast. It lived in his office. Sometimes, when he had been holding Consuella, I smelled it on her skin. He didn't look at me when he said, "For months I have wanted to tell you how lovely you are. I hope I don't alarm you." If he had looked at me, he would have seen that I was extremely alarmed. So much so I could not speak. I could not move. I said to myself, What is this? What is this going on here? Then a light spilled over the yard and I got up. Standing outside my room, in the half-light, Dr. Emmanuel Rodriguez looked at me as if we knew each other very well. I wanted to say, I don't know you. I thought I knew you, but I don't know you at all.

I COULDN'T SLEEP.

The following morning I got up early and laid the breakfast table. I was glad to see William. In the doorway, while he put on his yard boots, I asked him about his mother. I wanted to know if the rain had flooded the hill like before. And what about Solomon, I hadn't seen him in a couple of weeks, and were there any breadfruits growing at the back of the house. William was surprised. Smiling, he asked how come I want to know so much *now* when he's here every day. I told him I had been meaning to ask him these things but I hadn't had a chance; it didn't mean I hadn't been thinking about them.

Breakfast was as usual. Marva cooked black pudding which she had bought from a little shop in St. James. When I took in the hops bread, warm and fresh from the oven, Joe was telling his father about a teacher at school who had shown the children a collection of butterflies. He would like to collect butterflies, too, he said, in the same glass cases. "There are bright blue ones called Blue Emperors. Their wings are thin like tissue so you have to make sure when you catch them that they don't rip." Dr. Emmanuel Rodriguez said, "It's cruel to kill them just so you can look at them from time to time. Even if they're pretty." "They taste with their feet," Joe said. "They stand on their food to eat it." Joe climbed down from his chair and put his plate on the floor. Helen Rodriguez said, "Celia, can you bring some more milk?" I could tell that Dr. Emmanuel Rodriguez was in a good mood. From the kitchen I heard him tell his wife that he would like to go to the beach house again soon, maybe for the holidays. I didn't hear her answer; I didn't want to know.

THAT NIGHT HE came to my room. He knocked, and then let himself in. I was sitting on my bed in the dark, waiting.

"Celia," he said, "I'd like to sit with you." I wanted to say, Yes, only you don't just want to sit with me, but I couldn't speak. He put his hands on mine; they were folded in my lap. He stroked my arm, the lower arm near the wrist. I looked at the floor, and wished this was happening to somebody else.

"I have wanted you for months." He stared at me for what felt like a long time. Then he left.

THE FOLLOWING NIGHT he came again. The same thing happened. Only this time, before he went, he gently touched my hair as if I was a child who had woken after a bad dream, and then he kissed my forehead. "Good night, Celia. Sleep well."

But, of course, I didn't sleep.

ON THE THIRD night, he tried to kiss me on my mouth, as I knew he would. I closed my eyes. His mouth was Roman's mouth—a black hole sucking me in; I pulled away and started to breathe quickly, in a way that was more like panting. Like a kitten I once found, panting in the hot sun. It had skinny legs and a belly swollen with worms. When I took it home and Roman said we couldn't keep it, I tried to drown it in a bucket of water. But it didn't want to die. So I took it out, dried it off, and put it in a box under the breadfruit tree. Every day I brought the kitten food, and it got stronger. Then one day, I went to the tree and it wasn't there. That afternoon, Roman told me he saw a dead cat, "just like the little kitty you bring me," lying on the road to Buccoo. "Somebody must have run it over," he said, and his eyes were lit. I ran up to the Buccoo road. It was the same one. There was blood and vomit coming out of its mouth. Its neck was twisted, as if someone had wrung it.

Dr. Emmanuel Rodriguez got up. "What is it?"

I couldn't speak. I didn't want to tell him about Roman, and I didn't want to tell him about the kitten.

"You don't have to say anything. You don't have to speak if you don't want to. It's okay." He put his hand on my back.

Then he told me that when he came to the house in Laventille, he knew by the bruises on my legs that something had happened to me. He had mentioned this to Mrs. Shamiel and she had said she would talk to me about it.

"Who did it?"

I said, "It doesn't matter now, that's old news."

He said if I kept my eyes open, I would see it was him and not this other man.

"I'm not a beast, Celia. Open your eyes."

AT FIRST WE sat on the narrow bed; it had old springs, so he lifted up the mattress and put it on the floor. I lay on my back (he asked me to do this), and he lay on his side with his head propped up, and with a gap between us. In those early days, he stared at me in a strange way, as if I wasn't real. I didn't look into his eyes. I looked at the cracks on the wall, or at the patterns on his embroidered cotton shirts. After a while, I would turn on my side; I still wouldn't look at him. We hardly spoke. Once or twice he asked about my life in Black Rock, but I didn't give anything away. I didn't want him to know about my life. He seemed to understand this, and I was glad. But I wondered how long it would last, the silence and the looking. I didn't imagine it would last for long.

Then, after a week or so, he started touching me. I thought I would find this difficult, but for some reason I didn't. Perhaps because he was a doctor, because he had touched me before when I was sick, because his touch was soft and cool and with the tips of his fingers, along my neck, my shoulders, my arms. Perhaps because he spoke kindly to me. Perhaps because I was attracted to him. He said my skin was flawless, like when you peel away the bark of a tree and you see the soft new wood underneath. It is like that, he said. He knew that I was intelligent and that I would do very well for myself someday. "You are not just beautiful. You have something about you, Celia, something that won't get downtrodden like some of the girls in your position. You're different." I wanted to say, I'm glad you're so sure because sometimes I am not; sometimes I wonder if I'll make it through the week. Whenever he said my name, it was as if it was a new name, a foreign name, like someone learning a new language. He said it like this: *Seelee-ah.* I liked the way he said it. He told me that while at Avalon, more than once he came to my room and the door was open and he stood in the passageway watching me sleep. He wanted to wake me, but thought I might scream and alarm the whole house. "I would have," I said.

One night, he stroked only my legs, from above my knees and down to my ankles and my feet. He did not touch the top part of my legs. Every time his hand was near there, my body went stiff. He said, "Your legs are long. We must get you a new bed, a bigger bed for your long legs." I didn't expect him to buy it. But a week later, I was polishing silver on the steps of the house when a large van arrived outside and the driver got out. They were here to deliver a bed, the man said. At first I thought they had come to the wrong house and then I realized. In no time at all, the two delivery men carried my old bed out and then took the new one inside. Thankfully, Helen Rodriguez was resting upstairs; she never heard a thing. It was the most comfortable bed I had ever lain on.

That night, when the house was in darkness, Dr. Emmanuel Rodriguez came to my room, and he lay down. He leaned over and kissed me. I did not pull away; I did not want to pull away. He touched my face like it was made of glass. He put his arms around my shoulders and edged closer. Then he moved me to the middle of my new bed, and lay on me so that his legs were on my legs, and so that my legs had to open to let his fall through. I nearly called out when he pressed down, but he stopped and tilted my chin so I could see his eyes. They were mostly brown now, not small and mad and black like Roman's; but warm, alive, and tender. Then he touched me where he had not touched me before. Strangely I did not mind this part. I did not mind his hand; it did not feel enormous like the branch of a tree. It was gentle and slow; his soft fingers made my flesh tingle. And when he put himself inside me, the tip of him, and then the whole of him, it did not hurt as much as I had expected, perhaps because my body did not lock itself together. Perhaps because it was broken there now, unlike the first time, when I was sealed and new. Perhaps because part of me wanted him inside me. Soon he was breathing quicker and moving quicker. I kept my eyes fixed on him; I knew that if I closed them I would fall into the black hole that was Roman Bartholomew. Then Dr. Emmanuel Rodriguez made a deep noise, like a small groan, and I knew that it was over.

DR. RODRIGUEZ CAME to me three or four times a week. Unless I had my period, or it was a time when I could too easily fall pregnant, and I heard Aunt Tassi's voice, "Just now you're having a baby and you're still a baby yourself."

At first, I kept the door open. But then one night, a frog got inside. I didn't see it until I went into the bathroom. It was big and gray like a stone, and it seemed to be glaring at me. Aunt Tassi used to say that the souls of ill-fated people (those unable to leave the material world behind because they were attached to it in some way) could—on the point of death—inhabit an animal. A dog, a cow, a frog, a goat, a bird. If you look in the eyes you can usually tell if it is possessed.

"Why does a bird fly into a house?" she had said, one day. And how about the cow that came into the yard and followed her mother around after her sister died? I was staring at the frog in the bathroom, and these thoughts were going around in my head, when Dr. Emmanuel Rodriguez appeared.

He said, "Why on earth are you scared of a frog I thought you came from the bush in Tobago" (he said it all in a rush), and he took up the broom, prodded its back, and the frog jumped and jumped, until it went out and into the yard. I didn't like the way he said "I thought you came from the bush." But later, after he had been inside me, he said, "You are the prettiest flower in Trinidad," and I forgot about it.

From that day, we decided I would keep the door closed, he

would knock three times and I would know that it was him. "That way we don't have to deal with any toads!"

ON WEEKENDS, AFTER lunch, when Helen Rodriguez was resting, and if Joe was playing next door, he pressed the bell (all the rooms in the house had bells) and called me into his office. "Could I have some juice, please, Celia?" or "Would you fill up the water jug and bring it?" And then he would pull me to him. But I worried that someone would pass and peep through the shutters. Or Helen Rodriguez could come downstairs in her quiet way, like a wandering ghost, and she would want to know why in God's name the door was locked with Celia and her husband on the other side of it.

So, mostly, we went into the toolshed. It was a small, hot room and there wasn't much space to move around. I balanced myself on the bench, a smooth wooden bench with a metal vise. Dr. Emmanuel Rodriguez did not spend long stroking or kissing me, as he usually would. He quickly worked his way inside me, his trousers down around his ankles. From the bench, I could see William's tools, cutters, clippers, rope, a saw stuck on the wall, boxes of screws and pins and hooks, a hoe hanging. There was one small, high window. No one could see inside. When it was over, Dr. Emmanuel Rodriguez tore a piece of rag from the box of old sheets that were used to clean the tools, and he wiped himself clean.

Once, when we were in the middle of things, we heard something in the yard. He stopped, and put a finger to his lips. I kept very quiet, and, slowly, he drew himself out of me and pulled his trousers up. We waited for a few minutes, looking at one another. My heart was racing. I hid behind the cupboard while he opened the door. Whoever or whatever was there had gone.

"It could have been a lizard," he said, later, when he came to my room. "There are a lot of them about."

I imagined one of the big lizards that look like they're a thousand years old. The sort Roman used to pelt with a stone. He'd kill it in one strike, put it on a fire to roast, and peel off its black skin and eat it. I never ate the meat but Aunt Tassi said it was delicious. To cure Violet's asthma, she ground the skin into a fine powder, and sprinkled it over her food like salt.

"Did you know that a lizard's skin cures asthma?"

"Don't let my wife hear you say that or she will start to fret about obeah."

"Do you think it could have been Mrs. Rodriguez? I have often seen her there by the tree."

"No, it wasn't Helen. Not unless she went away very quickly."

DR. EMMANUEL RODRIGUEZ didn't always want to make love. Now and then, he lay down in my room without touching me. He put his hands under his head and looked up at the ceiling. He told me things about his life. I heard about his father who came from British Guiana, who died in a terrible fire in Georgetown when a burning pole fell and hit his head. And how his mother packed up their house and went back to Lisbon, where she quickly met and married another man. Dr. Emmanuel Rodriguez had not spoken to her since. His only brother was a hunchback who lived in Antigua, with a woman called Siri. They weren't married, but Dr. Emmanuel Rodriguez knew that his brother, George, was happy and that he loved Siri, and she took good care of him.

George Rodriguez had dreams of buried treasure. After such a dream, he took a boat or a donkey, and with his yard boy and Siri, went to the exact spot to look for it. There, the yard boy dug and dug and dug.

"The only treasure they had ever found was an old purse filled with worthless foreign coins!"

"I found a purse once, on the beach. There was nothing in it."

"In Tobago?"

"Yes. I kept it with my things under the house."

"Tell me about your house. Tell me about where you grew up."

"There's nothing to tell."

"Who was the first man you were with?"

I kept my eyes down on the crumpled sheets.

"One day I want you to tell me. It will be a sign that you trust me."

THERE WERE TIMES when Dr. Rodriguez fell asleep right there on my bed. And while he slept, I lay beside him and stared—at his tanned skin, the silky lids of his eyes, his small mouth, his almost perfect nose apart from the tiny mole on his left nostril, his chin with a dimple in the middle that he didn't like. And I imagined what it would be like to be with him every day, in this way. Eventually, I would have to wake him before he was missed. He'd quickly get up, fix his clothes, and leave.

Once while he was sleeping, I drew a picture of his face. I was surprised by how much it looked like him, although he did not look as kind as I knew him to be. In fact, he looked like a man who loved no one but himself! When I showed him the sketch, he was impressed. "Am I so handsome?" he said. I didn't say anything, but I wanted to say, You are *much* more handsome. He told me to put the portrait somewhere safe, in case Helen found it.

ON SUNDAYS, I went as usual to the Royal Botanical Gardens, but afterward, instead of going to church, I walked up Lady Chancellor Hill, as if I was going to the hotel. I started up the smooth road, which was flanked with dense bushes and trees; some of them were spindly and tall and tangled with vines like ropes. After rain, the pitch steamed and the road looked like it was breathing. Everything smelled alive. By the time I reached the second or third bend, the blue Hillman car appeared; Dr. Rodriguez stopped and I got in. Then he drove to the top, turned the car around, and if no one was at the point, we parked and looked down at Port of Spain, sprawled out and sparkling in the late afternoon light, with the Gulf of Paria rolling out behind it. It went so far you couldn't tell what was sky and what was sea. I could have looked at it for hours. But we never stayed long.

At the bottom of the hill, Dr. Emmanuel Rodriguez turned, taking the road that led to the beach. I liked the drive, with the high hills on the right, and the well-kept houses dotted here and there, with their driveways and verandas and beautifully tended gardens. The roads were quiet, and there were often girls, like me, but usually darker than me, walking with small children or pushing prams. We drove mainly in silence. "Better not to look too friendly," Dr. Emmanuel Rodriguez used to say, "in case we pass anyone I know. Make it seem like I'm dropping you somewhere."

After ten minutes or so, he drove off the main road and followed a track, and it went on for a little while. We parked under a Flamboyant tree. I liked this tree very much. It had bright red flowers and long black pods that rattled when you shook them. Once I took a pod home and offered it to Joe. "Where did you get it?" he asked, pleased. I made something up. (I soon got good at making things up.) At that particular spot, there was never anybody there. Now and again a car passed by on the main road, but none came our way, and even if they had, we were quite hidden in the tall grass. It was okay to push back the seat and lie all the way down, and that way, if Dr. Emmanuel Rodriguez was lying on top of me, he could see through the back window. We usually stayed in the car, but afterward, if I needed to pee, I walked along the track, to a dark and sheltered place where two trees met, and where there was a tiny stream. There were rocks on the other side, and I once saw clothes draped there to dry.

On the way home, he often seemed far away and I wondered what he was thinking. He was looking at the road, but at the same time, not looking at it.

One day I said, "When did you know that you wanted me, exactly?"

"I knew we would be together the first time I saw you in Laventille. You always know who you're going to sleep with the minute you put eyes on them."

"Even though I was sick with fever?"

"Yes," he said, "even though you were sick with fever."

AND ANOTHER TIME:

"Are English girls pretty?"

"Yes, but they don't understand Trinidad. When you tell somebody in England about Trinidad, they never know where it is."

"Have you ever thought you could live in England?"

"No. It's too cold and damp and it rains all the time. In winter it's so cold you can see your own breath."

"Aunt Sula told me so." Then, I said, "Can you eat snow?"

He laughed. "Yes, I'm sure you can, but I've never tried it."

HE ALWAYS STOPPED at the end of the road, and I got out and, slowly, walked back to the house as if I had just been to church. Once, though, near the house, we saw Joe walking with his friend from next door, and Mr. Scott, the boy's father. Dr. Emmanuel Rodriguez carried on driving. He said, "Don't say a word," and then he pulled up alongside them, cocking his head through the window as the car came to a standstill.

"Good evening, Dr. Rodriguez," said the tall, blond man. "We're bringing your son for you. He's spent the whole afternoon beating us at Scrabble."

"Very good. That's what I like to hear. Come on, Joe, climb in." Joe ran around to the other side and jumped in the back. Then, "Tonight I'm playing taxi driver. I found Celia here walking back from church."

I smiled at Mr. Scott, who gave me a funny, sideways glance.

THE FOLLOWING MORNING, I was sad. All day I went about the house with a long face. No one seemed to notice, not even William. I hardly spoke to anyone.

That night, after we had been together, I sat up and leaned against the wall. There was a firefly in the room, its tiny light flashing on and off.

"What is it, Celia?"

"It's my birthday. I've never had it go by like this before."

Dr. Emmanuel Rodriguez put his hand on my cheek. "Why didn't you say, you silly girl," he said, climbing out of bed. He started to put on his clothes. At first I thought he was cross but then he said, "Get dressed, I'm taking you somewhere."

"Where? It's too late to go out. What will you say to madam?"

"You don't have to worry about that."

"Someone might see us."

"Don't argue with me."

NEXT THING, WE were racing up the Saddle Road and the windows were down and the wind was blowing back my hair and I still didn't have any idea of where we were going. There were hardly any cars around, and apart from a couple of dogs barking, it was very quiet. By the time we reached the top of the twisty road that led up from the Long Circular Road, past the little tiny houses in the valley, and past the thick trees and the dark bush that covered most of the hillside, I had no idea where we would end up and I didn't care. And the steep road made me scared at first, and I wondered how we would get up it. But soon we were there, up at the top of it, and parking under a tree. He switched off the engine.

"Don't look," he said, "keep your eyes down." And with a torch that was barely needed in the moonlight, only where the branches of trees kept it hidden, Dr. Emmanuel Rodriguez took my hand and carefully led me over a small stone wall, and then up a narrow path. We crossed the grass. And then we stopped. It felt like we were on the edge of something. The breeze was cool like at Christmas. He put his arm around my shoulders and held me steady. "Now you can look."

The lights of Port of Spain were spread out and sparkling like a million diamonds on a black cloth and the sea beyond lit silver by the huge, white moon hanging there. I had never seen such a view. "This is your country," he said. "Isn't it something." Then, "Happy Birthday, Celia." Dr. Emmanuel Rodriguez put his mouth on mine and kissed me hard. Then he opened a paper bag I hadn't seen him carrying, and there was a bottle of something which he said might make me dizzy, but I had to try a little. "It's not quite champagne," he said, pouring it into a cup, "but it'll do.

"You never can tell what the future holds, Celia, but I'm sure you've got a lot to look forward to."

Yes, I thought, miracles can happen, they've happened before. I am living proof.

SIXTEEN

Helen Rodriguez didn't seem to notice anything different in her husband, which I found strange. On Sunday afternoons, for instance, she never questioned him when he said he was going to the office or the Portuguese club. Now and again, he made the excuse that he had to be at the hospital. This was sometimes true. A sudden burst of emergency operations and the hospital would telephone and ask for his help. Once and only once, I heard her ask in a suspicious way what time he would be home, and he said, "Oh Lord. I really hope you're not starting that nonsense with me again, Helen. What does a man have to do?" and that was the end of it. It didn't seem to occur to her that we were both out at the same time, or, if it did, she never said anything.

Sometimes I felt her watching me, or looking at me, when she thought I didn't know. She encouraged me to go to Tamana. "You had such a nice time with your aunt, Celia. You came back so refreshed. Please don't feel tied here every weekend." Dr. Emmanuel Rodriguez said I mustn't get paranoid. To me, she was like a person split in two; as if part of her soul was in Trinidad and the other part was living in another strange world I had no idea about. And that other part I didn't understand or trust. I never asked Dr. Emmanuel Rodriguez how he felt about her. I didn't feel I had the right.

There was nothing for her to do in the house and I imagined that she was bored. She liked to sew and sometimes spent a whole morning in her sewing room making things—cushion covers, dresses for Consuella, shorts and shirts for Joe. The elaborate flowery patterns she embroidered onto Consuella's dresses made them look like dresses you would buy in a store. She always stitched Dr. Emmanuel Rodriguez's initials on his handkerchiefs, and onto the pockets of his shirts. If I went into the room to call her for lunch, or to ask her something, I would see these things laid out on her cutting table.

One day, I said, "I wish I could sew like you, Mrs. Rodriguez."

And she said, "I'm sure you could if you put your mind to it. It's not so difficult. Any fool can sew."

The only time she was sure to be out was on Friday afternoons, when she went to the Queen's Park Hotel, where Gladys Richards washed and set her hair in the hotel beauty salon. On the way home, she might have tea with Mrs. Robinson from Barbados, who lived in St. Ann's, but that didn't happen every week because Mrs. Robinson was often busy. Now and then, she drove into town, shopping for material or patterns, or she'd go to the bank. In the early days, I'd often go with her. But later on, when Dr. Emmanuel Rodriguez started closing surgery early (Fridays, only), I made an excuse to stay at home. It was easy; there was always a lot to do.

As soon as William and Marva had left, he came to my room. We did it with the door locked and the louvers shut so it was dark like night. We didn't turn on the fan in case someone came and we couldn't hear them and that meant it was very hot. When the bed got damp with our sweat, I lay on the cool, hard floor. But the tiles were soon sticky and caught my skin, so we threw a sheet down there too and I lay on that—my legs up and out for him. Afterward the room looked wrecked. By the time Helen Rodriguez returned— pretty and fresh with her hair groomed like a model in one of the

American glossy magazines she sometimes brought home—her husband was bathed (the smell of me completely gone), dressed, and
working in his office; I was upstairs getting Consuella ready for her
afternoon walk. At first I found it hard to look at her but then I got
used to it.

SEVENTEEN

TAMANA WAS DIFFERENT IN THE WET SEASON; THE ESTATE was very green and wild, as if it was exploding with life. Even Solomon seemed to think so. "It nice up here at this time of year," he said as we drove through; the grass was long and the trees were thick and full. He dropped me off in the same place as before. "Wish me luck," he said. Nathaniel was taking him hunting.

"What kind of hunting?"

"Agouti, wild pig, manicou."

The idea of it made me feel uneasy.

"With a real gun?"

"No, Celia, with a toy."

"Well," I said, "I hope you're a good shot."

"I never miss my target."

AUNT SULA GREETED me at the bottom of the steps, and she put her arms around me. She had prepared a hot and delicious lunch, and while we ate, she asked me about the Rodriguez children, and about Helen Rodriguez, and the doctor. She wanted to know about the fashion in Port of Spain. Did I ever get out to restaurants or dance halls? It had been a while since she had been there. I knew that she was trying to keep the mood light and cheerful.

After we had eaten, she went inside and lay down, and I looked through some old *Reader's Digest* magazines she had there. I didn't realize how tired I was until I fell asleep. Aunt Sula said I should always rest after lunch. "Conserve your energy, child. You only have so much. One day you'll be old like me and you'll wonder where your life went."

While the cool breeze blew through her little house, I thought about Dr. Rodriguez. He had told me not to stay away too long. What would he do, especially in this rainy weather. I was his sunshine, he said, his light in the dark.

FOR THE FIRST time, Aunt Sula showed me properly around the estate. The main house where Mr. and Mrs. Carr Brown lived was much bigger than I had first thought. The windows were all open at the top, and the downstairs windows were also open, but I couldn't see inside. There was a small balcony that led from one part of the house to the other. A woman in uniform hurried across it. I wondered how many people worked here. The house needed paint and some of the fretwork was tatty but it was impressive. I liked the crocheted hammock strung across the large veranda, the planter's chairs with their flowery cushions. There were two huge pots on the side of the steps and they held palms with bright red trunks. A young, light-skinned girl was wiping them down. She looked up at us and waved.

"That's Cedar," Aunt Sula said. "See how her dress is always falling off her shoulder like a waif and stray." The girl looked like she was in a dream. "Her mind is peculiar. In some things she's dumb, and in others, sharp as a tack."

Then Aunt Sula took me around the back of the house and showed me the water well, and the three big outside sinks. We went into the cold room, where they kept ice, meat, butter, milk, and cheese. An overweight woman bustled through the door humming a familiar tune. "Morning, Sula, and who we have here?" She had a round, pleasant face.

"Dolly, this is Celia, my niece."

"She tall like you!" She looked me up and down in a friendly way. "How you feeling today, Sula?"

"I'm getting old, that's all that's wrong with me."

"You should take it easy; let your niece look after you." Then, to me, "Did you know your aunt was very sick just the other day?"

Aunt Sula rolled her eyes. "I had what all women have when they get to my age—aches and pains."

I said, "Did you go to the doctor?"

"No," said Dolly, and put her hands on her hips. "She didn't."

Aunt Sula sighed. "I didn't have to." Then, cheerfully she said, "Come, let's go see the chickens."

TWO CHILDREN WERE cleaning out the shed. All the chickens had been shooed to a corner and fenced in with a large piece of board. The boy and girl had brushes, brooms, and a bucket of water. I remembered the boy from my first visit to the estate. "This is Ruth and this is Tatton," said Aunt Sula, and they both stood up straight in their raggedy shorts and shirts. Ruth started to giggle.

"What is it?"

The little girl put her hand over her mouth. Then Tatton started giggling too.

"You haven't seen such a pretty lady in a while, huh?"

I didn't feel pretty, standing there in my housedress and the ugly boots Aunt Sula had given me.

In a whiny voice like a little cat, Ruth said, "Where you from, miss?"

"Port of Spain. I live in Port of Spain."

As if I'd said Paris or New York, her eyebrows shot up.

Aunt Sula said, "Maybe Celia will tell you about it someday. Not now because we have to go up to the stables."

We left them there, with Ruth staring after us.

ON THE OTHER side of the house there was a row of orange trees; their branches were full and heavy. This was the start of the small orchard, the one closest to the house. Apparently, there was another area of citrus which went on for three hundred acres. The workers picked and boxed the grapefruits and oranges and Mr. Carr Brown had them delivered to Port of Spain for distribution. I hadn't realized the estate was so enormous. Cocoa used to be the most important crop, but that had changed now, Aunt Sula said. We kept walking up, up, up, toward the land in the back. Some of the grass was long here; it was where the horses were brought out to feed. Now I was glad of the heavy yard boots.

"You can't walk about the place in sandals," Aunt Sula had said. "If a snake doesn't bite you a scorpion will."

"Does Mr. Carr Brown have a lot of money?" I asked.

"He used to. But these days cocoa hasn't been selling so well. He's put a lot of time and money into citrus fields. They export them now all over the place."

And then, as if he had heard us talking about him, he was suddenly there, cutlass in his hand.

"I was just showing Celia the chickens, and letting her meet everybody."

"Very good, very good. There are plenty of people to meet." Then, "I could show her the grapefruit fields. You'd like to see them, Celia?"

"Yes, sir."

"I'm assuming you know how to ride."

I didn't tell him that I had only ever ridden a donkey.

TATTON SHOWED ME how to climb onto the horse's back by using a small wooden block that the children used. Milo was the smallest horse. I hooked my boot into the stirrup and swung myself over. "It feels very high," I said quietly, looking down at the little boy. "I hope I don't fall off."

"No, miss," he whispered, "you make sure and hold on tight. Milo like the ride up there, he'll behave himself."

Joseph Carr Brown watched from the stable door. "Good," he said, climbing onto his horse, Seafer. "Keep your arms relaxed, so the reins stay at the same tightness. That's it." He rode alongside. Then, "Now, follow me."

He led the way, his back straight and broad, his right leg kicked gently against the belly of the red horse, and they started the climb up the side of the hill, passing through the cocoa trees where everything seemed darker. Shadow raced ahead, I could see his shape darting through the undergrowth. I tried to stay upright and get into some kind of rhythm, allowing myself to move with Milo, who seemed to know exactly where we were going. "Listen to the beat of his hooves," Joseph Carr Brown called. "One-two, one-two, one-two." We cut through tall bushes, and onto an uneven path, worn and rocky and muddy. Vines grew on the trees and there were huge black termite nests stuck to their trunks. I could see a strip of the stream and hear it as it trickled down the hill. "Don't let Milo near the water. He won't want to leave." When I looked up I saw the tops of the trees and the patches of sky in between, little slithers of gray and blue.

Soon we were out on the open space where the groves began, rows and rows of trees, and the horses slowed right down. "I don't know if your aunt told you, we have three hundred acres." He got down from his horse and examined the bark of a grapefruit tree, heavy with green, unripe fruit. He picked one of the leaves and handed it to me.

"See how it is. A perfect leaf. When they're diseased their leaves look mottled like cork. I come out here every afternoon to check on them." Then, "Did you try our grapefruits yet?"

"Yes, sir."

"They were sweet?"

"Yes, sir."

"So sweet you don't need sugar, right?" He smiled.

"Yes," I said.

He rode slowly in between the trees and I followed closely behind. I liked it out here, the huge rolling open field and the trees in neat and even rows; the silence. "Why don't you check the other side," he said, and pointed ahead.

I didn't know quite what to look for, but I went anyway. I rode along the edge of the field and stopped and looked at the branches and the leaves. From what I could tell, nothing was there that ought not to be there. Milo walked slowly, and I was grateful to him. Thank you, I said, and patted his long, shiny neck.

We made our way back through the forest. It was hot and still and the air was heavy with moisture. I was mostly behind him, but now and then, when the narrow path allowed it, Milo sidled up to Seafer and I found myself riding alongside Joseph Carr Brown.

"Nothing beats riding in this forest," he said. "Trinidad is a wonderful place, Celia. Everyone who lives here can't wait to leave. But once they go—to England or Canada or the U.S., they spend their whole lives trying to get back. I've seen it happen again and again. You might find that when you go to England, if you're still planning to leave. No sooner than you get to London, or wherever it is you want to go, you'll hear Trinidad calling you home."

"I hope to go one day, sir."

"And I'm sure you will. We usually get what we want most."

THAT NIGHT, THERE was a party in one of the little houses at the back of the estate. There were a lot of candles burning in the yard as it was dark and there was no moon. Dolly's son had returned from Sande Grande with his new wife and baby. Everyone who worked on the estate was there. I recognized some of the workers and they were friendly enough. Aunt Sula introduced me as her niece-from-Port-of-Spain. Cedar stood stiff as a post in front of me and in a stern voice said, "Good night." She stepped forward. "We have the same name."

"No, mine is Celia. Yours is Cedar like the tree."

Then she bowed like a tree, bowing in the wind.

"You're Sula's daughter."

"No, Cedar, I'm her niece."

Later, I watched her tie a white sheet around her shoulders and fly around the yard chasing the younger children like a ghoul. When they screamed Dolly clapped her hands and shouted, *"Ce-daaaaar!"*

There was a large pot of stew that someone said was agouti. I had never eaten agouti before and the meat was tender. There was curried turtle, which reminded me of curried beef. Aunt Sula said they must have caught it up at Grande Riviere. There was breadfruit, trays of buttery dasheen, large bowls of rice and peas. After we had eaten, someone started hitting drums and there was singing from one of the women. She had a deep, rolling voice that sounded like it came from under the ground. I wasn't sure I liked it. But then the music changed and people started clapping and singing songs more like the ones I knew in church.

I didn't expect to see Joseph Carr Brown. He arrived after

dinner, with Shadow, and a bottle of sorrell wine which he gave to
Dolly's son. He patted the young man on his back. "To wet the baby's
head," I heard him say. "Mrs. Carr Brown sent this," and he gave
him something, which I later learned was a christening gown.

Aunt Sula told me that Joseph Carr Brown had helped Dolly
with a small loan to send her son to study in San Fernando. "That's
how the boy come to be an engineer," she said. "Mr. Carr Brown
help a lot of people. His heart big like Trinidad."

BEFORE I LEFT, Aunt Sula asked me to take down an old milk tin
from the top kitchen shelf. She told me to take out five dollars. "For
next time," she said, "to make sure you come back."

ON THE WAY home, Solomon wanted to know if I'd brought fruits
or provisions, and I was about to show him the huge avocados in the
brown bag that Aunt Sula had given me when suddenly, just after the
turning on the road to Santa Cruz, thirteen miles from Port of
Spain, we hit something. I had never heard a sound like it. It was a
buh-buduh-buh.

"Shit," he said, and pulled over. Quickly, we got out and ran
back up the road to where a dog was lying on its back. It was twitching,
its mouth bloody and open, its eyes rolling back in its small brown
head. It was a mother, its teats big and dark and hanging. There was
no one around. But I could see some small houses farther up and I
wondered if the dog belonged to someone there. There would be
puppies somewhere.

"Get back in the truck," Solomon said.

"Why?"

"Get back in the truck." He said it like an order, so I did, thinking that he was going to pick up the dog and put it in the tray. But

next thing I knew, he had started the engine and we were reversing up the road to where the dog lay. Before I could ask him what he was doing, I felt its lumpy body underneath the wheels. And then again, as he drove forward—over it.

"Solomon!" I shouted, and put my hands up to my face.

For a few minutes he didn't say anything. He kept his foot down and carried on. Then, as we reached the turning in the road, he said, "I don't know why you're fretting so. The dog was going to die. Better it die quickly."

EIGHTEEN

THAT MORNING, HELEN RODRIGUEZ WAS IN A BRIGHT mood. She was taking Joe and Consuella to a birthday party in Cascade. I heard her tell Joe that when they came home, they would change and go to Maqueripe, the beach on the other side of town, on the American base.

"We can take a picnic," she said, as they came into the kitchen.

Joe looked pleased. "Will Daddy come too?"

"Of course."

"And Celia?"

"I think Celia probably has a lot to do here," she said, and looked up. "Celia, will you tell my husband to be ready for around three o'clock?" It was now 11:00 a.m.

I followed them outside. Through the car window, she asked if I would prepare tea. "Just some ham sandwiches, and fresh juice. That should be enough. She smiled, as if she was fond of me.

I was closing the gates when I heard Dr. Emmanuel Rodriguez call out. *"Seelee-ah! Seelee-ah!"* I ran inside and hurried up the stairs, sure that something was wrong.

"I'm in here," he said. "In my bedroom."

I was surprised to find him standing wet and naked in the doorway of their bathroom. I had never seen him fully naked. I had seen him wearing swimming trunks, and I had seen bits of him naked, but not like this, where I could see all of him. His body hair was dark and it looked like there was nowhere on his skin that it was not. His penis was slack and soft and long. He looked up, and smiled, and then took up a towel and tied it around his waist.

"It's rude to stare," he said, and told me to get undressed. "We are lucky this morning with the house empty. She should be gone for at least three hours."

I looked around the room. A skirt was thrown on the chair, things were scattered over the dressing table; there was talcum powder on the floor and I realized I had stepped in it and walked it across the room. I went quickly to fetch a cloth. When I came back, he was lying under the mosquito net, sprawled out.

"There are so many mosquitoes at this time of year. Make sure you don't let them in." Then, "Do you know that only the females bite? Isn't that typical?"

It felt odd undressing in the room Dr. Emmanuel Rodriguez shared with his wife. I must have looked uncomfortable but he kept on talking as if it was the most natural thing in the world, as if I *was* his wife.

"When I was a baby, my mother left me in my pram under a mosquito net while she went off to play tennis. She didn't know there was a mosquito trapped under the canopy. When she came back, I was screaming and covered in bites. It had feasted on me."

I stood there looking at him, not sure what to do.

"Come on." He patted the place beside him.

I climbed up and into the bed, sliding onto the cool sheet. He rested on his elbow and stared at me.

"I feel strange."

"Don't think about it. Pretend you're in a hotel."

"I've never been in a hotel; I'd feel strange there too."

"Then I will take you to one and it won't be strange anymore."

He bit my neck, not hard. (Dr. Emmanuel Rodriguez was never

rough.) And then he put his mouth on my breast. This was something he liked to do. Next he moved lower, onto my stomach, where
he stayed for a moment, looking, smelling my skin. He took a pillow,
with its embroidered linen cover, and put it under me so that the
bottom half of me was raised. He had never done this before. Then
he went lower, again, until his head was down between my legs, and I
could only see his thick, dark hair. Gently, he pushed my legs up and
pressed them back so they were opened wide and I felt as if the whole
world could see me. I wanted him to stop. But he stayed there. He
stayed there for a while, holding my legs, and licking as if he was a dog
eating something off the ground. And then I no longer wanted him
to stop. I had never known pleasure like this. He turned me over and
lifted me up by my waist and I dropped onto my hands. I could see
the wall and through the white net, the photograph of Helen Rodriguez. He put himself in and up inside me, and we did it like this,
with his small jutting movements.

"Come here," he said, and tugged at my hair band, until it came
away. Then, running his hands through my long hair, "It's like a
lion's mane." And he rolled back on the mattress and pulled me to
him. He liked it when I was above him, because I looked serious, he
said. He liked the angle; when I leaned forward and he could hold my
breasts in his hands. He'd say, "If only you could see what I can see."
It was better for me if, rather than kneeling, I squatted with my feet
on either side of him. For some reason, my legs didn't get tired. A
sign of youth, he said.

When it was over, I lay down next to him. I had just put my head
on his chest, and I was thinking how his hair there was soft like feathers, and how I would like to have it next to me for a long time. And I
was feeling warm and high with love, as if I was floating, and I was
thinking of how much I loved Dr. Rodriguez, when I heard the un-
mistakable sound of the Hillman car pull up outside in the road, the
car door slam, and then the familiar creaking of the gates.

"That can't be Helen. They've only just left."

I ran from the room, and into the children's bathroom and locked the door. I pulled my dress over my head at the same time that I heard the car driving into the garage. I climbed onto the ledge of the basin and looked through the shutters. Joe was closing the gate. Again, I heard a car door slam.

HELEN RODRIGUEZ WAS standing in the hallway, pale like milk. Dr. Emmanuel Rodriguez had his arm around her narrow shoulders. He was helping her to a chair. Consuella was still in the car, he said, with Joe. I ran outside; she had just started to cry. "Mummy has a migraine," Joe said, in a flat voice. "Are we still going to the beach?" Then he pulled a face. "What have you done to your hair? It looks a mess."

Now Helen Rodriguez was sitting at the table, sipping water. "Can you close the shutters in our room, Celia," Dr. Emmanuel Rodriguez said, and gave me a look. With Consuella in my arms, I went quickly upstairs. She was crying and crying, her little face red and wet with tears. I put her down in the cot.

"Hush," I said, straightening the covers. "I'm coming back just now."

In their bedroom, I closed all the shutters and turned up the fan. I quickly fixed the sheets and searched the floor for my hair band but I couldn't find it. I thought about changing all the bed linen, but then I thought she would *know*.

In the corridor, I heard Dr. Emmanuel Rodriguez say, "We must keep the house quiet. Voices, music, any noise in fact will be painful for your mother. Do you understand, Joe?"

Joe looked as if he was about to cry.

"All done, Celia?"

Helen Rodriguez was shading her eyes.

"Yes, sir."

Then Dr. Emmanuel Rodriguez disappeared into the bedroom with his wife and the door closed. Very quickly they started to argue about something and her voice grew high and strained. And while I tried to get Joe away—pulling gently on his hand, asking him to please come with me to check on his sister because I'd left her crying in her cot—there was no hiding the sound of his mother's inconsolable weeping pouring out into the passageway.

LATER, SHE RANG the bell. The room was dark like a tomb, and she was curled up with her head underneath the pillow. I wondered how she was breathing, and I wondered, too, if she could smell me on the linen cover. At first she didn't know I was there. I touched her arm; it was a thin white stick. She lifted the pillow and opened her eyes. They were narrow and intense like two cuts. She spoke so softly I could barely hear. Would I go with Dr. Emmanuel Rodriguez and the children to the beach? She had been promising them a swim for so long.

"Joe has been looking forward to it. I know you like the beach." Then, "You do like it, don't you?"

I said, "Of course. Can I get you something?"

"No," she said, "just go. I want all of you to go."

AT MAQUERIPE, THE water was green and calm. Consuella lay on the large towel I had put under the tree; she seemed happy in the shade. Earlier, I had taken her down to the water's edge and let her put her feet in it. I splashed it on her legs and on her small body. She had cried a bit but then she seemed to like it. The sea air made her tired; she was soon asleep.

I watched Joe and his father digging a hole big enough to climb inside. Then Dr. Emmanuel Rodriguez sat in the hole; his son started to cover him up, at first pouring the sand onto him, then scooping it up in his small hands and dropping it in. Joe got excited, and he started using his foot to push the sand onto his father. Dr. Emmanuel Rodriguez shouted, "Not in my eyes, Joe." By the time he had finished, the sand reached Dr. Emmanuel Rodriguez's neck, so that just his face was sticking out. The little boy patted it down, like it was a grave, and smoothed it over. He was laughing as he ran off into the sea. His father waited for a moment, then gave a huge roar, burst out of the sand, and ran after him.

I followed them in. I walked until the water was up to my waist, and then I dipped my head underneath the surface. I swam a little, to the start of the rocks, and I turned and looked back at the bay. It wasn't big, but it wasn't small either. There was a family on the left and they were having a picnic; they were all looking out. I was sure they were watching us. In the end, we didn't bring a picnic. There hadn't been enough time, because when Helen Rodriguez asked me to go to the beach with her husband and her children, I wanted to get out of the house as quickly as possible before I did something "immature" (Dr. Emmanuel Rodriguez's word) like tell her what I had done, what *we* had been doing for these past months, so I forgot all about a picnic. Now I remembered the ham sandwiches I was supposed to make. And I was thinking about the fresh juice, too, when Joe appeared like a star floating beside me. I said, "Are you hungry, Joe?" But suddenly he was gone again, under the water. I could see his shape wriggling toward the rocks.

Dr. Emmanuel Rodriguez swam toward me and rested for a moment.

"We have to be more careful," I said. "We nearly got caught today."

To the sky he said "yes," and then he turned and rolled onto his back and started swimming away as if we didn't know each other. I tipped my head to one side and let the sea chop the world in half. It looked strange, like my life.

HELEN RODRIGUEZ STAYED in bed for a week. At her request, Dr. Emmanuel Rodriguez slept in the spare room, in case he disturbed her. He was concerned; it was unlike her to get migraines, it hadn't happened for a long time. She didn't come downstairs; she didn't leave her room. When she needed anything, she rang the bell. I carried up tea and juice, but she only ever wanted water, and dry biscuits broken into little bits like you might feed a bird. Also at her request, I kept the children away. For some reason she didn't want to see them. I didn't know if I was imagining it, but when she looked at me, it was as if she didn't want to see me either.

NINETEEN

WILLIAM AND I STROLLED TO THE BOTTOM OF MARY
Street. Like a gentleman, he stayed on the outside; walking, not too
slowly, because we needed to arrive in time to find a good seat. All
the same, he said, there was no point in rushing either. It was a cool
evening; the sky was powder blue with puffs of yellow cloud floating
here and there, like cotton you see in the fields. The grass was dark
green in that light; hedges were tall and clipped; typical of the manicured gardens in St. Clair, where, it seemed, nothing was ever allowed to grow wild. In the park, a young couple were sitting on the
swings, holding hands. I wondered how we might look to them. Me
in my cotton dress with a hoop print (given to me by Helen Rodriguez because, she said, it was too big for her and "you must have
something nice") and flat leather slippers, and William in a lime
green shirt I had never seen before, dark slacks, and sandals. He was
wearing a cologne that smelled of limes.

He was quiet and I guessed that he was feeling shy. This was a
date, after all. Marva said he had probably been looking forward to it
for two whole weeks. "He's like a puppy," she said, that morning. "I
never see him so excited. Usually William so laid-back."

It was true, he was definitely more lively; although I wouldn't
have noticed if Marva hadn't pointed it out. These days my head was
elsewhere.

I said, "How is your mother?"

"She say you must come up to the house and have dinner." Then, "I tell her how you always busy."

"I've been waiting for an invitation."

"You would come back to Laventille?"

"Of course. It's just difficult to get away. Mrs. Rodriguez doesn't like to be alone with the children. She can't cope. You know how she is."

"Solomon says you're one of those girls who take what they want and move on. Mother says that's because that's how he is. Always looking for a chance."

"Solomon can say what he wants. I like your mother. She was kind to me. So were *you*." I smiled, and William's face lit up.

WE SAT IN the upper level, rather than in the pit, which was where William usually sat. The seats were comfortable and we were right in the middle of the row, looking at the big, blank screen and the curtains on either side of it. Some people were sitting underneath the projector at the back, and they were making a lot of noise. William said they didn't come here to watch the picture.

At first, when the lights were dimmed, I felt anxious, and I wondered what in God's name I was doing sitting in the Deluxe cinema and I wished the night would pass quickly so that I could get home to Dr. Emmanuel Rodriguez. But then the huge, glorious Technicolor images appeared—the grand white house, the very green fields; the shining, galloping horses, the girls in their beautiful lacy gowns; and the orchestra boomed and crashed and filled me up and I felt as if I was right there in the Deep South of the United States of America—and I soon forgot.

The film was so long, when the lights came on at the interval, I

got up to leave. William looked worried. "You don't like the show?"
Then we both realized, and I laughed, and then William laughed too.

"HE SHOULD HAVE left her long ago," I said, as we started our
walk home around the Savannah. There were colored lights under
the trees, and a lot of people were out that night. I saw a group of
sailors standing on the corner. They stared at me, and I could tell
they liked the way I looked. For the first time in as long as I could remember, I felt light and free.

"Who?"

"The Butler man. And how come that girl—Melanie—was so
nice to Scarlett when she was always chasing down her husband."

"Some women are like that."

"And he wasn't even handsome."

"You liked the movie, Celia?"

"Yes. But if I was her, I wouldn't have let him get away like that."
And so it went, the whole way home.

AT THE BACK door, I quickly turned and went inside. "Good
night," I said, through the screen.

"See you Monday," William said, "please God."

I passed through the kitchen turning out the lights. I could feel
his eyes watching through the net. Dr. Emmanuel Rodriguez was in
his study, waiting up; wanting to know all about my date.

WILLIAM AND I started going to the cinema every other week. We
saw *Casablanca*, *Prince of Peace*, *South Pacific*, *Walking in the Rain*, *Pillow Talk*, *Ben
Hur*, *Strangers on a Train*, *Enchanted Evening*, *Affair in Trinidad*. These are the

films I remember. We always sat on the upper level, and stayed until the credits had rolled and the lights were up. And then we walked home along Queen's Park West, Marli Street, and up Maraval Road and then around the back of the college, and the whole way I talked about the movie—why I liked it or didn't like it, and who was good and who wasn't good. Apart from once, when it was raining, William never so much as touched me. We were running for shelter under the eaves of the Roman Catholic church and he put his arm protectively around my shoulders. And that same night, before he said goodbye, he tilted his face and I was sure he was going to try to kiss me. I said, "William, I'd like to take things very slowly." "I understand," he said, and looked down at his feet.

That was the week after the projector broke in the middle of the movie, and we went to a bar called The Cricket, and I drank a Coca-Cola, and before ordering a beer, he asked if I minded if he drank alcohol. I said, "Of course not, as long as you don't go and get drunk and I have to call the police." He laughed at this. "Sometimes Solomon and I come in here and we don't remember how we get home."

WE WALKED BACK the long way round, and stopped to look in the windows of the department stores. There was always something I wanted. A dress, a pair of shoes, a piece of jewelry, a new cream to rub on my skin.

"I wish I had a lot of money, William. I'd buy so many things."

"Money doesn't buy you everything. Look at Mrs. Rodriguez; she has a lot and she still unhappy."

"Do you think so? Do you think she's that unhappy?"

"I hear her. Her window is right there."

"Crying?"

"Yes, like a little child."

I said, "Maybe she knows you're there and she does it on pur-
pose."

"Why would she do that?"

THE WOMEN IN the films we saw were beautiful and I often wished
I could look like them. Rita Hayworth, Elizabeth Taylor, Audrey
Hepburn, Greta Garbo. They were perfect, I thought, and if I was a
man, I imagined that they were the kind of women I would want to
marry. William said they were okay, nothing to shout about.
"Trinidadian girls are the most beautiful girls in the world," he said.
"Anybody will tell you that." Then he said, "I think you're prettier
than all of them."

DR. EMMANUEL RODRIGUEZ didn't agree with William's idea
about Trinidadian girls. Yes, he said, they have beautiful women here
in Trinidad, because of the different racial mixtures, but they have
them all over the Caribbean too. And how could he say that English
girls weren't pretty when he'd married one. "You can't get more English than my wife. And she was a typical English rose."

We were lying on my bed, and it was getting late.

"Is she still a typical English rose?"

He didn't answer. Then, "What about Trinidadian men? Do
you like them?"

I knew he was talking about William.

"I like some of them. Not all of them."

"Who was the first man you were with, Celia?"

DR. EMMANUEL RODRIGUEZ didn't seem to mind when I went
out with William. How could he, when he was the one who suggested

it. When he first came up with the idea, that a date now and then with
"Gardener" (as he often called him) would put a stop to any suspi-
cions his wife or anyone else might have about our relationship, I was
dismayed. "How can I go out with someone else?" He said, "It's not
about going out with someone else. You don't have to do anything
with him. It's about making sure people don't talk. It's a way of
throwing them off the scent."

I SOON LEARNED that he was right.

The morning after our first date, Helen Rodriguez hurried
into the kitchen wearing her dressing gown and slippers, her face not
yet washed.

"How was it, Celia?" she asked, in a hushed voice. "Did you
enjoy yourself?"

I carried on wiping down the parlor shelves.

"I had a nice time, thank you, Mrs. Rodriguez."

"Oh good," she said, obviously wanting to know more. "That is
good news." Then, "Did you go to the cinema?"

Without looking at her, I said, "Yes, madam. We saw *Gone With the
Wind* at the Deluxe."

"What a romantic film to see!" Some hair had escaped from her
bun, she pushed it back and pinned it in place. "Do you think you'll
go out with him again?" This said like we were friends sharing our
private thoughts.

I rinsed the cloth in a bowl of water and squeezed it out. Then I
started on the large ceramic containers, cleaning off the grubby han-
dles and lids. They hadn't been cleaned in a long while.

"We'll see," I said. "I don't want to rush anything."

"Of course. But now he's on the hook, you mustn't let him
wriggle away. William is a good catch."

She was grinning.

"No, madam," I said, wiping my hands on my apron, looking her straight in the eyes. "I won't let him wriggle away."

AND FROM THEN on, it was always the same. "Did he say anything special?" "Did he look after you?" "Did you go somewhere afterward?" I never said much. Usually, I smiled and nodded, allowing her to imagine whatever she wanted. She wasn't put off by my withholding; if anything it seemed to encourage her. If Marva was there, she would look across and nod, or wink. Marva would say, "This girl like to keep her cards close to her chest." Or, "Getting anything out of her is like pulling teeth." I wanted to ask Marva why she was suddenly so interested in my life.

"The thing is," I said one day when they were both quizzing me, "talking about it too much might bring me bad luck."

"You mustn't be so superstitious, Celia. If it's the Lord's wish that you and William are together, then there's nothing you can do to stop it from happening."

HELEN RODRIGUEZ STARTED giving me clothes. She had lost so much weight, she said, and these were dresses and skirts she would never wear again; it was a shame to throw them away. "Please have them," she'd say, and she'd lay them out in her sewing room. "It's important to feel special when you have a boyfriend." I felt bad at first. But then I thought, Why not, I could never afford to buy such things. On the nights that William came to collect me and while he waited outside, she often came to see what I was wearing. She might fix a strap, or the collar, or check a hem. If Dr. Emmanuel Rodriguez was there he would tell her to stop fussing. "Leave her be, Helen. She knows how to dress herself."

Marva said I should count my lucky stars. "I never see her do that with anybody else. Look at how much clothes she give you. She treat you like a daughter."

When I got home, I often saw her light on or heard her moving around upstairs, and I knew that she was waiting to hear me come in. This was annoying for Dr. Emmanuel Rodriguez, who preferred to visit my room when he knew his wife was asleep. "You're keeping the lady up," he'd say in a half-playful way. "And me too."

THAT NIGHT, WE had just got home after seeing the eight o'clock showing of *The Bad and the Beautiful* with Lana Turner and Kirk Douglas, and William was in the kitchen drinking a glass of water, when Helen Rodriguez called down to tell me that there was a letter for me on the table. It had gone to the wrong house and someone had dropped it by hand, late this afternoon. I went at once to the dining room and picked it up. It was from Aunt Tassi. For some reason, I knew it was good news.

IT WAS MORE than I had hoped for.

AUNT TASSI WAS "writing to inform" me "that a terrible thing had happened." Roman was wrongly accused of doing "something," and the police had gotten involved. They'd put Roman in jail and she had to "find money for his bail." The whole thing was a misunderstanding and it had made Roman very upset. The night they let him out, Roman stayed home and got real drunk, more drunk than usual. After everybody went to bed, he left the house and decided to take a walk on Courland Bay. Aunt Tassi was sure he went down there to think about things. Because now and then we all need to be alone and think about things. Some men, and they still don't know who the

men were, but they might have been the fishermen we used to see—
the badjohns, the good-for-nothings. Well, they must have heard
about the lies people spreading, because they beat Roman. They beat
him with sticks. They beat him hard. They beat him so you wouldn't
know it was Roman. Next day two little children find him on the sand
and all around him black with blood. Aunt Tassi said she should have
known, because just that night, she had seen a huge scorpion crawl
out of one of Roman's shoes, a sure sign of death.

Aunt Tassi didn't know what she "feel right now," because she so
shocked. Everybody know how she love Roman. Vera and Violet were
in a terrible state. They can't believe their daddy dead. She hoped
that at some point I would come home to Black Rock and we could
patch up our differences. "Blood is thicker than water," she said. She
wanted to know where her friends were now. In her heart, she know
that Roman would *never* do what they say he did. And she know the
Mackenzie girl like to tell stories. Why did no one believe her?
"Friends carry you," she wrote at the bottom of the page, "but they
will not bring you back."

When I had read it, I called out, "Praise God! Praise God!" and
William came running inside. "What happen?" he said. "What happen?" I said, "It doesn't matter, it doesn't matter, this is a time to
celebrate." He was glad to hear this, he said, because tomorrow night
he had wanted to take me out to hear the New Town Singers play in
Charlotte Street. The whole way home, he wanted to ask me but was
so sure I would say no that he hadn't dared ask. I said, "Yes! Let's go
and hear the New Town Singers in Charlotte Street."

From the doorway, Helen Rodriguez said, "What is it, Celia?
Good news?"

LATER, DR. EMMANUEL Rodriguez came to my room, and he
wanted to know why I was in such good spirits. "Your eyes are

sparkling, Celia. I have never seen you like this before. What happened, is it something to do with your aunt? The one in Tobago?"

That's when I told him: "You are always asking me about the first man I was with. Well, the first man I knew was called Roman Bartholomew, and tonight I found out he's dead. And I'm happy because it means God never sleeps."

TWENTY

ON THE PORCH, WHILE THE DAY COOLED RIGHT DOWN
and we drank a cup of English tea, Aunt Sula taught me how to cro-
chet. I quickly got the hang of it and this pleased her; bringing the
yarn over, from back to front, then plucking it with the hook, bringing it through the slipknot . . .

"You're like me. I learned it very quickly too, and I've been
making things all these years." Then, "When you get married you will
want things for your home. Better start now." "You can make things
for children too; babies' clothes are quick and easy to make."

I couldn't imagine a day when I would be married.

"Why didn't you get married, Aunt Sula?"

"You have to meet the right man."

"Have you ever been in love?"

She half smiled.

"Who with?"

"Questions, questions! That was a long, long time ago."

"How did you know you were in love?"

"Well, I suppose I wanted to be with him all the time. When I
saw him my heart would beat hard like a drum." She thumped her
chest.

"Did he love you too?"

"He said so."

"Then why didn't he ask you to marry him?"

"You can love somebody but they might not be right for you."

Yes, I thought, that is exactly how I am.

WE WERE GOING to walk up to the stream, but Aunt Sula wasn't feeling well. She didn't complain but when Joseph Carr Brown arrived with some special herbs that he'd picked up in Four Roads, I could see that she was glad. While she mixed them together with powdered milk and warm water, he told me the herbs had come from Hazra. "The lady we gave the lift to; she said it's a cure-all. Hazra's not just a pretty face." I couldn't tell whether or not he thought they were worthwhile. "She grows them in the yard and dries them out to make tea." Then he said, "How does it taste, Sula? Like mud, I bet."

"Yes, Mr. Carr Brown, just like mud, only worse."

He was about to leave, but then the sky opened up and rain came lashing down. The wind blew hard through the little porch, so we went inside. And I was wondering what to say to him, because Aunt Sula was in her bedroom and apart from Shadow we were alone together, when he pulled out from his pocket a silver oblong box which he put to his mouth, and started to blow. Later Aunt Sula told me that Joseph Carr Brown's family had come from Scotland, and he had learned to play this instrument from his grandfather. I had never heard anybody play a mouth organ before. Shadow looked up at his master, ears cocked, and Aunt Sula came and stood in the doorway of her room. The music was sweet and sad and it made you want to smile and cry at the same time. When it was finished, she said, "Will you play that for me at my funeral?"

"Well," he said, "if nature takes its rightful course, I'll be gone long before you, Sula."

And then I thought about Roman, and wondered if he would be buried near his mother in Speyside. Earlier, when I arrived at

Tamana, Aunt Sula said, "Celia, we don't have to talk about Roman, but let's at least acknowledge that he's gone."

"Yes," I said, "and may his soul burn in hell."

AFTER SUPPER, AS usual, Aunt Sula insisted on washing the dishes. I was her guest, she said, I wasn't there to work. I thought how straight and slim her back was, not like Aunt Tassi, who was always heavy, no matter how she tried to lose weight.

That night, I asked, "Was my mother pretty?"

She looked up from the sink and out at the yard.

"Of course."

"Did people stare at her when she walked by?"

"I'm sure they did."

A small lizard stuck his head from behind a painting, and slipped back behind it. His tail was still poking out.

"Was she fun?"

"Oh yes."

The lizard made a run for it, darting across the wall to the window where he paused, then flipped himself over the edge and disappeared.

"Do I look like her?"

Aunt Sula turned around, and studied my face; then she shook her head. "A little." For a moment, I thought she looked sad.

"I must look like my father then," I said, and sat back in the rocking chair, sliding my hands over the smooth, polished arms. The back and seat were cooling rattan that left little patterns on your skin.

"Did you know your father, Aunt Sula?"

"I didn't know him well at all. He was a difficult man."

"Well, one day I'm going to meet mine," I said.

"And when will that be?"

"Not for a while. I don't have enough money saved. As soon

as I do, I'll go to England and find him. It's not so hard to get to England these days."

"I hope you'll tell me when you're going." Aunt Sula wiped her hands on her apron. Then from the drawer, she took up a fresh tea towel and started to dry the little pile of pots. "These things have a habit of coming together at the right time. You know what they say: If you want to make God laugh, tell Him your plans."

WHEN IT WAS dark, she put on the radio. I was always glad to lie down early in the bed she had set up for me in the living room. And I always slept well. Aunt Sula said it was the country air.

When it was time to leave, she filled a basket with mangoes, grapefruit, plums, and pineapples.

"Won't he mind that you've given me these things?"

"Mr. Carr Brown? Not at all."

TWENTY-ONE

I DON'T KNOW WHICH I NOTICED FIRST: THE CHANGE IN Dr. Emmanuel Rodriguez or the change in his wife. At that time, Helen Rodriguez was spending long hours in her bedroom. She complained about the rain, the heat, and the flies. From the newspaper she read out stories of robberies, murders, corruption. One particular case had troubled her: a brutal murder of two young women. When they were found, their eyes had been sewn shut, their private parts mutilated.

"This place is the opposite of paradise," she said one day, to no one in particular. "Hell on earth." She was also troubled by a murderer called Boysie Singh, known to cut out the hearts of his female victims, and rub them on the shoes of his racehorse, to guarantee a win. "These small islands breed monsters. No one is safe."

Some days she was quiet and withdrawn as if she was disappearing inside herself. Others, she was bright and gay as a butterfly. But this never lasted long. And I wondered on these good days, if she was trying very hard to make everything all right between herself and her husband.

"It's been ages since we went out for dinner," she said to him one morning, when I was clearing the breakfast table. "We could try that new place by the hotel."

"Whatever you want, Helen," Dr. Emmanuel Rodriguez said,

without looking up from his journal. "We can go out, we can stay home. Usually you want to stay home, that's why I never ask."

I felt sorry for her then.

"Well, why don't I book it, and we can go. It will make a nice change."

"Yes," he said. "Why don't you."

ONE DAY, SHE decided to take Joe shopping. He needed school shoes, she said. I asked if she would like me to go with her, and she said no. It was very hot, the dry air crackling with heat. "Why not go tomorrow morning," I said, "when it's cooler." But Helen Rodriguez drifted outside as if she hadn't heard a word, calling Joe, Joe.

They were gone all afternoon. It wasn't until dusk that I heard the car pulling in. Joe ran into the kitchen, and I could tell at once that he was upset. His mother followed, her arms laden with large shopping bags. "There's more in the car," she said, in a breathy voice. They had been all over Port of Spain buying shoes, driving as far as Chaguanas. Joe and I carried the bags upstairs and laid out the shoes in a line; we counted eight pairs.

When Dr. Emmanuel Rodriguez saw them, he threw up his hands. "What were you thinking?" Helen Rodriguez looked blank, as if she could not understand. "You must take these shoes back to the stores tomorrow." Then, "Celia, please put them back in their boxes, and place them in their correct bags." His wife let out a little cry, ran into her bedroom, and slammed the door.

ANOTHER TIME, SHE came home from the hairdresser's wearing a lot of makeup. There was a new beauty consultant based at the salon. Her eyelashes were black and thick, her eyes shaded in silvery blues and grays, her lips a deep red. Marva said she looked like a film star. But when Dr. Emmanuel Rodriguez came home at noon, he sat across from his newly made-up wife and ate his entire lunch without noticing. "Can *you* see the difference?" she asked Marva afterward, her eyes moist with tears. "Can you?" Marva said, "Yes, madam. Yes I can."

With me he was the opposite. Recently I had noticed that he was asking more questions about my whereabouts, particularly after I came back from Tamana. For the first time since I had started working there, I was taking time off. "What is it with Tamana?" he asked. "You're not thinking of living there?" "I like going to see my aunt," I said, surprised. "And Joseph Carr Brown is nice to me."

"Don't mention me to them, okay. Do you understand that? Carr Brown knows people I know."

Also, I had been going more often to the cinema, and it seemed to make him irritable. I had actually started to enjoy going out with William. And more than that, I loved watching the films; I came home wanting to talk about the movie I had seen.

"You act as if these people are real, as if you know them. You can't live in a movie, you know. They're actors paid to say lines."

"I don't want to live in one, I like watching them."

DR. EMMANUEL RODRIGUEZ no longer told me when he was coming to my room; instead of knocking on my door, he walked straight in. If I was doing something—bathing or brushing my hair or sweeping the floor or putting away clothes—he sat on my bed and waited until I had finished. I didn't ask about his wife and guessed that she was asleep early. When he was inside me, it was as if he was in a hurry, like when a man who has not eaten for days has a plate of food put in front of him. He started getting up earlier, and sometimes he came looking for me. Like that cloudy morning when I was outside cutting thyme, and William was there, and we were wondering if it might rain. We looked up at the sky and saw Dr. Emmanuel Rodriguez staring down at us from his window. William waved but he didn't wave back.

There were more questions: Had William ever tried to kiss me? I told him, William had more manners than any man I'd known. He would only try to kiss me if I said he could. If I took off my clothes and stood in front of him, would he know what to do? William is a man, I said, so of course he would know what to do! I tried to say these things in a lighthearted way but Dr. Emmanuel Rodriguez was insistent. Had William had girlfriends before? How about Mrs. Shamiel, was she encouraging her son? Who owned the house in Laventille?

I answered as best I could. I didn't understand why he was behaving in this way. I couldn't believe that my relationship with William would make Dr. Emmanuel Rodriguez jealous.

But there were other things. He had heard that his brother in Antigua was ill; Siri had telephoned to tell him that he might have to come if his condition worsened. Apart from his wife and children (and his mother), George was his only surviving family. When it came to sickness at home, Dr. Emmanuel Rodriguez found it difficult to cope. Marva had told me this.

"When Alexander die, Dr. Rodriguez did some things I sure he sorry for."

"Like what?"

"Never mind. All that's in the past now. All that's gone."

"Tell me, Marva."

"Let's just say, he hurt some people very badly."

THEN ONE NIGHT, he came to my room with a tiny black box. Inside, was a pair of sparkling silver earrings. "I hope you like them. I bought them in De Lima's." I tried them on, and lifted up my hair to show him. He said, "They're something else, aren't they. I knew the minute I saw them they would be perfect for you. I never see you wear earrings." I checked in the mirror, took them off, and put them away in my dresser. Someone was bound to ask where I got them.

"Tell Helen your aunt sent them from Tobago."

"She'd have seen them arrive in the post."

"Well, tell her you got them from an admirer. Or you saved up and bought them yourself."

"How would I ever have saved enough for these?"

"I want you to wear them, Celia." He said this like it was an instruction, an order. "You don't have to tell her they're real. A lot of shops sell costume jewelry made to look exactly like these."

It was almost as though he wanted to get found out.

THAT SATURDAY AFTERNOON, he insisted I drive south with him to the refinery camp, where he had to make a visit to the hospital. As it turned out, Helen Rodriguez had been invited to a lunch in town. She was taking the children and it was an all-day event. The Robinsons had recently built a swimming pool so everyone was bringing their bath suits. Even Consuella had a little cotton bikini of her own. Mrs. Scott had offered to collect Helen and the children, and drop them back at the end of the day; that way Dr. Emmanuel Rodriguez could have the car.

"You should have the rest of the day off," she told me, while packing their towels into a large basket. "I'm sure William would like to take you somewhere."

IT WAS A long drive on the old road toward San Fernando. Even though it was a chance to spend time alone together, I didn't think that we should be going so far from home. If the car broke down, or we got stuck for some reason, how would we explain it. "Life is very short," Dr. Emmanuel Rodriguez said, his eyes fixed straight ahead. "You'll understand this one day. When you're young you think it will last forever. There's no such thing as forever."

Soon green fields were on either side of us, the sugarcane as tall as people. The fires had started and we could smell the sweet burning. In the distance, there were clouds of smoke puffing up into the sky.

"It's partly to get rid of all the spiders and bugs," Dr. Emmanuel Rodriguez said. "And the leaves. Afterward they crush it up and make sugar." I already knew this but I didn't say anything. Sometimes he spoke to me like I was a child, as if he was my teacher or my father. "And you know they make rum from sugar." "Yes," I said. "And this is one of Trinidad's best exports." Again, "Yes."

He dropped me at the jetty, near a small yacht club.

"Go and look at the sea and I'll be back for you in a while." He pointed straight ahead where the water was blue-gray and flat. "If you look hard, you can see Venezuela."

UP ON THE hill, Pointe-a-Pierre Yacht Club was decorated with balloons, streamers, and bunting. People were drinking at the bar. One of the children who were playing on the beach came running along the jetty to where I was sitting, watching the sailing boats. There were three or four boats and they were tipping in the wind.

The little girl was staring at me. "Where are you from?"

"Who wants to know?" I said, in a friendly way.

"Everybody is wondering who you are." She glanced up at the bar.

"I'm from Port of Spain."

"My mother comes from Port of Spain," she said. "You might know her. They said you shouldn't be here unless you know someone."

"Well maybe you shouldn't be here either," I said. "You're annoying me."

She looked confused as she walked away, her blond hair trailing down her back. I watched her run up the hill, and speak to someone. Next thing they would be calling security. What kind of a place was this?

I was glad when Dr. Emmanuel Rodriguez arrived.

WE DROVE AROUND the camp. It was strange; all the residential houses looked the same, big brick houses with white walls and green galvanized roofs. The gardens and land around were immaculate. There was a golf course and tennis courts and a swimming pool. We parked outside the entrance and walked up a path cut between a high hedge, like a wall. The pool was big. I thought how lucky the young people were, all day diving off the high board, and swimming up and down in the turquoise water. Some tanned girls were perched on wrought-iron chairs under umbrellas, eating and drinking and talking. They were having a good time. Almost everyone I saw was white, unless they were minding little children and then they were black and in uniform.

"This is another world," I said. "They have everything here, these people."

We stopped at the lake and parked under a huge samaan tree. The water was low and there were two or three alligators lying like logs on the bank. Dr. Emmanuel Rodriguez leaned over and kissed me hard. Something told me he wanted to do it right there. He put his hand up my dress, and found his way to the top of my legs. Next thing, his fingers were inside me, and he started to rub himself with his other hand, over and over. There was an older couple and two young children strolling alongside the lake.

I said, "There are people coming this way. Don't you see them?"

"Yes, I see them. I want to finish." He was breathy now, coming to the end. I knew when this was going to happen.

Afterward, he reached for a bottle of water in the back, poured some of it on the seat where he had spilled, and rubbed it with his handkerchief. "Let's hope it doesn't leave a stain. It should be dry by tomorrow."

Then, just as I thought we were about to leave, Dr. Emmanuel Rodriguez insisted that we drive to a shop in Vistabella called Charlie's that sold the best black pudding in Trinidad. We could take some back for dinner.

I said, "Are you sure we have time? Isn't it in the opposite direction?"

He didn't answer.

WE DROVE BACK in the dark, the car full of the smell of fresh hops bread and peppery black pudding. We hardly spoke. I didn't ask Dr. Emmanuel Rodriguez what he was thinking about as I usually would, or what he was going to tell his wife. It was almost 8:30 p.m. I had my own story ready. I would say that I had been alone to the early showing of *Bridge on the River Kwai* at the cinema. Helen Rodriguez wouldn't have any reason to doubt it. On Monday, in case she mentioned it to William and Marva, I would tell them the same thing.

At the docks I saw the boat from Tobago was in; the same boat I had arrived on. People were hovering outside the Port Authority gates, looking for a ride; some were queuing for the tram. We stopped to let a woman cross the road. She was wrapped in a sheet like a vagrant. Halfway across the road, she looked at the car and put up her hand. In the bright headlamps, I could see her hand was disfigured, a bundle of tangled flesh, and I suddenly recognized the woman from outside the post office more than two years ago. She fastened her eyes on me. So much so that Dr. Emmanuel Rodriguez said, "Do you know her?" He tooted the horn once, then twice, and the woman shuffled away. I suddenly felt cold and tired. More than anything, I wanted to get home.

But when we arrived, the house was in darkness. In the garage, Dr. Emmanuel Rodriguez kept the car lights on while he looked for keys. No sooner had we walked in the front door than the telephone rang. I *knew* it was Mrs. Robinson. She wanted to let Dr. Rodriguez know that his wife was fine, and they had had a lovely afternoon. But Helen wasn't feeling too well. Mrs. Robinson called it a "nervous attack." It was probably nothing to worry about, and in fact, Mr. Robinson was going to drive her back earlier, but everyone thought it best that she wait until someone was home. She must have said, "What's your maid's name?" because I heard him say, "Celia. She's called Celia." Then he said, "Yes, I think she was out all afternoon, too. I have just returned myself."

JOE WAS PALE and tired. After supper at the Robinsons', he had fallen asleep on their sofa. Now he staggered upstairs, weary and irritable. Meanwhile, Helen looked like she had been awake for days; her eyes were red and dark underneath like someone had punched her. She handed me Consuella, and I carried her upstairs.

When I went to tell Joe good night, he was staring up at the airplane suspended from the ceiling. He said, "What's wrong with Mummy?"

"She gets very tired, Joe."

"Why? I don't know anyone else who gets tired like that."

"I'm not exactly sure but you can ask your daddy. It's very useful having a doctor for a father."

"She wants to go to England. She told me today; she hates it here." Then he looked straight at me. "She hates you too."

· · ·

IN THE MORNING, I was about to go into the kitchen when I caught sight of Helen Rodriguez standing at the sink. I quickly stepped away and then I saw Dr. Emmanuel Rodriguez, his back against the wall.

I heard him say, "Do you want to talk to somebody?" Then, "You have to tell me what's going on, Helen. You can't barricade me out of our room."

She was getting something out of the cupboard.

"Is it that you're missing England?"

Silence.

"What is it that you feel anxious about? There is no reason to feel that way. Everything is good. We have two beautiful children, and we have a lovely home."

Now she was filling the kettle.

"If this is about England and you want a trip away, then we can sort it out. Perhaps you want to see Isobel."

Her figure disappeared into the living room.

WHEN HELEN RODRIGUEZ telephoned Marva and asked her to come to work (Marva never worked on Sundays), I wondered what was going on. Then she started getting everything out of the pantry: flour, sugar, butter, pans, bowls, in a cheerful way. Joe hovered around her, watching. She said, "We're going to have a tea party. You pick whichever friends you'd like to come. As if it's your birthday." Her voice was definite and clear.

He looked up. "Why?"

"Don't ask why, Joe. Just go and make a list. Tell them to come for three o'clock."

"Aren't we going to church?"

"We don't have time to go to church." She was getting irritated. He glanced over at me. I nodded as if to say: Make the list.

BY THE TIME Marva arrived, I was feeling uneasy. Helen Rodriguez, who had never cared for baking, had mixed up three different cakes: chocolate, marble, lemon, and was now starting on gingerbread. She was following recipes from a book; something I had never seen her do. There weren't enough pans, and there weren't enough mixing bowls. She wore an apron over her nightdress and her hair was like a scruffy nest on the top of her head. She never left us alone together, but whenever Marva had a chance, she glanced over at me and I knew that we were thinking the same thing.

In the hallway, I could hear Joe speaking on the telephone. "No special reason," he said to someone. "Just a party." I thought how grown-up he sounded and I felt sorry for him. He would soon be old enough to compare his mother with his friends' mothers, and see that she was different. When he had finished, he came back into the kitchen and told Helen Rodriguez that most of his friends already had plans. Some were down the islands. Only six could definitely come, he said. He didn't look happy; he looked confused.

Then, unusually, Dr. Emmanuel Rodriguez was called out on a visit. A patient had gone into labor, the midwife hadn't shown up, and the woman couldn't get to the hospital. She lived in Diego Martin. Before he left, Dr. Emmanuel Rodriguez stood in the doorway and ran his eyes over the growing chaos.

"I don't know what is going on in here but I'm assuming somebody does."

WE MADE ENOUGH sandwiches for ten guests, just in case, and there were three cakes in all, plus gingerbread. At the last minute, Helen Rodriguez decided to make biscuits, cut into stars and moons. "There's no point in doing things halfheartedly."

While they were baking, she found some balloons in the cupboard under the stairs. "From three years ago," she said. "We got them for Alexander's christening."

Marva and I blew them up, tied them into bundles, and pinned them in the corners of the dining room. She looked pleased. Then she said, "What about the piñata?" I had heard about piñata. I knew that it was a game involving a shape made out of papier-mâché that was filled with sweets and hung from the ceiling. A blindfolded child would be spun around by the other children, and then, with a big stick, set the challenge of breaking the thing open to get the sweets out.

Helen Rodriguez threw up her hands, "Well, you're not very enthusiastic today, the two of you."

We followed her outside. There on the lawn was a big, round shape covered in newspaper. "I made it early this morning. It needs a little longer to dry."

She was beaming; happier than I had ever seen her.

By the time I came back from the store carrying five large bags of sweets, she had popped the balloon inside the ball, and was covering it with blue tissue paper. It was going to be a fish, she said, to represent Christ. She had thought about making a donkey; the creature that carried Mary to Bethlehem, but this was easier.

I fed the sweets inside the blue shape and Helen Rodriguez brought the ladder. Marva climbed up it and tied the piñata to the beam.

"What about a stick," she said. "Celia, let's go to the tool room and find one."

I didn't want to go to the tool room with her.

"Come on, no time to delay," and off she marched barefoot

into the yard. The ground was still wet in parts from the rain that had fallen in the night. She didn't seem to mind the mud on her bare feet.

I WAS GLAD to quickly find an old wooden pole that William once used for picking fruit. There was no longer a hook on it, which was just as well.

"It gets hot in here, doesn't it," she said, fanning herself. "I wonder how William can stand it. You really can't have more than two people in here at once." She ran her hand along the bench. "My husband had this made when we moved here. He used to come out here a lot. He still does, I think." She glanced at me and I shrugged my shoulders as if to say, How would I know? Then she dipped her hand in the box where the old sheet was kept and ripped away a strip of it. "This is useful. We can use it for a blindfold."

At the ficus tree, Helen Rodriguez stopped. She took a deep breath, then made the sign of the cross.

"Did you know my boy died?"

I said, "Yes, madam. Yes, I did know."

And she looked at me in a way that made me feel small and low, like I was no better than a cockroach crawling in the dirt, so much so that I couldn't bear to look at her and I turned and ran toward the house as if I had seen something there. She didn't call me back.

AT 2:00 P.M. Helen Rodriguez told Marva and me to shower and change. "By the time they arrive, we should all be clean and dressed." Then at last, she went upstairs. Marva and I looked at each other. It was hard to know what to say or do. If only Dr. Emmanuel Rodriguez was at home. Marva said, "I think we should try to find him."

"But where is he?" I said. "No one knows where this patient lives. You could drive all over Diego Martin and never find him."

· · ·

WE HEARD THE first car pull up just before three. It was Mrs. Robinson and her son, Damien. I went out to greet them. She was standing next to her yellow car with the engine running. She was a large blond woman with a deep, raspy voice.

"How is Mrs. Rodriguez? Is she better?"

I might have asked her to come inside, but I didn't like the way Mrs. Robinson looked at me. So I said that madam was getting ready, and she was feeling much brighter, thank you. When she asked what time she should collect Damien, I said 5:00 p.m. was fine. She jingled her car keys. "I might come a little earlier, I would like to see her." Then Mrs. Robinson kissed her son on his forehead, said goodbye, and left.

Joe ran outside and took Damien into the yard and they started to play on the wooden swing that hung from the tree. Then Emily arrived with her father. Nelson Scott, from our road, came with Dinah, his maid. No one brought a gift; it wasn't a birthday party. Mark and Kitty Aleong, who were twins and both a little younger than Joe, arrived as a rain shower began to fall. Soon it started coming down heavy, and everyone ran inside. Including Joe, I counted seven children.

I asked everyone to sit at the table. Marva made sure they each had a napkin and a glass for their lime juice, which I poured. Marva had just brought out the sandwiches when we heard Helen Rodriguez coming down the stairs. She was singing an old-time song. It went, "Oh the girls are so pretty, Waiting at the docks for the boys to come in. Oh the girls are so pretty . . ." All the children turned and looked at her. Marva put her hand up to her mouth.

She wore a long silver dress, with a silky train. The neck was square and elegant. Her hair was pinned in a bun and she was wearing makeup; the same makeup she'd bought at the beauty salon. Only it didn't look the same. Her eyes were two dark holes and her lipstick was thick and uneven. When she picked up her dress, I saw her feet were bare and filthy.

"Hello, children," she said, and found a seat at the table.

Emily started giggling, but Helen didn't seem to notice. I was relieved when Marva said, "Come on, everyone, let's eat."

Helen Rodriguez helped herself to a little pile of sandwiches. She must have been hungry; I hadn't seen her eat all day. Then, to Nelson Scott, as if he was an adult, she said, "And how are things with you, Nelson?" Her voice was strained.

"I'm very well, thank you, Auntie Helen."

And she went around all the children, taking turns to ask them how they were, as if they were her friends or acquaintances and it was a grown-up dinner party. Mark, who thought she was playing some sort of game, answered in the same way. Kitty must have kicked him under the table because he then started shifting around in his seat, and before we knew what was going on, there was a lot of moving about in seats. Then Emily said something and laughed.

In a high voice, Helen Rodriguez said, "Share the joke. Come on, it's not fair to keep it to yourselves." Everyone was silent and I wondered what they were thinking. Then Nelson spoke. "It's just that Emily said you were like someone out of a book."

"Who is that someone, Emily?"

"I don't remember her name," said Emily, looking puzzled.

I BROUGHT IN the cakes, and Marva cut up slices and I cut up slices. And the whole time, I prayed that Dr. Emmanuel Rodriguez would come. He had been gone for more than four hours. And I wished, too, that William was there. Marva rolled her eyes and I knew that she was worried. Trying to keep things light, I said, "Come on, everyone, there's plenty of cake!" Helen Rodriguez was watching the children, carefully. When most of them had finished eating she got up.

"Now," she said, "we'll play piñata. Plenty of time for cake later."

The children looked at one another, and then everyone got up and rushed noisily into the living room. Helen Rodriguez sat in the nearby armchair and drew up her legs so her dirty feet were on the seat. The children stared at the big blue shape hanging from the ceiling.

She said, "Give out the stick, Celia."

From the corner, I took up the long wooden pole.

"Whoever puts up their hand first can have a go."

Emily's arm shot up.

I tied the cloth around Emily's eyes. Then everyone gathered around the little girl, and they started to turn her. Her two plaits twirled as they spun her in a circle. I had to say, "Not too rough, be careful," and adjust the rope so the fish came lower and almost within her reach. I took hold of her shoulders and she raised the stick and I guided her a little. Everyone shouted out: Up, Up, To the left, and then Up to the right, Forward, and all the while the stick was hitting the air and then coming down on the floor. When she finally hit the piñata it wasn't hard enough, nothing fell out. She took off the blindfold and sat down.

Next it was Mark's turn. He was a small child, with fair curly hair. He was stronger than Emily, and when he hit with the stick, he hit it hard and with his whole body, so much so that he fell forward and onto the floor and I had to help him up. He said he didn't want to do it anymore.

Damien put up his hand. "Let me have a chance."

We spun the skinny boy round and round, and he, too, lashed hard with the stick, cracking it down on the floor. He hit the piñata in the middle and it looked as if it might break and everybody cheered, but then it didn't break, and the boy lost his patience and pulled off the blindfold. Joe was going to go next, but his mother stood up.

"Let me try," Helen Rodriguez said, in a way that no one would argue with.

Marva tied the blindfold, and like before, the children gathered around. It was difficult to spin her at first, because she was so much taller than them, but then they got the hang of it and she went easily with their pushing. Light was coming through the shutters now, and her dress was sparkling. She lifted up the stick and thrashed it in front of her, whacking it hard, smashing the top of the piñata. Everyone cheered. "Do it again," said Mark. But then she stumbled a little on the train of her dress, and when the stick came down, she hit the floor. She kept moving off to the right; the children yelled, Left. Left, Left, Left. But she wasn't listening. Next thing, she smashed the stick down on the shelf and a vase fell and broke. Someone (it might have been Nelson) said, Mrs. Rodriguez! We all thought it was an accident, but then she brought the stick down again, and little ornaments and picture frames flew off. Emily screamed and then Kitty screamed too. It must have alarmed Helen Rodriguez because she took off the blindfold, went to the cabinet, opened the doors, and dragged the stick over the shelves, throwing down glasses, dinner plates, serving dishes. By now all the children were crying out and I could see they were afraid. Finally, she went to the piñata and hit it so hard that it came down like a bomb on the floor and all the sweets fell out and scattered and the children didn't know whether to grab them or to run away. Some of them did run toward the door.

Mrs. Robinson and Dr. Emmanuel Rodriguez must have arrived at the same time; when I looked up I saw both of them at once: their shocked white faces like two masks. Dr. Emmanuel Rodriguez ran to his wife, wrapped his arms around her like a straitjacket, forcing her to drop the stick, and lowered her onto the floor. She said No, No, No, over and over. Then, Leave me alone. Leave me alone.

Her voice sounded more like her own. Marva and Mrs. Robinson had already taken the children out of the room, but Joe was still standing in the doorway. His eyes were big and frightened. I said, Joe, go with Marva. Go with Marva. But he didn't move. So I took his hand and pulled him away from his mother, who was now staring at the floor as if it was alive with snakes.

THAT NIGHT DR. Emmanuel Rodriguez stayed by his wife's bedside. I brought him soup and bread. He had given her a sleeping tablet but thought she might wake up when it had worn off. Together we carried a single bed into their room and he lay on it. Then he told me to leave; if she woke and saw me there she might be angry.

Downstairs, Marva was sweeping the floor. "I never see anything like this," she said, wiping her forehead. "Something happen today, something bad happen. Like somebody flick a switch in her mind."

"I saw it this morning, in the kitchen."

"Yes. Well, Mrs. Robinson say something going on with the two of you." She stopped sweeping and looked at me.

My heart was beating fast. "Going on with what?"

Marva's eyes turned dark and narrow. "Dr. Rodriguez. She say you have something with him."

"I was at the cinema yesterday. I swear to God. I swear on my father's life."

"I never said anything about *yesterday*."

THAT NIGHT, THE house had a strange feeling, as if someone had died.

I stayed awake for a long while, wondering what would happen tomorrow. It was like a nightmare, the whole thing. Through my dreams, I heard Dr. Emmanuel Rodriguez knock three times and then come into the room. I shifted onto the other side of the bed, to make space for him. He usually took a few moments to undress. I was glad that he had come to me now. I hadn't expected him. So when I felt him sit on the side of the bed, and then lift up the sheet and climb inside next to me, I said, "I'm so glad you came," and I moved back into him. I needed him to hold me in his arms, to say it was going to be all right. Cool fingers ran from my shoulder to my wrist. I said, "I was afraid of her today." But he didn't say anything so I moved farther into him. Then I half turned—to look at him, to find his mouth. It was difficult to see in the dark, and at first I thought I was dreaming but even in the dark there was no mistaking Mrs. Rodriguez's silhouette.

I jumped up from the bed, and ran to the light. She had no expression; if anything she looked like herself when she was calm, and yet her eyes were not calm, they were two screws holding me in place. Slowly, she got up and started to walk toward me. Her white dressing gown gaped open so that I could see her small breasts, with their tiny dark nipples. I could see the brown hair between her legs. For the first time, I was frightened of her. "I never meant to hurt you, Mrs. Rodriguez."

When the door opened and I saw Dr. Emmanuel Rodriguez, I cried out with relief.

TWENTY-TWO

WE NEVER SPOKE BEFORE SHE LEFT. I WATCHED HER KISS
the children goodbye, as if they belonged to somebody else. Joe tried
to hold on to her hand but she let go of him and went to the mirror
to adjust her hat and her immaculate hair. That morning, Dr. Emmanuel Rodriguez had taken her to the beauty salon to have her hair
fixed. He waited there in case anything happened. He had chosen her
traveling outfit: a stylish skirt and jacket in pale pink gabardine. At
first she didn't want to wear it. In the softest voice, I heard him say,
"Darling, you have to wear smart clothes in first class." Even though
her eyes were tired and vacant, she actually looked pretty. William
carried the trunk outside and put it in the boot of the car. Then he
opened the gate. From the upstairs landing, I watched the car drive
away. Mrs. Rodriguez didn't look back.

I HAD HARDLY seen Dr. Emmanuel Rodriguez in the last week.
His wife was too sick to be left alone, he had said. The drugs were
strong and made her sleep. There was no danger as long as she took
them. All day and night he stayed with her, either in their bedroom
or in the living room where she sat and stared at nothing and he read
his medical journals. He had hired a nurse to travel with her to
England.

Now, he would relax a little. Once Marva and William left and he was home from surgery, apart from the children, there was nothing to stop us from being together. And after Joe had gone to bed, it was easier again. He could come to my room whenever he pleased, or I could sleep in his bedroom and we'd lock the door. Perhaps, what we needed more than anything was a weekend down the islands at Avalon. No one would think anything of it. Places to go ran through my mind: the Botanical Gardens, the beach, the cinema, church. We could go as a family. As long as we weren't too friendly, it would be okay. People would say, "Oh his wife was taken ill, and his maid is very helpful." By then the rumors would have died down.

This is how I thought it would be. I couldn't have been more wrong.

WHEN HE CAME home that morning, Dr. Emmanuel Rodriguez disappeared into his office, asking not to be disturbed under any circumstances, unless it was "something to do with Helen." I was disappointed, and thought he would come looking for me later. He didn't. In fact, I didn't see him again until the following morning.

Usually at breakfast, he would ask about the post or say something nice about the fruit juice, or the fresh bread Marva had brought from that "terrific bakery in St. James," but that morning, it was as if he couldn't see me. I came and went, carrying this and that, and he never once said a word to me or looked my way. He talked to Joe a little about school, homework, plans for the weekend. But that was all. He left the house early to get to Mass before surgery. I had never known him to go to church in the week. The next day was the same. And the day after. When I tried to ask him what was going on, he didn't seem to want to talk and I eventually realized that he was avoiding me. Then he stopped coming home for lunch and instead bought something at the hotel restaurant next door to his office. I heard him telling Marva, "Nothing against your cooking. I have a lot to catch up on."

But more than this: he stopped coming to my room in the night, except to tell me that he was going out and I was to listen for the children. And even then, he didn't come inside, he spoke through the window like I was a servant. I don't know where he went on those evenings. He left around eight and got back after midnight. When I asked him to come to my room, or if I touched him in any way—like one time when we were in the kitchen and no one else was there and I put my face close to his—he pushed me away. "Not now, Celia. Please, not now." He said I would have to wait for a while. It was too soon.

I said, "Too soon for what?"

THEN JOE TOOK to sleeping in his father's bed. At first he lay next to him and listened to a story. But then he stopped wanting to go to his own bed when the story was over. When I told Joe that it was important to give his daddy some time to be alone and to rest, Dr. Emmanuel Rodriguez said, "It's fine for Joe to sleep with me. It's hard enough with his mother away. Isn't that right, Joe?"

WHEN WILLIAM ASKED if we could go out that weekend, I made an excuse that since Helen Rodriguez had gone, it didn't seem right to leave the children. We were sitting outside on the bench. The sky was darkening as if rain was coming, but here and there were streaks the color of flames. He had brought me a piece of pineapple from the yard; a sign, I hoped, that he hadn't turned against me. By now, William seemed like my only true friend.

"Thank you," I said. "You're good to me, you know."

"Mrs. Rodriguez liked pineapple. It was the only fruit she really like. I wonder if she can buy it up in England."

"I'm sure you can get everything in England."

"But what she really want she can't get there."

It was warm and there was a sweet smell and I wondered if it was the Lady of the Night. It made me think of Aunt Sula.

"William," I said, "I know that Marva thinks her going away might have something to do with me. But it's not true. Mrs. Rodriguez was like this long before I came to live here. Remember how you used to tell me things when I was in Laventille? About Consuella getting her head caught in the bars of the cot? Remember when something happened with Brigid. I don't know what that was. But she was always strange, wasn't she?"

He stretched out his long legs in front of him.

I said, "Mrs. Rodriguez hates Trinidad. It doesn't matter what anyone says or does, she will always hate Trinidad. You should marry someone from your own town, and if you can't, then marry someone from the same country or at least from the same part of the world."

He was looking ahead through the trees.

"Mrs. Rodriguez wasn't well," I said. "That's the truth."

William cleared his throat. "I told Marva, I don't believe what everybody say about you. You fit in here like they your own family, and just because you and the doctor get along good, it doesn't mean you are carrying on with him. People always ready to throw stones. They should look in their own backyards first. Marva not so perfect herself."

"Exactly," I said, relieved.

HELEN RODRIGUEZ HAD been gone three weeks when Dr. Emmanuel Rodriguez received a telephone call from her sister, Isobel, in Warwickshire. It was the second telephone call since she had left. The first was to let Dr. Emmanuel Rodriguez know that his wife had arrived safely and that she would be in contact again soon. Their conversation was brief. But now Isobel had a lot more to say. I heard him telling Marva: Helen was doing well. She had been to the nearby hospital, and the doctor had given her some medication that was definitely working. But it seemed to her (Isobel) that the countryside was the best medicine her sister could want. Every day they were walking in the nearby woods. Isobel hadn't got to the bottom of what had happened yet; when the time was right she would ask. But for now, he mustn't worry. Helen Rodriguez was thriving. She was taking good care of his wife! She sent her love to him and to the children.

After this news, Dr. Emmanuel Rodriguez's mood was noticeably brighter. The next day, he took Joe for a drive to Macqueripe, and they swam for most of the afternoon. When they came back with sweet buns and coffee cake, I made tea and they sat on the veranda and Joe asked me to join them, and I did. I really thought it was going to be okay.

But that night Dr. Emmanuel Rodriguez came to where I was washing clothes in the outside sink, and in a calm voice, he told me that he had some decisions to make, and it might be better for me if I didn't expect anything from him right now.

"I need time to think. Why don't you go and visit your aunt in Tamana? Or you could go to Tobago? I will manage with the children. Marva has offered to help out."

"Yes, Marva would love nothing more than that."

"Marva is concerned about you as well. I think you should go away for a little while, then we can see where we are with everything."

I knew that Marva had been keeping an eye on me. Whenever I was anywhere near Dr. Emmanuel Rodriguez, I could feel her burning eyes. The seeds of doubt had been sown and they were now growing tall.

"How long for?"

"Three weeks or so. As long as it takes. I will get a message to you somehow, and let you know."

TWENTY-THREE

WHEN I SAW AUNT SULA'S FACE I WANTED TO CRY.

"Child, what happen?" she said, and put her arms around me. "What happen?"

And then she asked me again at the table when I couldn't eat, and again when I was sitting outside on the steps staring at nothing.

"Celia, what is it?"

I wanted to tell her my life was hanging on a thread; that I was in love with a man who—as far as I could see—no longer loved me; a man I couldn't have, a man I had no right loving. But I thought she wouldn't understand.

"Is it your job? Has the English woman been unkind to you?"

Each time I shook my head.

"Is it a money problem?" Then, "Are you pregnant?"

And later, when she grew tired of asking, she said, "How long will you stay?"

"I don't know. Three or four weeks. I hope that's okay."

"Of course," she said. "You stay as long as you need to. My home is your home, you must always remember that."

"If somebody wanted to reach me, would they send a telegram?"

"Yes, it would come to the house and one of the children would bring it here for you. Are you expecting something?"

.   .   .

THOSE FIRST FEW days at Tamana I felt faraway, as if I was outside the world looking in. I watched Aunt Sula while she cooked and cleaned and crocheted. I watched her sweep, and fold clothes, and wash dishes. I often caught her looking at me with a sideways glance. I tried to eat a little to please her, but my appetite had gone. Now and then, to break the silence, she spoke about something that had happened on the estate. Sudden heavy rain; a worker who had cut himself; a parrot found with a broken wing. She talked about Joseph Carr Brown—the news that a citrus disease had broken out in South Trinidad, somewhere near Central. "If you're wondering why you haven't seen him, he's been up in the orchard covering the trees with nets." Apparently, it might not stop infection but it would help. It had been a terrible time. Aunt Sula said these things as if they mattered at all to me.

AT NIGHT I lay on the mattress and listened to the wind in the bamboo. I listened to the crickets in the grass. I listened to the gentle rumble of my aunt's breath. And I longed with every bone in my body to be back in my bed in St. Clair with Dr. Emmanuel Rodriguez above me; to smell his hair, to feel his mouth on mine. And I berated myself for wasting time with William, time that I could have spent with him. I had become complacent. It was my fault that he had turned away from me.

In the morning Aunt Sula would ask, "How did you sleep?"

"Same," I'd say. "Hardly at all."

And so it went. I soon lost weight and the dark circles under my eyes got darker.

.   .   .

THEN, AFTER FOUR or five days, she said, "Mr. Carr Brown want to know if you could help out at the stables."

My heart sank. "I'm not sure how helpful I will be."

"The stable boy is sick and we don't know when he's coming back. Mr. Carr Brown will show you what to do. Right now he has too many other things to think about to do it himself; everybody busy with something."

THE SUN WAS low when we started on the track. It was cool and still and there was mist on the ground. I looked up at the big house, pretty like a painting. I said, "How come some people have so much, and some people have to struggle all their lives just to get by?"

"It's only a struggle if you make it a struggle." She put her hand on my back.

AUNT SULA STOOD by and watched as Joseph Carr Brown took me into the stables. "You came at just the right time, Celia. Marlon is sick with yellow fever."

"I heard so, sir."

"The trouble when you get ill up here in the country, is finding a doctor. It takes three hours as you know to get into Port of Spain. Not all of us are lucky enough to live in the same house as one."

"Yes, sir," I said, my heart heavy as clay.

"Now, remember, we have three horses and a mule. And the workmen always tell me before they take them out. Unless it's something urgent. We don't like them to get overworked. The horses, that is."

I realized he had made a joke and smiled. But I was a little late.

The wooden sheds were large, cool, and dark, except for where there were holes in the roof and sunlight jetted in. I followed him to each stable door and he told me the name of each horse. He showed me a large box of brushes, combs, and the special cream I must use when their skin was bruised or sore. "Sometimes they get open wounds or the skin breaks where the girth pinches. You have to watch out for that." At one point, he stepped out and called down the hill to Tatton, who was playing right there by the oleander tree. He came running up. Apparently, he knew how to "muck out," but Joseph Carr Brown thought it best if he didn't do it alone.

They left me there with Tatton.

TOGETHER, WE GOT the horses from inside to outside, letting them roam a bit under the trees. At first I felt unsure about holding their ropes, and their size frightened me, but then I saw the boy calmly leading them here and there. "They'll get used to you," he said. "Sometimes they get in a bad mood and you have to leave them. Especially Cocoa. She doesn't like anyone except Mr. Carr Brown."

We swept out the stables and mopped the floors. It was hard work and I soon got hot and tired. Once it was clean, we brought the horses back in and Tatton showed me how to check the bottom of their feet, where "things" got stuck, and how to clean them out. We carried water from the pump up the path. Bucket after bucket. And they drank quickly as if these buckets were small like thimbles. Then we glanced over their coats to make sure there weren't any cuts or sores or parasites. And, finally, we brushed them down. Their bodies, their tails, their manes. By the time we had finished it was almost midday.

On the way back to Aunt Sula's house I realized, for the first time in days, I was hungry. I could tell my aunt was pleased.

"It's good to take your mind off things," she said. "You'll do the same tomorrow?"

·   ·   ·

BY THE END of my first week, I was taking out the horses on my own. Tatton was impressed. I had such an "easy way" with them, he said, it must be in my blood. When I told him that was doubtful, he said, "Then your mother must've ridden a horse when she was pregnant." Truth was, I wasn't sure that I liked horses. I liked Milo because he was smaller, and there was a gentleness about him. But the other two were big and unfriendly. Their dark eyes followed me around and made me wonder if they knew things. When I was stuck, when they bucked, or jerked their heads from side to side, or refused to move, I called Tatton and he quickly came to help. They were always keen to get outside. Seafer and Cocoa were the most impatient; I half expected them to break away and run out onto the field, but they didn't. They waited in the sun until we took them to the shaded parts and fastened them to the trees. Once the gate was up, we untied their ropes and let them go. They stayed quite still, particularly Diamond, the mule who seemed weary like an old man. Diamond, Tatton said, was a friend for Cocoa when she was young. They need a friend when they're foals," he said. "Like children."

We swept out the sheds together. They were often hot and damp, especially when the rain came in through the roof. It made a narrow funnel of water which seeped through the partition. When this happened, Tatton brought the mop and soaked it up. At times there was a strong and unpleasant smell. He said the dogs were to blame; they got in when the stable door was left open, and slept in the passageway. "Sometimes they make a mess. Don't tell Mr. Carr Brown. He'll say it's my fault for not closing the door."

"Who else could have left it open?"

"Soldier Ghost."

I must have looked confused.

"Soldier Ghost was a pilot. His plane crashed in the hills." The little boy pointed behind him. "When they found him he was so mashed up you could fit him in a bucket. And now he walks around Tamana looking for his plane and the passengers."

I said, "Have you seen him?"

He lowered his voice. "No, but Cedar saw him in the yard one night, walking around the back of the house, in a blue uniform with stripes and boots, and a white hat."

"Does Mr. Carr Brown know about Soldier Ghost?"

"Yes, miss. He say it's nonsense and superstition."

EVERY MORNING, JOSEPH Carr Brown stopped off on his way back to the house. I'd hear him whistling all the way down the track. For some reason, I often felt shy with him, and this made me awkward. Like that time, a few days after I had started, when he asked, "You like the horses, Celia?" and I said, "Yes, sir."

"Which one is your favorite?"

"Diamond," I said, suddenly unsure.

"But Diamond's a mule, not a horse."

I said, "Are they so different?"

He narrowed his dark blue eyes, as if he wasn't quite sure if to believe that I was serious. Then, "Well, the head is bigger, the tail is short like the tail of a cow. The eyes are larger, the ears longer. They're completely different beasts!"

More than once he caught me using a brush instead of a comb. My strokes were going in the wrong direction, he said. "Follow the growth of the hair," and he took my hand and ran it over the long back of the horse. "See how it grows. You have to use your instincts with these things, too."

TATTON SAID, NICE as Mr. Carr Brown seemed, he didn't stand for fools or cowards. When he found him and Ruth behind the shed making a fire, he took a switch from the mango tree and beat them both. Now the boy was quite frightened of him. Tatton told me of at least three people who had been caught stealing at Tamana. "All of them were fired, even though Mr. Carr Brown knew them since they were small like me. One of them was in his fifties. His whole life all he ever knew was Tamana. And Mr. Carr Brown throw him off the land like he a stranger trespassing. No matter how the man beg, he wouldn't let him come back. When Mr. Carr Brown finish, he finish."

After the stables, Tatton and I made our way back together. I stopped off at the main house and looked in at the kitchen where Dolly was preparing lunch. She cooked a hot meal for Mr. and Mrs. Carr Brown and it had to be on the table by 12:30 p.m. Cedar served the meal. If there was anything extra, a piece of meat or some pie or an extra loaf of bread, she sent it for Aunt Sula and we had it for lunch. Dolly said, "They don't have the children here anymore, so who gonna eat it? I cook all this food and for who? Madam eat like a bird."

Before I left, I'd ask if the mail had come.

"No, child. Nothing for you," she'd say. "Check again in the morning. Tomorrow another day." And half of me would feel wretched, and the other half relieved; no news was better than bad news.

NOW AND THEN, when Mr. Carr Brown said I could, I took Milo and rode slowly up to the fields. There was another route around the forest, and it meant riding on the road, which was easier. The hills were right there, covered with vines and huge ferns; there were red, hard, hanging flowers. For some reason, they made me feel sad. After I had ridden through the fields and checked the citrus trees, I started back. Sometimes, my heart ached so much I felt like carrying on into Arima, and riding on horseback all the way to Port of Spain.

EVEN THOUGH I was unhappy, there was something about the land at Tamana that calmed me, maybe because there was so much of it. Nothing here changed, and yet everything changed.

Every afternoon, Joseph Carr Brown dropped by. He sat on the veranda, his long legs stretched out. Aunt Sula made a pot of tea and offered him something to eat: shortbread, cake, biscuits. Mr. Carr Brown had a sweet tooth, she said. They sat and talked like friends who had known each other for a long time. It was easy, comfortable. Sometimes, Aunt Sula took out a pack of cards and the three of us played a simple game called hearts.

"Hold up your hand," Joseph Carr Brown would say. "I don't want to see what you have." And I'd hold my cards right up to my face, but then as the game went on, I'd forget and the cards would drop.

"Why does this girl want to show me everything she has," he'd say, and Aunt Sula and I would laugh. Sometimes, when he gave a joke, Aunt Sula laughed so much tears rolled down her face.

He taught me how to shuffle the cards, splitting them equally into three, pressing down with my fingers, using my thumbs to lift the corners, arching my palms to create a bridge. "Your hotshot friends in Port of Spain will want to know where you learned to do this. You can tell them, in Sula's gambling parlor."

Aunt Sula told me that when his children were young, Joseph Carr Brown played marbles with them every afternoon. They sat underneath the house where he'd laid a smooth flat patch of stone, perfect for the game. He carved giant pickup sticks and painted them in bright colors; he marked up a cricket pitch. He built a wooden house in the mahogany tree, nearly good enough to live in. Now and then he packed them in his car and drove to Ballandra where he swam with them in the Atlantic ocean. "They clung to his back like a raft. That sea can be rough."

I WAS HEADING home that morning when I remembered that Aunt Sula had asked me to stop off at the chicken shed and pick up some eggs for supper. Through the wire fence, I could see Ruth playing with her doll.

"Hello, miss," she said, her little face beaming.

"Now it's holidays, you're happy not to go to school," I said, bending down by the wooden gate. There were about twenty chickens in all and they were mostly walking about, pecking at seed on the ground. They didn't seem to bother her.

"Yes, miss." Then, "Will you play jacks with me?"

"Maybe," I said, not seeing the snake that had crawled into the pen right where the little girl was playing. But then I did see it: a thick black and yellow snake and it was crawling toward a hen just inches from Ruth's feet. The hen was sitting on its nest and could not move, as though the snake had put a spell on it, and then Ruth saw it too. They say this about snakes—that they can hypnotize animals and children. Then suddenly, as if the spell snapped, there was a screeching and squawking. I ran around the edge of the pen, dived inside, and grabbed Ruth, who, terrified, climbed onto my back and clung like a crab on a rock. From the safety of the fence, both of us watched at where the hen was jumping, flapping its little wings. And we watched in horror as the snake opened up its mouth and swallowed each and every one of its seven eggs. And in no time at all, all the eggs were gone from the nest and the snake was sliding itself over the dusty earth toward the corner of the pen. There, it curled its body into a ring and quickly fell asleep.

Next thing, Joseph Carr Brown came outside. "Why didn't you

call me?" he said, surprised. Then he did something that shocked me: from over his shoulder, he took up a fouling piece with a duck shot, held it out, and fired and blew the snake's head into pieces. I held Ruth's head so she would not see the fleshy mess. He told me to collect the eggs. So I walked over to the dead snake and plucked out each egg (not one of them was broken) from its throat and put them back in the nest. That evening, the hen was sitting on them again and four days later chicks started to hatch.

When I told Aunt Sula what had happened, she said it took courage to go inside the pen and rescue Ruth. "Not everyone could have done such a thing. You're brave," she said, "like Mr. Carr Brown."

NEXT DAY, AT the stables, Joseph Carr Brown asked if I was feeling better. "Sula told me you haven't been yourself for a while. I thought so, too."

I felt my face grow hot.

"Your aunt is a good person to talk to."

"Yes, sir."

I didn't tell him that I felt like I was dying inside.

DURING THE DAY I could just about cope, but at night, my longing for Dr. Emmanuel Rodriguez left me exhausted and unable to sleep at the same time. I tried hard to imagine what he was doing. I tried to picture him in his study, sitting at his desk and working. I saw him in his bed, lying on his back, his eyes open. I talked to him, softly, so Aunt Sula wouldn't hear. I asked him to come for me or to send for me. I told him I was sorry and that I missed him with all my heart. I thought about the children and wondered if they had asked where I was and what he would say to them. I counted the days I had been at Tamana, and I counted how many there were before I could leave. And when I lay there thinking about all that had happened to bring me to this place, I didn't know how I would last. I knew that Aunt Sula was glad to have me there. More than once she said, "I don't know why you came and I never want to see you unhappy, but I—for one—am very glad to have you here."

And this is how it was every day at Tamana. And the days passed. And I waited, and I waited, and I waited. But I didn't hear anything from Dr. Emmanuel Rodriguez.

THEN, ONE AFTERNOON, Dolly came rushing down the hill to Aunt Sula's house calling, Celia! Celia! I had just finished bathing; my hair was wet, my dress not yet buttoned. Aunt Sula was lightly sleeping in the chair when Dolly arrived in the living room, her face hot and shiny. "Look what came," she said, waving an envelope. I felt my whole heart flutter like a bird in a cage.

There was no postmark; my name was written in black ink. I tore it open; it didn't matter that Aunt Sula and Dolly were there.

> *Dear Celia*
>
> *Please forgive my handwriting. This is my third try. The others were not correct and you will see from this why I did no good at school. I am writing to ask how you are. I ask Marva when you coming but she don't know. So I hope you will tell me.*
>
> *Yours, William*
>
> *P.S. Last week I saw* Gigi. *The girl was called Leslie Caron and she remind me of you.*

Aunt Sula got up from her chair. "Is everything okay?" In a sharp voice (a voice I never meant to use) I told her no, and why should I ever expect it to be any different. Then I hurried from the house. I heard Dolly call out, but I didn't stop. I ran up toward the stables, along the side of the main house; I ran around the back where the cocoa sheds were. I climbed up and through the shady cocoa trees, and out of the gate at the top of the estate. Out on the road, I began to walk. I walked fast, as if someone was following. I passed an almond tree and a rocky part where angel trumpets were hanging. I passed the waterfall; people were sitting on the ground eating and I could see smoke from a fire burning. Somebody said, Good afternoon, but I didn't answer; I kept on walking; walking until I came to the tiny stream where I had once seen children bathing. I walked until I saw the edges of the night sky and I knew that I had no choice but to go back.

By the time I reached the estate it was almost dark. Aunt Sula was waiting on the porch, looking out; in the lamplight, I could see her face was anxious. Joseph Carr Brown was drinking a glass of beer, his legs stretched out, as usual. I heard him say, "Ah, she returns." Then, "I told your aunt not to worry. Port of Spain is a long way from here on foot."

ON SUNDAYS WE went to church. It was a long walk and we all wore hats and tried to stay in the shade. Cedar walked with Dolly, and as she walked Cedar sang. Her voice was beautiful and strange, like it came from another world. The old folk songs reminded me of Black Rock, and the songs Mrs. Maingot used to sing: "When Me Baby Born" and "Ine Ine Katuke," "Old Lady." There were three other families who slept in the barracks and worked on the land. They all had children, two of whom were Tatton and Ruth. All in all, there were nineteen of us on the road. When the Carr Browns drove by, everybody waved like the king and queen of England were passing.

The church was plain and narrow and there weren't any stained glass windows. It was like St. John's church in Black Rock. But for all its plainness, it was always full; the congregation was mostly made up of country folk. The Carr Browns usually stood near the front. Mr. Carr Brown wore a white suit, and his tiny wife a long dress and a little hat like a box that sat on her head. I had only ever glimpsed her in the house. She looked more Spanish than anything; her olive skin, her brown eyes deeply set.

THAT MORNING, MR. and Mrs. Carr Brown were strolling out ahead, and Aunt Sula and I were walking, slowly, behind them. We stopped there by the palm tree with the red berries and watched them get into their car. They didn't seem to notice us. I asked Aunt Sula if she liked Mrs. Carr Brown. She told me that in all these years, she had never really got to know her. People said she was shy and private, but Aunt Sula wasn't sure. "She was always a little miserable." And these days, she was more so because the children had left home; they visited often and they brought the grandchildren.

"I wonder how anyone could be like that when they have their children and their grandchildren visiting so often." Aunt Sula shook her head, as if she really couldn't quite understand such a thing.

I said, "I haven't even spoken to her yet."

"I'm sure you'll meet her before long."

I DIDN'T EXPECT to meet her in the way that I did.

I WAS PASSING the main house when I heard Cedar call out. "Miss," she said, and put out her hand, "I want to show you something. Come, quick."

I was wondering what it could be and why she was so excited. I ran across the grass and up the veranda steps. The girl was bent over,

staring at something on the floor. At first I couldn't see it because the
wooden boards were so dark and there were lines on the wood. But
when I got closer, I realized she was staring at a large black scorpion,
the biggest scorpion I had ever seen by far, with a long black body and
a thick tail—up, arched, and ready to strike. I screamed. And that
made Cedar scream too: a terrible high-pitched yell that went right
through me. Suddenly, the scorpion started running toward Cedar's
feet, her bare, splayed feet (I knew that scorpions liked to sting between the toes), so I ran to her and slammed my boot down on top of
the thing. Over and over until I had completely crushed it. Cedar
cried, "She kill it, she kill it." And, to my amazement, she burst into
tears and started to bawl—as if I had just slaughtered her friend. And
I was so angry that she was crying and bawling because I had killed the
creature that was about to *bite* her, the creature that could have made
her very sick and might have killed her, that I did something I should
never have done: I slapped her. I slapped her across her face. Next
thing Mrs. Carr Brown came outside, and she said, "What happen,
Cedar? What happen?" It seemed to me that this lady was blaming
me for the way Cedar was behaving. "It might have bitten her," I said.
Then Joseph Carr Brown came outside too. He was eating his breakfast when he heard the terrible noise.

"What in God's name," he said. "It sounds like someone is
being murdered!"

I said, "Someone nearly was murdered, sir." Cedar was holding
her face and glaring at me. Mrs. Carr Brown put her arm around her
bare shoulder. She said, "This is Sula's niece?" And Joseph Carr
Brown said, Yes, yes it's her niece. Both his wife and Cedar were
looking at me as if I was a rotten fruit. I turned and ran away back
down the path to Aunt Sula's house. He shouted my name, but I
didn't look back.

I found my aunt lying on her bed. "Don't worry," Aunt Sula
said. "These things happen; everyone know Cedar not quite right in

her head. And don't worry with Mrs. Carr Brown, either. She would look for a reason to dislike you. Tell Cedar you're sorry, it will be okay." I was so upset I never thought to ask *why* Mrs. Carr Brown would look for a reason to dislike me, or *why* my aunt was lying down in the middle of the morning, at a time when she was usually working.

THAT EVENING, I had just gone inside when Tatton arrived at the door. He was out of breath. He said he didn't know who the letter was from because he don't know how to read yet, but "Mrs. Carr Brown say it for Sula's niece."

I examined the stamp and the postmark. It had come from Port of Spain; the address was typed. "Thank you, Tatton," I said, and stood there, until he realized I wasn't going to open it. I waited until he was out of sight, and I could hear Aunt Sula preparing supper. Then I sat on the steps in the half-light, and with my heart thumping, opened the small white envelope. The slip of paper read: "Please come to the house as soon as is convenient. Dr. Emmanuel Rodriguez."

TWENTY-FOUR

I HAD PLANNED TO LEAVE FOR PORT OF SPAIN straight after lunch, but as soon as I got back from the stables, I knew something was wrong. Aunt Sula was sitting at the table in her nightdress. The pain, she said, had been coming on and off for a while.

"What kind of pain?"

She put her hand on her womb. "Just here." She had noticed some bleeding, and it was painful for her to pee. She pressed on her lower back.

"It feels very sore." She didn't have a fever right now. But in the night it was quite high. And like the pain, the fever seemed to come and go.

"Is this what you were sick with before?"

She nodded. "Yes, and I was back on my feet in a day or so." Then, "Are you going back to Port of Spain? You must tell Mr. Carr Brown you're leaving so someone else can do the horses."

"I can't go now. Somebody has to take care of you."

"Nobody has to take care of me. I can look after myself."

As soon as she said it, we both knew it wasn't true. I helped her up, and together we walked to her bedroom and she lay down. She didn't want to get under the sheets.

"I'll just rest here for a while."

"Mr. Carr Brown came this morning. He brought some things. He will look in later."

"What things did he bring?"

"They're on the sideboard. Please don't worry, child. You eat something and go. There's no point in you being here. Where's the driver? Take some money from the milk tin."

There were supplies in the bag, soap, juice, two bowls with cooked rice, stewed chicken, onions, bread, oil, sugar. I put everything away and then I chopped some vegetables and put them on the stove to make broth. Later, when I looked in on her, Aunt Sula was lying on her back with her mouth open, breathing heavily.

JOSEPH CARR BROWN arrived just as I had finished watering the plants. I was washing my hands when I heard his boots on the steps. I looked out and saw Seafer tied to the avocado tree. He pulled back the beaded curtain hanging in the doorway. "Sula," he said, softly. Then he saw me. "Hey, how is the patient?"

I said, "She's in bed."

"Is she feeling any better?"

"I don't know, sir, she's sleeping. She was in a lot of pain."

He walked through the kitchen and into Aunt Sula's bedroom. From there, I watched him. He looked at her, he opened the windows right out; he fixed the covers and then went to the top of the bed where he touched her forehead. Lastly, he took her hand in his, and because his back was turned, I couldn't tell if he was feeling her pulse or holding her hand.

"She has a fever again. If it's there tomorrow, or it gets worse, we'll take her to hospital. This thing seems to come and go."

"Perhaps she should go to hospital now."

"No. I don't think we should panic. She hates hospitals. It's good that you're here, you can keep an eye on her." He said this like it was a fact. But he must have seen something in my eyes, because he then said, "You will be here, won't you?"

"Sir, I was planning to go back to Port of Spain. I'm supposed to go back." I was about to explain that now Aunt Sula was sick my plans had changed but he jumped in.

"With respect, Celia, your aunt is quite ill. She needs care." He glanced around the room and saw my suitcase propped up. "Surely Rodriguez can wait a few days. Didn't he send you away for a month?"

I suddenly felt ashamed and angry. "He sent me here for a rest, but I haven't had a rest."

Joseph Carr Brown's eyes flashed, and in a firm, cool voice he said, "Let me know what you decide. If you're leaving, I'll see someone's here to look after her."

THROUGHOUT THE NIGHT, I got up to check on Aunt Sula. Mostly, she seemed to sleep quite deeply. At one point, though, she had to use the toilet. Neither of us could see very well; there wasn't much of a moon and apart from a few stars, the sky was black as pitch. I helped her down the steps, holding a candle in one hand, her arm in the other. Then, slowly, we made our way over the damp black grass.

"Do you remember when you and my mother used to pretend to be bushes called Pilil and Lala?"

"Who told you so?"

"Aunt Tassi. And she told me how one night you waited behind the guava tree and sprang on her like a couple of cats. She played dead and frightened you both. She said you shook her like a flour bag!"

"Yes, child," Aunt Sula said, "I remember. I didn't realize you knew all that."

·   ·   ·

UNABLE TO SLEEP, I watched a firefly blinking on and off in the dark, and I started thinking about Dr. Emmanuel Rodriguez. And then I was thinking of how we had met, in Laventille; remembering how sick I was, how I almost died, and if it hadn't been for him I probably would have. And it was while recalling something Joseph Carr Brown had said—about the nearest doctor being three hours away, and trying to guess where in the room the little firefly's light would next appear—that the idea came to me. If Aunt Sula needs to see a doctor, then she must see Dr. Emmanuel Rodriguez. He had cured me of yellow fever, so surely he could heal my aunt of this illness. Why didn't I think of it before!

IN THE MORNING, Aunt Sula was feeling a little bit brighter. I made her a sandwich and a cup of tea and then went up to the main house. Dolly said she didn't mind looking in on her while I was gone. It was no trouble at all. She would stay the night too. A couple of nights if necessary.

"Are you worried you'll lose your job?"

"Yes," I said. "They asked me to return yesterday." Then, "When Mr. Carr Brown asks where I am, tell him I'll be back tomorrow."

I WALKED QUICKLY through the back of the estate and cut into the path that led to the main road. I hadn't seen anyone so far, apart from two workers clipping the rotten branches of the cocoa trees, and they did not look at me. If I was quick, I could catch the bus to Arima, and from there, another bus to Port of Spain. It would take all morning, and depending on when I could get a connecting bus, perhaps all afternoon too. I felt excited; my heart was fluttery and light.

But in Arima, I noticed a dead bat lying on the side of the road. Its dark brown wings were thin like silk; its little teeth exposed and yellow. It looked as if its neck was broken. I was sorry I had seen it; a dead bat was never a good omen.

TWENTY-FIVE

By the time I arrived at the Rodriguez house, it was almost dark. I didn't expect to find Marva still there. But the minute I went to the back door and saw her in the kitchen, I knew at once that she had fully taken over the running of the house. She had her back to me, pulling out clothes from the laundry basket and folding them. I thought she was alone, until I heard his voice.

"The specialist says the only thing she really needs now is a good rest."

"Isn't that something, sir," Marva said, like it was a miracle.

"Isobel likes having her sister around. It's the first time in years they've spent so much time together."

I had planned to breeze in as if I had been there just yesterday, but my legs were suddenly heavy. I crept along the wall so they could not see me.

"She must be getting to know her nephews and nieces," I heard Marva say. "And eating all that English fruit. Madam was always talking about her English fruits."

"Yes, she's already put on weight. I imagine she's eating a lot of chocolate!"

They laughed.

"That's good, sir," said Marva. "And will she meet you at the airport?"

"Yes, and we'll travel back together to the countryside."

My heart dropped like a stone in a river.

"It will be good for the children to spend some time with their cousins."

"Of course, sir."

Now Marva was filling the sink. I could hear plates, the clanking of cutlery. Then she said, "It's time for the family to be together, sir."

"Hello, Marva," I said, from the doorway. "Sir."

Dr. Emmanuel Rodriguez looked startled as if he had seen an intruder.

"I'm sorry," I said. "I didn't mean to alarm you."

I turned and went to my room, half expecting to find my belongings packed away and Marva's in their place, just like when I first came to the house and the maid's clothes were in the drawer. But to my surprise, the room was as I'd left it.

THAT NIGHT, WHEN Marva had gone and I knew the children were asleep, I went to Dr. Emmanuel Rodriguez's office.

"When were you going to tell me?"

He looked confused, as if he didn't know quite what I was talking about.

"Tell you what, Celia?"

"I hear you're going to England."

His eyes ran over his desk. "I was going to talk to you about it tomorrow. We do need to talk. That's why I wrote to you."

"When are you going?"

"On the weekend."

That was just four days away.

"For how long?"

"Two months." His voice was matter-of-fact, as if he was talking to someone he didn't know, someone he didn't particularly like. He straightened a pile of papers and put them on one side.

I hadn't imagined he would go for quite so long. I felt sick.

"And what am I supposed to do?"

I was shaking inside like when you have a fever and a cool wind blows.

Dr. Emmanuel Rodriguez got up.

I said it again. "What am I supposed to do?"

"I need you to leave here by the time we get back, Celia. I can't have you here when Helen comes home." He put his hand to his forehead, as if speaking about this was causing him great difficulty. "It's because of you that she had this breakdown." He quickly corrected himself. "It was because of both of us." He walked round to the other side of the desk and leaned against it. "She knew about it for a long time. I can't do it to her again. She has promised to come back on condition that you won't be here when she does. I have to accept that; she is the mother of my children. My wife."

We stood there looking at each other. Then he came toward me, and I took a step back. He put his hands on my shoulders; it was not sexual; it was comforting, like a father would have done.

"It just can't happen again under this roof. Helen is four months pregnant."

"Pregnant?"

"Yes, we had no idea. The children will have a brother or sister."

He actually sounded happy. Now my eyes were fixed and steady, but they were filling up. Tears spilled out and slid down my face.

"You can stay here while you get something else sorted out. I don't know if you like it up at Tamana or if you'll look around for another job." His voice was softer now. "Either way, by the time we're back you must be gone."

Hearing "Tamana" reminded me of Aunt Sula.

"My aunt is sick. I wanted you to come with me to the country. That's partly why I came back."

I knew he wasn't sure if to believe me. "It will be impossible to get up there before we leave. There's too much to do. I can speak to Dr. Anderson and see if he can help."

I didn't hear what else he had to say.

NEXT MORNING, I got up early and cleaned my room. There was a lot of dust and there were half a dozen cockroaches dead in the bathroom. I opened all the jalousies to let the air in.

William was surprised and glad to see me.

"When did you come? No one told me." Then, "Did you get my letter?"

"Yes, William. I'm sorry. I meant to write you."

I explained that I had only come to pick up clothes and that I had to get back to the estate in a couple of days. I told him my aunt was ill.

He looked as if the roof was falling in. "Are you going to live on the estate?"

"I'm not sure what else I can do right now. Could you ask Solomon to drive me back?"

He nodded. "I wish I could drive."

"I'm not taking everything. I'll come for it when I know where I'm going to live."

"You have a home in Laventille," William said, "please remember that."

I STAYED IN Port of Spain for two days. I kept around the house and waited for a chance to speak with Dr. Emmanuel Rodriguez. But it was impossible. If he wasn't working late, he was out on a call, or

picking up the children from somewhere or dropping them some-
place else; he was visiting friends in Maraval, St. Ann's, Diego Martin. I caught him on the stairs. I said, Please, please can we talk. He
pressed himself into the banister as if he'd rather fall over the railings than be near me. I went to the surgery and asked for an appoint-
ment to see him. The receptionist gave me forms to fill in and told
me I'd have to wait. She suggested I see the new doctor who was starting next Monday. That night, I went to his bedroom door and said
his name. Softly at first and then louder. He came out, finger to his
lips, and told me to hush. Joe was inside sleeping, he said. I thought
I was going to explode.

In the early hours of that morning, I called Dr. Emmanuel
Rodriguez. I called in a way that would make him believe there was
something wrong. By the time he got to my room, I was lying under
the sheet, naked, just like I used to be. At first he was angry, but then
he seemed to let go, and he allowed me to kiss him, and help him take
off his robe, and before long he was in my bed. When he was inside
me, though, he had a distant look. It was a look I had never seen before; a look I didn't like. As soon as it was over, he put on his robe and
left. From the doorway I said, "What can I do?" He didn't answer.

Meanwhile, during the day, Marva was hurrying about the
place, getting the holiday trunks packed with warm clothes and ready
for the early morning flight on Saturday. I tried to keep away from
William; for some reason he made me feel sad and irritable. And in
all this time, at the back of my head like a door banging in the wind,
I remembered my sick Aunt Sula.

ON FRIDAY AFTERNOON, I packed my bag and said goodbye to
the children. Marva had gone to the drugstore and I was glad for time
alone with them. Consuella didn't understand that she would not see
me for a long time, perhaps never again. "You're a big girl now," I

said, and held her until she wriggled free. She ran to where her doll was lying on the step, picked it up, and held it like a baby.

"You know when I came here you weren't much bigger than your dolly."

"She needs to go to bed now," she said. Then, waving goodbye, Consuella started up the stairs.

I knew that Joe understood more of what was happening. In the kitchen, he leaned against the sideboard where there was a bowl of oranges. He picked one out and rolled it between his small hands.

"I don't know why Mummy hates you. I don't hate you, I like you."

"And I like you, Joe."

"She hated Brigid as well."

This surprised me. I knew that Brigid had left suddenly but I didn't think there was such bad feeling. "Why did she hate Brigid?"

"Because of Daddy."

I said, "How do you know that?"

"She was always following him around. I saw her in the car with him one day and they looked like they were kissing. I never told Mummy."

"Why didn't you tell her?"

"Because Daddy said it would only make her unhappy. Marva said Mummy heard them."

"Marva told you this?"

"No, she told Brigid. I was right there by the door when she said it. She said they were in the tool room."

I NEVER SAID goodbye to Dr. Emmanuel Rodriguez because he was at the office. He left me fifty dollars in a small "good luck" card. William said that I would be seeing him soon, so there was no need for goodbyes. He carried my bag out to the truck where Solomon was waiting, stood at the gate, and watched us drive away.

And on that hot, gray afternoon, while the heavy clouds hung over the Northern Range Mountains threatening thunder and rain and I was numb and tired with pain, Solomon drove me back along the busy main road leading out of Port of Spain, up through Arima, which was swarming with people for some reason, and on to San Rafael, through Brazil and Talparo, and along the El Quemado road to Tamana.

TWENTY-SIX

I COULD SEE FROM THE LOOK ON HIS FACE THAT JOSEPH Carr Brown was angry. He was sitting in the rocking chair, reading. When I told him good evening, he replied in a polite but clipped way.

"Sir," I said, "where's Dolly?"

"She's where she's supposed to be. In her house."

His eyes were hard like glass.

"She said she would keep an eye on Aunt Sula."

"And you told her you'd be back the next day. I'm surprised; you knew how sick Sula was."

"Is she all right?"

"We almost lost her on Wednesday night. She had a kind of fit and then she came out of it. Everybody was waiting for you. She kept asking for you. I tried to telephone Rodriguez but the lines were down. Tomorrow I'm taking her to hospital."

He got up and walked out.

LIKE A MIRACLE, soon after I returned, Aunt Sula took a turn for the better, and for a few days, I really believed she might be okay. There was no need for her to go to hospital now. I think even Joseph Carr Brown was surprised at how well she seemed, though he never said. She got herself up and bathed; she pottered about the house.

When she was tired, she sat in the comfortable chair on the veranda and I brought a stool for her feet. At first she didn't want me to do anything for her. "Celia, please relax, you came here for a little holiday. I don't want you rushing about." I didn't say that I had nowhere else to go.

I boiled leaves from the bush, and made a tea which she drank throughout the day. She'd sip it slowly. I kept the pot boiling on the stove from dawn to dusk. It gave the house a strange smell, but I was sure it was helping her. It seemed to bring down the fever. I sat by her bed and read to her from the large Bible she kept on her bedside table. Or I spoke to her, about things. "You remember when you found that giant turtle in the river and it was dead?" Aunt Sula said, "Yes, yes, I remember." "And how you used to throw coins in the water and dive down to find them?" "We were good swimmers then," she said. Then I reminded her about the time the baby was born in the schoolyard and how Grace cut the cord. But she couldn't remember this part. She closed her eyes. I knew she was sleeping when her breathing changed.

Joseph Carr Brown visited two or three times in a day. He always came in without knocking and went into her bedroom and stood beside the bed, like a giant looking down at the long, withering shape that was my Aunt Sula. He would often feel her brow, and he might sit down and talk to her quietly; so quietly that even if I stood by the door and concentrated very hard, I couldn't hear what he was saying.

With me he was not the same. There was a coolness I hadn't known before. Once when he was leaving, he said, "You're Grace's daughter, is that right?"

"Yes, sir. My mother was Grace D'Abadie. She is dead."

"Yes," he said. "I heard about Grace."

"She died when I was born."

He looked away as if to say, All this talk of sickness and death is too much.

. . .

THAT SAME AFTERNOON, Aunt Sula called me inside. She wanted to talk to me, she said. I helped her to sit up. She looked drawn and pale, as if her spirit was already on its way. I sat on the side of the bed; she put her hand on mine.

"You never told me why you were so sad."

I looked down; her fingers were slender and long, the nails still strong.

"I'm guessing it was something to do with a boyfriend?"

I didn't say anything, but I felt my face grow hot.

"You don't have to tell me."

I knew that she meant this; Aunt Sula had never pressed me to tell her anything.

"You know, Celia, when we feel pain like that, it's not always such a bad thing. It shows we can feel. It shows us we can love." She gently squeezed my hand. "I think of the heart a bit like a piece of land. We don't want it to be dusty and dry. Sometimes a little rain is good, it makes things grow and come alive. Maybe for the next time. Do you understand what I mean?"

"Yes," I said, quietly.

"People know if a heart is full and moist. Of course we don't want it to flood!"

At this, she smiled. I smiled, too.

"I don't want you to be afraid. One day you'll look back and say, I'm glad that happened, it's made me who I am. Your feelings can tell you which way to go, like a compass."

LATER, A SMALL brown bird flew into the house. It perched for a moment on the gramophone, then it flew to the window and settled on the ledge. It had yellow eyes. It seemed to look right at me; it wasn't at all afraid. I wondered if it was a sign that my aunt would soon die.

NEXT DAY, AUNT Sula asked me to wash her down, and I did. Then I helped her put on a fresh dress. She wanted to come outside, she said. At the top of the steps, we looked out at the grounds of the estate. The big house in the distance, the tall green hill where the grass was growing long; we could see the track and the stream.

"That grass needs cutting back," she said. "I must tell Mr. Carr Brown."

I took her slowly down the steps. I showed her how pretty her garden was looking. She didn't say anything but I thought she looked pleased. On her brow were dots of sweat like raindrops. She told me she was glad I liked her garden. Before she fell asleep, she said I was a good girl. "Please make it up with Tassi. Don't let Roman win, Celia. There's so few of us left."

EARLY NEXT MORNING, when Aunt Sula woke in terrible pain, I ran up to the main house and called out to Cedar. "Tell Mr. Carr Brown to come at once."

She shook her head. "He's out by the shed. He not back till lunchtime."

I said, "I don't care where he is, find him and tell him to come now. Before it's too late. Aunt Sula is dying."

WHEN HE SAW Aunt Sula lying there, her body bent over with pain, he told me to quickly pack a bag. "There's no time to waste."

I found myself looking in her wardrobe without knowing what I was looking for. I wanted to cry but I knew there wasn't time for tears.

In a paper bag, I put a nightdress, some clean underwear, tooth-brush, a towel. This was all she would need.

A man from the estate drove us to Port of Spain. I sat in the front and Aunt Sula lay down in the back with a blanket. Joseph Carr Brown said that he would follow in half an hour or so.

"Make sure she drinks water, she needs to keep hydrated."

For the first few minutes, Aunt Sula kept saying she was okay, and that she didn't need a doctor, but as we got near to Arima, she drifted away into a deep sleep. By the time we reached Port of Spain General Hospital, the nurses couldn't wake her up.

AUNT SULA DIED on February 5, 1958. The tumor in her womb was large, the size of a nine-month-old baby, and the surgeon was surprised that she had gone for so long without some kind of medical intervention.

"She must have been very brave. This condition usually makes people sing with pain."

"Sing?" I said.

"Yes," he said. "If you ever come by the hospital at night, you often hear patients crying out with pain. It almost sounds like they're singing."

THE FUNERAL WAS on a Saturday. Solomon drove William up from Port of Spain, and I was grateful to have him there. Aunt Tassi couldn't make it; she said it was impossible to leave Black Rock in time for the boat as it was Vera and Violet's graduation the day be-fore. And she, too, had been unwell with some kind of sickness; the doctor had told her not to travel. She begged me to put a flower in the grave with her sister; she was crying when I spoke to her. It was the first time I had heard her voice in more than three years. It sounded

broken and thin. "Come and visit me soon, Celia. Let's put everything behind us now. There's only us left." I wanted to say, What
good are you to anybody if you can't even get here for your sister's
funeral. But I wondered if it wasn't time to forget our differences.

Joseph Carr Brown read from Corinthians. From the way he
spoke about Aunt Sula, I knew that he cared for her. He talked about
her "fortitude," and dedication to his family. He used words like dig-
nity and loyalty. She had worked for them for twenty-five years, and
never had a day gone by when Sula hadn't been of some help to them.
None of these things surprised me. But what did surprise me was how
sad he looked, and how his wife stood beside him and she didn't look
sad at all. There were prayers; Cedar sang "Ave Maria." Her voice went
through me like a cool whirr of air. I knew that if I cried I would not be
able to stop, so I counted the rows of colored floor tiles from left to
right and then from right to left. Then they sang "The Lord Is My
Shepherd," and when it was over, a young white boy made an announcement: there were sandwiches and drinks up on the veranda at
the main house. I didn't want to go but I knew that I should. For my
aunt.

William wanted to see Aunt Sula's house, so we stopped off on
the way. For some reason, I suddenly felt very tired. I sat in the rocking chair while he fetched me a glass of water. "So this is where you
come to hide," he said, and grinned. Meanwhile, Solomon went
from room to room. "Sula was a classy lady," he said, looking
around. Then he wandered out to the porch and lit a cigarette. I felt
irritated. "Let's go," I said, and got up. "We shouldn't be late."

ON THE VERANDA, there was a long table with benches and several other smaller tables, covered with cloths, and trays of sandwiches
and chips and cakes. There were cold beers in buckets and jugs of
planter's punch, and large containers of fresh juices. William,

Solomon, and I sat on a small round table by the cotton tree. I looked up at the black branches like a roof of lace; they seemed to stretch over the whole yard. We're all caught in something, I thought. No matter who we are. From there I could see people gathered in little groups, talking. The crowd was mixed: young people and old people, some white and some black. I could make out the other Carr Brown children, or so I thought. There were young ones there too; the grandchildren. A lot of people looked upset, even little Ruth, carrying trays back and forth to the house. I thought how popular Aunt Sula must have been, in her quiet way.

"Celia could have a very nice life here. I don't know why she likes Port of Spain." Solomon stretched out his legs. "Well, their loss is our gain." He raised his glass and swallowed the rest of his drink. "We're very glad to have her, aren't we William. As is Dr. Rodriguez." He looked at me and winked.

And so it went. I don't know why Solomon drank so much that afternoon. No one would have known that he was drunk, because he hid it well. But I knew. And I knew that when he was seen in the main house, upstairs on the landing, "admiring" a valuable silver tray, he was up to no good. Solomon was "hovering" outside the bedroom door at exactly the moment Mrs. Carr Brown came out from fixing her hair. It was obvious to her that he was up to something. Apparently, she said, Who did you come with? and he said Celia, and then asked if her room was the bathroom because he "busting for a piss." So no matter how I might have defended him to Joseph Carr Brown, I knew that he was right to be angry.

"You frightened my wife," Joseph Carr Brown said. "What were you doing upstairs?" Shadow got up.

"She must be easily frightened," Solomon said, as if he couldn't care less.

Now the dog's ears were flat and his lips pulled right up so you could see his teeth. Solomon hissed at Shadow, and Shadow snarled; saliva was dripping from his mouth. I had never seen him like this.

"Dogs don't bother me," he said to no one in particular.

"They might not bother you. But you bother me." Joseph Carr Brown looked flushed. He held Shadow by his collar.

Then William said, "Come, come," and he took his brother's arm, and I said how late it was and what a long drive they had ahead.

"I don't want to *ever* see you on this land again. Do you understand?"

Solomon looked at Joseph Carr Brown as if he wanted to harm him. Then William dragged him off, which was exactly the right thing to do. I heard Solomon say, One day he would show these fucking white cockroaches.

LATER, AFTER EVERYBODY had left, I saw Joseph Carr Brown sitting on the steps, Shadow lay like a black log at his feet. He was smoking; something I had never seen him do. I asked if he would like me to help clear the house. "From what I can tell, Aunt Sula didn't like to throw things away." I said this lightheartedly.

"That's okay. I'll do it with a couple of my helpers." Anything he thought I might want he'd send on to me in Port of Spain. "When are you leaving?"

"I'm not sure, sir. I'd like to stay on a couple days if that's all right."

TWO DAYS LATER, he slid a note under Aunt Sula's door.

"Tomorrow I shall be coming with Dolly and Cedar to go through the house. Let me know your plans. JCB."

.   .   .

No ONE SAW me leave the stables. I rode up toward the back and slowly climbed the hill, passing through the cocoa trees, where I knew the forest started. For some reason, the forest trees seemed bigger than before; they hid the sky and the light. The thick green vines were like tentacles, ready to hook around my legs and loop around my neck. I found the uneven path and let Milo lead me up it. It was slippery after the early afternoon rain and there was a dank earthy smell. Ahead I saw the stream, and remembering what Joseph Carr Brown always said, tried to steer Milo from it, but I couldn't. He clip-clopped to where it was widest, stopped, and dipped his head so low into the water, I thought I might slide down his neck. All around there were unfamiliar sounds, hissing and rustling and a clicking that I couldn't quite figure out. At one point some birds flew out of the bushes and screamed so loud I almost fell off with fright. When Milo had finished, he moved off slowly through the bushes, back onto the path, and headed out toward the bright light.

I stayed in the shade, at the first row of grapefruit trees. I had almost fallen asleep when I heard the thudding of Seafer's hooves. I opened my eyes and saw Joseph Carr Brown riding into the field where the orange trees grew. When he saw Milo, he turned the horse around and came galloping toward me.

"Sir, I came to check on the trees," I said, getting up. "The grapefruits are okay. I looked at the leaves and bark and there weren't any white stains."

Seafer's red coat was gleaming in the sun.

I said, "I haven't checked the orange trees yet."

"I told you I don't like anyone taking the horses unless they tell me first. You took Milo without asking."

He jumped down, and brushed the mud from his trousers.

"Did you wonder if Soldier Ghost had taken him?"

His face was serious. "I thought you were going back to Port of

Spain." He took out a handkerchief and wiped his forehead. "I thought you had a job there. Isn't that why you left when Sula was sick?"

"They gave my job to someone else."

A kiskidee bird said, "*Qu'est-ce qu'elle dit! Qu'est-ce qu'elle dit!*"

"I hear Rodriguez threw you out. Rumors are flying around Port of Spain."

"That's not true. Mrs. Rodriguez is crazy."

Then, "*Wheep-wheep! Qu'est-ce qu'elle dit!*"

"Did you think that with his wife gone you'd become the next Mrs. Rodriguez?" He said this with a kind of pity, and I suddenly felt ashamed. Then, "Celia, I don't think this place is for you. If it wasn't for Sula you would never have chosen to come to Tamana. People who love the country live here."

"I'll work hard," I said, but even as the words left my mouth, I knew it was pointless.

"You should stay away from Solomon Shamiel; everybody knows he's trouble." His eyes were deep blue like the far-out sea where big ships sail. "You have your whole life ahead of you, Celia. Try to do something good with it; make something of it."

IN THE MORNING, there was a truck leaving for Port of Spain. The tray was filled with grapefruit, piled high in a hill. I could sit up front, Joseph Carr Brown said. The driver was called Dummy, because he could not speak or hear. (I was relieved that I would not have to speak to him.) He would carry me safely back to town.

Joseph Carr Brown watched us leave, along with Ruth, Tatton, and Dolly, standing in a line against the chicken fence. Tatton waved; there was sadness in his eyes, as if he knew I'd never return.

At the top of the muddy track, Cedar was swinging back and forth on the gate. As we passed, she stood up tall and bowed like a tree in the wind.

TWENTY-SEVEN

DUMMY DROPPED ME AT THE DOCKS. FROM THERE, I took a tram up to the top of town. I got off at the corner, and then walked slowly along the edge of the Savannah. It would soon be carnival; streamers and flags hung between trees, carts were parked here and there; men were carrying wooden blocks across the yellow-brown grass, ready to build the stand for the players to cross. Red dust was everywhere. Meanwhile, the sun beat down; it was hot enough to die.

THE RODRIGUEZ HOUSE was locked up, at least the veranda doors and the front shutters. The outside furniture had been put away. It looked like no one lived there. I walked around the side of the house, and under the eaves to the back where I could hear water running. "You?" Marva said, as if I was a ghost, her long face at the kitchen window. She came out and stood on the step, hands on her bony hips. "You can't stay here, you know that."

"Dr. Rodriguez told me I could stay until I found somewhere else." Then I said, "Is William here?" and put down my bag.

"He cutting the hedge. He has a lot to do before the end of the day, so don't go troubling him."

I said, "I'd forgotten how miserable you are."

Marva sucked her teeth. "Well you better not forget because Dr. Rodriguez phoning here tonight, and when he ask me what goin' on, I'll tell him."

WHEN HE SAW me, William put down the shears and quickly made his way across the grass. He was wearing overalls and boots and they made him look even taller. "I was worried," he said, wiping his forehead. "I thought you might stay in Tamana. I thought I might have to come up there and get you." He smiled.

"Tamana's not for me. People who love the country live there."

"You staying here?"

"I don't know where I'm staying," and I suddenly felt sad and hopeless about everything. "I hate Marva."

"Come home with me." He said it without question, as if it was the most natural and simple thing to do. "I told you before, you have a place in Laventille."

"What about your mother? I'm sure she's angry with me for not visiting her."

"I'll talk to her."

"Solomon?"

"He could say what he likes. It has nothing to do with him."

I would rather go to Laventille than stay with Marva.

"Are you sure?"

"As sure as that is sky," he said, and pointed at the sky. Then, "You want me to help you pack?"

And while Marva stood like a guard, we emptied my belongings—dresses, skirts, blouses, and books and toiletries—into boxes. I was surprised by how much I had collected. Many of these clothes had come from Helen Rodriguez. I took down the pictures I had stuck to the wall, the photographs of Hollywood movie stars, the postcard of

Southampton I had taken from Aunt Tassi, a little map of England with the port marked in ink. Together, William and I carried the boxes out to the gate.

"So where you going?" Marva asked, scanning the room, which, apart from the bed, looked exactly the same as when I had arrived. "Tobago?"

"Where I go and what I do has absolutely nothing to do with you."

"You'll never get work here in Port of Spain, you know that."

Then, to William, "I thought you had things to do? The yard needs water."

He rolled his eyes. "I'll see you in the morning, Marva."

In the doorway, I saw an upside-down broom, its bristles white with salt. I knew what this meant, this obeah spell; Marva was making sure I would never come back. I had once seen Aunt Tassi do the same thing, when she feared her first husband would return to Black Rock to steal the twins.

"Don't worry, Marva," I said, "I'm not coming back here."

I told William we could wait for Solomon in the park, but he said there was no point hanging about. On the corner, he hailed a taxi. Next minute, my belongings were in the trunk of an old American car and we were driving away.

TWENTY-EIGHT

I CANNOT SAY THAT EDNA SHAMIEL WAS PLEASED TO have me in her house. Yes, she greeted me, her round face friendly and bright, but I knew her show of warmth was for William. There was no doubt, to forgive my long absence, I would have to work hard. And I knew, like everyone, she must have heard the rumors. "You're very bad for not coming to see me," she said, wagging her finger. "All this time I hear from William how busy you are. I wait and wait. I say, Celia D'Abadie will visit me one day. That girl wouldn't let me down." For some reason, when she said, "That girl wouldn't let me down," I wanted to cry. She realized, and quickly softened. "I forget your aunt die just the other day. William say you were close like two peas." Then, "Come, come," and she led me up the brick steps.

The house had changed; there had been a small extension to the back, and this allowed for a larger dining area and another bedroom. The new bedroom was tiny, but there was a narrow mattress which was just about long enough. Mrs. Shamiel gave me two clean sheets and showed me hooks where I could hang my dresses. Meanwhile, William put the rest of my belongings in a crate, under the house. Apart from this extension, everything else was just as I remembered it; the porch with the two wooden chairs, the picture of the Virgin Mary, the cluster of banana trees, the breadfruit tree in the back, the larder with its stacked plates and pots.

That night, Mrs. Shamiel cooked breadfruit and coconut, with baked chicken. We sat around the table, her, William, and I, and it struck me that although many things were exactly the same, others were very different. I was not the same person who had sat here three years ago. I ran my finger over the tablecloth pattern of apples and pears. I wished I was hungry; since the funeral my appetite had vanished. Mrs. Shamiel said it was because I was sad.

"Nothing kill your appetite like grief. Sometimes God take away things we love and we don't know why."

After supper, William got up and cleared the table, and then he gave me a lamp to take to my room. "Don't worry," he said, "you'll be okay." His eyes were soft and watery, like two dark pools.

LATER, MRS. SHAMIEL knocked on my door. Her face was calm and not unkind. She spoke quietly, so quietly, had someone stood right there, they would not have heard what she said.

"You and me need to have a little talk." She sat on the edge of the mattress. Then, "William tell me it's not true what people say. He say Mrs. Rodriguez go back to England because she sick and it have nothing to do with you. But we both know there's no smoke without fire."

I drew up the sheet; I felt for the piece of black rock under my pillow.

"These things happen," she said, "these men in high positions think they could do what they like." Her eyes were dark, but for the lamp that flickered them with gold.

"It's not the first time. Rodriguez should be struck off. One minute, he's here examining you, and the next, he's up to no good."

On the wall, her shadow was enormous.

"This kind of thing goes on all the time. I've seen it again and again. It doesn't make it right."

I looked down at the folds of cotton. "It's not like you think," I said.

Mrs. Shamiel put her finger to her lips.

"I want you to understand something, Celia. I'm not here to judge you. If anything I feel sorry for you. I know you had a hard time. I know when you came to Trinidad, something bad happen to you, and I pitied you for that. You've had some bad luck. So I don't mind you coming here to stay in my house. But"—and here she made her eyes small like beads—"you and I both know how William feel about you. From the first day he put eyes on you he fall in love. You and me both know that."

I nodded.

"So, I say this: if you hurt William, if you play games with my son, my precious son who would not hurt an ant, I will throw you out in the street like that," she snapped her fingers. "You understand, Celia?"

Again, I nodded.

"Good," she said, in a louder and more cheerful voice. "Now, let's forget this little conversation, put it to the back of our minds." She got up and she was suddenly very tall.

"Sleep well. Remember that tomorrow is another day. Remember God is good."

IN THE MORNING, after William and Mrs. Shamiel had left (Solomon had not come home that night), I walked down the hill to the stand and bought a newspaper. I took it home, poured over the classified sections, marking up any jobs I thought I could do. Before the sun was too hot, I made my way to the post office where I telephoned several "domestic" vacancies. Mostly, though, as soon as I told them my name and where I had last been employed, they lost interest. That was probably because the jobs were all in Port of

Spain. I heard Marva's words, "Everybody know everybody in this place."

Over the following week, I applied for a cashier job in Hi-Lo grocery. The manager seemed to like me, but, for some reason, his assistant manager didn't. "Where did you go to school? Why did you leave your last job? Where are you living?" The questions came fast as if she was trying to catch me out.

I dropped off a handwritten résumé at the Queen's Park Hotel, and it looked as if I might get a position as a chambermaid, but they insisted on a reference, which of course I couldn't get, at least, not until Dr. Emmanuel Rodriguez was back. I asked for clerical work at the main post office, but they said there was nothing. One morning, I went to St. Peter's primary school in Woodbrook and explained that I had high standards of English and arithmetic and wanted to offer my services as a teacher. I showed the principal my handwriting, which she said was excellent. I offered to sit an exam, to read to her from the Bible so she could hear how well I read. "Perhaps you should think of going to university," she said, her face sympathetic. "With references and a diploma, we'd be delighted to give you a try."

That afternoon I left the school and walked in the blistering sun up to the Botanical Gardens, where I sat under the African tree until dusk.

What to do. What to do.

I HELPED IN the house, preparing meals and tidying up the place. Mrs. Shamiel was grateful. She didn't have time, she said. The bakery had been taken over and business was good. I swept the floors, and polished the furniture. I washed and ironed clothes, it was a way to earn my keep. It was better than doing nothing; it was better than sitting around thinking about my life.

William came home from work as usual. He hardly talked about

Marva or mentioned the Rodriguez family, but I knew they must be due back anytime. He always looked glad to see me. He told me, "Every day like Christmas now you're here."

Solomon was out a lot; and when he was home, he seemed restless. Apparently, he was trying to buy a boat, to start a ferry service between Trinidad and Venezuela. He was looking for sponsorship. But William said, Any person in their right mind will see at once Solomon is up to no good. "They have plenty drugs in Venezuela. I hope he's not getting into that." Mrs. Shamiel must have told Solomon something, because he never asked about my plans, although I sometimes saw him looking at me, as if to say, Yes, she desperate now.

Days passed. And then more days passed.

THAT EVENING, WILLIAM asked if I would like to go out. "I could take you to The Black Hat," he said. "The food is real good." I didn't want to go, but I didn't want to stay at home either. Tonight Mrs. Shamiel was working late. Across the hill, just last week, a young woman had been found dead in her yard, her throat cut. Solomon said he knew who did it. "The baby father. They say she sleeping with some other man and he get jealous." These kinds of murders happened often in Laventille.

I didn't bother to dress up. I wore a skirt and blouse that I'd had for some time, and a pair of leather sandals. William said I looked nice.

As we walked through Woodbrook, he talked about a new movie opening next week. It was a western with an actor called John Wayne. Everybody like John Wayne, William said. I half listened to him, but mostly I was far away. I watched people out and about—young people—just like me. Only they seemed happier, somehow, like they were living, and not crawling through their lives.

The Black Hat was on the corner of two streets. It was dark

inside. Low lamps hung over wooden tables, and there was a horse-shoe bar. It wasn't yet busy, but I knew it wouldn't be quiet for long. It had a lively reputation. William said you couldn't book a table; you just had to turn up.

"Sometimes it's good to take a chance," he said.

"Is it?"

And he smiled, as if I was making a joke. He asked if I would like a beer.

"Yes," I said, "why not. I'll try it."

Next thing, we were sitting together near the window, and the place was filling up. William was smoking a cigarette. His eyes were shining, his face bright and open. The beer was refreshing and I liked the bitter taste; it soon went to my head. He asked if I would like another and I said yes! Then somebody put a coin in the jukebox and "Matilda" came on.

"This is a great song." William looked uncertain, but then he got up.

"Would you like to dance, Celia?" He reached out his hand.

"Why not," I said, again.

I let him gently pull me up from my seat, and lead me onto the small dance floor. We took a place in the middle and we started to dance, twisting our hips, moving down toward the floor, and back up again. William knew what to do. The song went, "Ma-tild-a, Ma-tild-a, Matilda she take me money and gone Venezuela!" He twirled me around and then tipped me back toward the ground, then back up again, and round and round; slow, quick quick, slow, quick quick. At arm's length, he pulled me to him and let me go, in and out, in and out. And then he put his hand on my waist, and mine was on his shoulder, and our bodies were pressed closely together like pages in a book. And there were cheers and whoops from the crowd, and somebody said, Pampalam! Pampalam!

French fries arrived with steak and fried vegetables. There was so much of it, the plates with covers, and the huge steaming dishes with huge spoons, and the rich smells of onion and pepper and oil. I ate all I could, which wasn't very much. William asked if I liked the food and I told him, yes. But then I suddenly felt sick, so I went to the ladies' bathroom where I threw up. I waited for a while before returning to the table. "I'm sorry," I said, "it must be the beer." William said maybe we should go home. I was glad to step out into the night air.

But the following morning I was sick again. Solomon had just come back after an all-night fête. In the kitchen, as he passed, I caught the smell of stale rum and cigarettes, and next thing, I was suddenly hit by a wave of nausea as if I was on a boat. He followed me outside. "What happen to you? Like every time you come here, you sick?" I went inside my room, lay on my bed and closed my eyes. The next day, the same thing happened.

After a week of this nausea, sometimes in the afternoon, sometimes in the morning, I knew it wasn't a virus I had, and I knew by the soreness of my breasts and the new hardness of my belly, that it would not go away; not unless I saw a special doctor like Mrs. Jeremiah, who could give me a potion to drink; not unless somebody placed a pouch of chicken liver and aniseed inside me and fed it to the top of my womb with a piece of wire. Aunt Tassi's words spun around my head: "Just now you're a baby and you're having a baby yourself." Only I wasn't a baby anymore. I was nineteen years old.

THAT NIGHT I asked William, "Are they back from England, yet?"

"Yes, Celia." Then, carefully, as if he wasn't sure whether he was saying the right thing, "Mrs. Rodriguez get big with the next child."

Mrs. Shamiel threw me a look; I pretended not to notice.

TWENTY-NINE

I TOOK A TRAM FROM THE BOTTOM OF THE HILL. I SAT near where the doors opened, so I could catch a bit of breeze. In the glass my face was thin. These past few days, I had made myself eat because I didn't want Mrs. Shamiel to become suspicious, but mostly, the thought of anything but dry bread made me feel ill.

The tram filled up as we got closer to town. Some young children were dressed like kings and queens, wearing glittery crowns and cloaks of bright colors. They were talking loudly, excitedly. I had forgotten it was the first day of carnival. Port of Spain would be busy.

I got off early and cut through the back streets of Woodbrook. Even here, there were people walking in the road; some in sailors' costumes—blue wide trousers with striped shirts and white caps. They were probably going to find their band; hundreds would dance in the streets today. "Hey baby," one of them called, and from a pouch he pulled out a handful of white powder and threw it at me. "You're going in the wrong direction!" I could hear music coming from somewhere, and somebody was loudly beating a drum. As I turned the corner, a man appeared on high stilts, dressed like a robber, wearing an enormous hat with a wide brim, and a terrifying mask. He pointed a gun at me.

"Hand over your money, girl," he shouted, leering forward. I tried to walk closer to the wall, but he lifted his long wooden legs and, like a giant spider, straddled his way toward me.

"I drown my grandmother in a teaspoon of water. I steal little children and decorate my house with their faces. Their brains make my supper. Give me money or I'll shoot your ears from your head."

Then he laughed, as if he had just heard the best joke in the world. I hurried down the street.

THE SURGERY DOOR was held ajar with a large piece of coral. Inside, there was a small queue of people. The receptionist was friendly enough. "Yes," she said, "Dr. Rodriguez is the only doctor working today. He's just back from his vacation." She said this as if I was lucky to catch him fresh from England, especially at carnival. She asked me to fill in a form, which I did. I called myself Grace Carr Brown; he would not know this name. In the tiny bathroom, I washed my hot face; dusted the white powder from my hair; I put on lipstick. Then I sat near the waiting room window. There was a ceiling fan, and every time it reached a certain place it made a clicking sound: *tuck—tuck—tuck.* It made me want to fall asleep. It was almost noon before she told me I could go in. "He's in the first office," she said, "no need to knock."

I walked in, and without a word, Dr. Emmanuel Rodriguez stood up. He came around and closed the door behind me. He had put on weight; his tan had gone.

I said, "You probably know why I'm here."

"No, Celia. I don't have a clue." He sat down opposite me. I could see that he was nervous.

"Helen is due much sooner than me. There's still time to get rid of it."

He looked me up and down. "Are you sure?"

"I'm sure." For some reason, I did not want to cry. I was far
from that place of tears. "I need you to help me. I have no money, no
way of making a living. You have to help me." My voice was small and
the words all sounded like the same note.

For a moment, he leaned back in his chair. Then he rubbed his
face as if to wake himself up.

I noticed a recent photograph on his desk. The family was
standing outside a castle. Helen Rodriguez was wearing a pink mater-
nity coat, her hair tucked up in a hat. A proper English rose.

He said, "How do I know it's mine?"

I did not understand this question.

"How do I know it's not William's?" Then, "Or another man
you might have been with in the last couple of months?"

"There's been no one else." Now my voice was about to crack.

"And I have to take your word for that."

I stared at him; he must know I wasn't lying.

"I gave you money when you left, Celia. If you're in trouble, use
the money I gave you to get rid of it."

"What if I want to keep it?"

Dr. Emmanuel Rodriguez drew a deep breath and sighed. For
the first time, he looked at me with kindness and, perhaps, pity. His
eyes were more green than brown; green like green sea. "I can't help
you, Celia. I'm sorry. If you decide to have it, and I hope you won't,
then that's your choice. I can give you the name of somebody, he's
very good. He's right here in town."

"I hear girls die in these operations."

"Not when they're done properly, professionally. It takes no
time at all. I wouldn't recommend somebody who wasn't profes-
sional."

"Do you ever think about us?"

He looked down at his hands.

"Yes," he said, "but not in the way you might want me to."

"And how do I want you to think of me?"

There was a tap at the door, and the voice of the receptionist said, "Dr. Rodriguez, there is a telephone call for you. Shall I put it through?"

"Yes," he said, "give me two minutes, thank you."

"I don't know, Celia. With some kind of need or desire. It doesn't really matter, does it." He got up and put his fingers through his hair. "I really hope you'll make things easy for yourself and go to see Charles. You met him, down the islands at Avalon. Charles Smith, the gynecologist, remember?" He scribbled a number on a piece of paper, and gave it to me. Then he opened his wallet and pulled out three twenty-dollar bills. "Just don't go saying it's my child you're getting rid of." He smiled.

"Is this what you did with Brigid?"

"I'm sorry, Celia. I'm sorry this has happened to you." And with that he walked around his desk. He opened the door and held it wide.

I wanted to say something more. But I couldn't.

THIRTY

Now I knew for sure: all roads lead to nowhere.
Mrs. Jeremiah was right. My life was not to be happy. My life was miserable and it would always be miserable. I escaped one monster to meet a different kind of monster. Only this one was much more dangerous because I loved him. He did not love me. He had never loved me. Like rum, he drank me up and peed me out. His child told me he had done this before and the moment I heard it I knew in my bones it was true. I was not the first. I would not be the last. If I saw him in the street, he would cross over to the other side and pretend he did not know me. Pretend he did not know what my skin tasted like, how I smelled, how my thighs felt around his waist. I was not his sunshine, his light in the dark. He will break your heart in two, Mrs. Jeremiah said. She was right.

Tamana, a place where nothing changes, and yet everything changed. I thought I could live there, when I saw there was nowhere else to go. This white man will look out for me. My aunt would take care of me. Her home was my home. I could ride the horse up to the fields, play games with the children, clean out the stables. That could have been my life. But I disappointed him. The woman I loved, my beloved aunt, died. I wasn't welcome there anymore.

I had nothing. There was nowhere to go. If I went to Black Rock, everybody would say, Oh yes, Celia run away to make her life and come back when it all go sour. Look where she reach! With no father for the baby and no money to take care of it.

So I live in Laventille with two men—one ugly, the other a handsome crook—and their mother, and eventually I will marry the ugly one and wait for the mother to die so we can say the shacky little house is ours? Where did the baby come from, they'll say. The little half-white pickney child?

Money buys you freedom. I had little money. I was not free. I told myself I do not want to live. All roads lead to nowhere. Money. Money. If only I could have more money. If I could get to England I would find my father. He might be a rich man, he might be a pauper. It wouldn't matter. He would want to see me. I was his flesh and blood. If my skin was too dark for him, I would scrub it with lime to make it pale. In England I could start again. I could be a cook in a restaurant, or a seamstress, or a nanny. I could go to university. I'd teach in a school. Just because you're pretty doesn't mean you shouldn't study and do something with your life. Money. If only I had money. With money I would start all over again. You will not die in this place. That's what she said. Mrs. Jeremiah said, Celia does what Celia want. You don't care what happen to get what you want. You must get what you want.

You will die in a foreign place. But somehow I had to get to the foreign place.

THIRTY-ONE

WILLIAM CAME HOME FIRST. HIS MOTHER HAD GONE TO visit Ruby in the General Hospital, so she wouldn't be back until early evening. I had a memory of this, something she had mentioned that morning. By then it wouldn't have mattered if Queen Elizabeth of England was coming to Laventille.

Apparently, William heard me as he was walking up the hill. At first he thought the cry came from a dog or a cat trapped somewhere. And then something told him it was Celia. He ran up the steps and flew into the house; when he opened my door, I looked up at him, my eyes frightened and swollen, my face wet and red. (Later he said, "You didn't look like yourself.") He thought something terrible had happened. "What happen, Celia? What happen?" He tried to lift me up from where I was curled over. But I was heavy like rock. Everything in me wanted to go down, down, down. He called my name. It made no difference; I was at the end of a place I had never visited before. There was no light and no sound. He put his arms around my back; he swayed me gently from side to side like a child. Until, at last, I heard my breath slow right down, and the sobs become laps, not waves. And then, finally, they stopped. "Tell me, Celia," William said, his dark eyes searching. "You can tell me. Whatever it is."

.   .   .

WE LEFT THE house and made our way through the back of the village. I had never been this way before. I followed William up toward the top. We passed little shacks that looked like they might fall down. And some of the people we saw stopped what they were doing and looked at us. Some said good afternoon or waved, and I realized they must know William. A man asked, "You play Mass today, William? I hear Port of Spain heaving with people." Another said, "Tell your mother I bring black pudding for her tomorrow." William made it clear he couldn't stop to talk.

And so it went. And we kept on walking in that golden light, weaving along the narrow path lined with wild, dry bush, until we reached an open concrete area. Rubbish was scattered there—broken chairs, torn mattresses, old clothes. Ahead was a large church, and in the grounds of this church, a stone statue of Our Lady of Laventille towered thirty feet high. I had never seen her so closely. I had glimpsed her from the highway. But she had not looked like this. Her robe was long and flowed down to her bare feet. She wore a crown; her face was kind and serious. She did not appear sad; her eyes were filled with pity—pity for me, pity for William; pity for the whole world.

It was here, on the dusty ground at the feet of the Virgin Mary, that I told William I was pregnant. At first he was shocked. He stared at me as if I was speaking a foreign language.

"Since when?"

"I don't know. Maybe eight or ten weeks. I'm not sure."

"Is it someone from the estate?"

I shook my head.

"Someone you've met in town?"

"No."

William looked confused. Then, and I saw the thought take shape, "Not Dr. Rodriguez?"

"Yes."

He stared at me, his eyes dark and wide. He was absolutely still, as if he wasn't breathing.

"I'm sorry," I said.

William got up and walked to where the concrete stopped and long grass grew. He bent over like somebody who has taken a blow to the stomach; he put his hands on his knees. I wondered how long he would stay like that. He might lose his balance and fall down the hill. On the other side, some children were playing with a bicycle wheel and a stick. They hadn't noticed us. One of them shouted something and William stood up. He wrapped his arms around himself as if he was cold.

There were questions: When did it start? Soon after you got the job?

"No," I said. "It was later, it was much later."

"You were together in the house?"

"Yes. Sometimes we went out in the car. She was often in her room."

I could see that he was thinking, trying to remember. "Did you go in the toolshed?"

I nodded.

He shook his head. "That's why it was always messed up." He made a strange grunt, like a kind of laugh. "I always blamed Joe."

Then he said, "Were you in love with him?"

"Yes."

Now William looked at me as if he was in a kind of trance, and I knew that he was trying to make sense of it. He pressed his fingers into his forehead.

"Does he know?"

"He wants nothing to do with me or the child."

"You saw him?"

"Yes," I said. "Today I went to the surgery."

"And Mrs. Rodriguez?"

"She doesn't know. She won't ever know."

William looked away at the tiny lights in the distance. We could see the main road to the east, and straight ahead the flat gray sea. Those who did not like carnival would sail their boats down the islands. In town, celebrations would be winding down, with masqueraders going home to rest up for tomorrow. Another day of drinking and dancing in the streets, and then it would all be over.

"That's why she went crazy."

"Yes," I said.

"Same thing with Brigid."

"Yes."

By now the sun was low, the golden glow had vanished. It would soon be dark.

"Do you want the baby?"

"I don't know," I said. "Yesterday I didn't, but today I do." I surprised myself to hear this. Then, "I beg you, William, please don't say anything to your mother. I don't want her or Solomon to know. I just want some time to sort myself out. He gave me the name of someone."

"For what?"

"To get rid of it. They say it doesn't take long."

Two stray dogs had come to the edge of the grass, they were fighting over a chicken bone. They were so thin their stomachs were bloated. One of the dogs growled, and chased after the other dog; I saw it had only three legs.

"You wonder if they'd be better off dead," I said. But William was no longer there.

"Where are you going?" I shouted.

He didn't answer. I watched him disappear into the jungle of houses.

I SAT THERE for a few minutes. I was so tired, I could have lain down on the ground and slept. I looked up at the statue looming now in silhouette. And for a moment, I could imagine that she was real, and not made of stone at all.

THIRTY-TWO

NEXT DAY, I HAD JUST FINISHED SWEEPING THE FLOOR, and it was around noon when William arrived home unexpectedly. Apparently, he had left the Rodriguez house without saying anything; he'd put down his tools and walked out.

"Why?" I asked. "Did someone say something?"

"Not really. Nothing in particular." He seemed dazed, bothered.

"You can't quit your job now. You've worked there all these years. Nothing has changed."

"Everything has changed," he said, looking at me as if I was crazy.

"That's not true," I said. "The only difference is that you know something today you didn't know yesterday."

He sat down on the old wicker chair. "I can't work for Dr. Rodriguez anymore. I can hardly look at him. I want to help you, Celia."

"Well it won't help when your mother starts asking why you've given up your job and you tell her it's because of me. And then there's two of us here."

Outside the light was bright and glaring. The banana leaves were shiny as if they'd been polished; two large hands needed picking.

William got up. "We could go away; you could have the baby. If we were somewhere else it wouldn't matter. Somewhere nobody knows us. Jamaica or Barbados. Even England. Look how many people going to England now and making a fresh start. Isn't your father in England?"

"With what, William?" I felt my face getting hot. "You can't live on air. We have nothing; that's what we have. Nothing. You can't start a new life with that."

FOR A FEW days, William went back to work, but he never stayed a full day. He went in late, and left in the early afternoon; Solomon picked him up at the gate and they took off somewhere. Apparently, Marva asked if he was sick and he told her, Yes, sick of her, sick of the whole Rodriguez family. At home he was distracted and quiet. His mother soon noticed. She said, "You feeling all right?" and for the first time I heard him snap at her. "Don't fuss so," he said. "Everything's okay." She looked at me, I pretended I hadn't noticed.

One night, he went out with Solomon and he came back drunk. I had never seen him like that. From my window I watched him staggering in the half-light of the moon, trying to find his keys, calling out to nobody in particular. Eventually, Mrs. Shamiel went outside; she told him to go in his bed and sleep. I noticed them talking on the porch until late. Their conversations were hushed and serious. Something was going on. I said, "Since when were you and Solomon so close?"

EVERYWHERE WAS HOT and dry. Dust blew through the windows and fell on everything—shelves, furniture, crockery. The skies were clear: a bright, holy blue; the land was splitting and cracking with heat. All day cicadas rattled their song so loud I felt to scream. Meanwhile, *The Gazette* reported terrible fires raging through the hills.

AT THE END of the week, William came to where I was washing clothes in the outside sink. He leaned against the wall. "I have a plan," he said, and half smiled.

"What plan is that, William?" I carried on rinsing the garments, swilling out the water, filling up the bucket.

"It doesn't matter. You don't have to know what it is."

"Does it involve Solomon? Because if it does, I can tell you right now I don't want anything to do with it."

"I don't want you to worry about him."

For the first time in days, he looked calm and sure. He turned off the tap. He was closer now; I could smell the lime cologne he had taken to wearing. "I've been trying to find a way for us to be together. I'll do all I can to take care of you, Celia, whatever it takes." His eyes were full of tenderness.

"You're not going to steal money from somewhere? You're not going to kill anybody."

"Don't be silly," he said. "I want us to have a new start. I want this baby to have a proper home."

For some reason, I felt the opposite of calm.

"Remember what you told me the other day. You can't start a new life with nothing. That's the truth."

"Yes," I said, "but I don't want anybody getting into trouble."

"No one is getting into trouble, Celia."

From his pocket, William pulled out a travel brochure. On it was a photograph of a ship and a small map of the Caribbean islands.

"We can buy a ticket to England. We can go wherever we want. The travel agent told me a ship sails to Plymouth every week." William was excited.

I was looking at the pictures and I was about to ask how much a ticket would cost when we heard: "Good afternoon," and Mrs. Shamiel appeared in the doorway. She was wearing her uniform dress, a green scarf over her silver hair. "The power went so the boss sent us home early. I hope I didn't frighten you."

"Just a little," I said, catching my breath. "We didn't hear you come in."

William gave me a look, and then followed his mother inside; I heard her ask him to go to the store to buy some milk. "I don't know how I forget it." She was going now to wash and change. "Pick up some tea, too," she said, her voice trailing off.

I FINISHED WRINGING out the clothes, carried them into the yard, and started to hang them on the washing line. The light was softer now, and there was a warm breeze. The clothes would soon be dry, and then I would iron them. And while I was putting the wooden pegs in place, I was thinking about all that William had said, and wondering if there really might be a way to leave Trinidad and start over. And if so, where would we go? And I was wondering, too, if it would ever be possible to love William.

"So the baby is William's or Rodriguez's?"

Mrs. Shamiel was standing on the steps.

My face flushed with heat.

"Don't pretend with me. You're taking a long time to answer, that tells me all I need to know."

I could see through the underneath of the house to the gate; I would have to pass her to get to it.

"I warned you, Celia."

"William wants to be with me. I can't help that."

"Then he can be with you somewhere else. But not in my house. Not under my roof. Not as long as you're pregnant with another man's child."

She was looking at me as if she hated me.

"I want you gone by the end of the week. You understand?" Then, "And if you care about my son at all"—and these words came like knives—"don't tell him about this conversation." She suddenly looked dismayed. "Trouble seems to follow you around like a bad smell. I don't know why that is. But I don't want it destroying my son's life." Her voice was breaking now. "He's all I have."

Mrs. Shamiel walked back up the steps and into her house.

ALL NIGHT SHE stayed close. William didn't seem to notice, although at one point, he asked her if she was going to see Ruby. Mrs. Shamiel said no, Ruby had visitors from San Fernando; she wanted to stay home and finish some chores.

Mrs. Shamiel served corn soup for dinner. There were dumplings in between bits of meat and bone in the yellow liquid. I didn't want to eat it, there was something about the soup that tasted odd. I remembered Aunt Tassi telling me how some people put human bones in their soups to make unwanted guests sick.

I made an excuse to leave the table, saying I would eat the soup later. I went to my room, lay on my bed, and stared at the ceiling. I felt anxious, as if something very bad was about to happen. It was hot and still. I got up and stood by the window, hoping for a little breeze. Outside, I could hear a hissing noise, and I was sure it was a snake. The yard was filled with strange, black shapes.

LATER, WILLIAM KNOCKED on my door. He had brought a glass of sorrell juice.

"Are you okay?"

I sat up and took the drink. "Yes," I said, knowing his mother was probably listening. "I'm feeling so tired; it must be the heat."

"The heat getting to everyone tonight."

He glanced down at my stomach where my hands were folded. "You shouldn't live in a place like Trinidad. You belong in

America or Europe. Somewhere else. Somewhere with a real future. I'll help you." Then, "I believe I was born to care for you."

William looked at me with such kindness, I almost felt ashamed. I had always known that his affections were strong, but hearing "I believe I was born to care for you" made his feelings more real and somehow, shocking. And I felt dizzy with this realization. Like when you start up a hill, and you climb higher, and higher, then you look back and the ground rushes up toward you. And I knew in that moment, that I would never love him as he loved me now. I had loved only Dr. Emmanuel Rodriguez. His mother was right; Mrs. Jeremiah was right.

I was suddenly very afraid; I could not stay here anymore.

What to do. What to do.

THIRTY-THREE

I TELEPHONED AUNT TASSI AND TOLD HER I WAS COMING home. She was thrilled. "I was hoping you'd come. I had a feeling. I must fix up the place; if you see how bad it looking. Since Roman I haven't felt to do anything. What would you like to eat? I will get something nice ready. And tell me exactly what time the boat getting in. Violet and Vera will be so excited," she said. "Wait 'til you see how grown-up they are."

THE BOAT WAS leaving at 9:00 p.m., which meant checking in at 7:00 p.m. I was glad to be traveling at night, it would be cooler. We arrived at the docks in good time. While William went to the ticket office, I stood in the queue of passengers. A large ship from Miami was moored and there were some American guards gathered at the gangway. Strangely, I thought I recognized one of them; his tanned and pointed face was familiar. It was the guard from the security post at Chaguaramas. A dark-skinned girl was on his arm; she looked no more than fifteen years old. A song floated back to me: *If Yankees come to Trinidad, Some of de girls go more than mad, Young girls say they treat dem nice, Make Trinidad like a paradise . . .*

Passengers for Scarborough were told to get in line. William and I waited near to where a lady was selling popping corn.

"You want some, Celia?"

"No, I'll get something on the boat." Then I said, "You know what, maybe you should go now. We'll be leaving soon, anyway." I could make out Solomon's truck parked outside the gates.

"I'd rather stay here with you." His eyes were dreamy and sad. "I still don't know why you have to go. It seems so rushed."

"I need to see Aunt Tassi. I want to see my cousins, swim in the sea." I smiled as if I was happy about it.

"Everything will work out, please God. I'll come to Tobago as soon as I can."

"William," I said, looking straight at him, "whatever it is you're doing, please don't do it for me. I can't promise you anything. I don't know what I want anymore. I wish you'd forget about me."

And with that, I kissed him quickly goodbye. "Go, William," I said, "please be careful." For a moment he looked confused. But then he smiled, made his hand into a fist, and pressed it to his heart. I watched him slip into the crowd and disappear in the darkness; I didn't feel sad or fearful, I felt numb.

THE BOAT WAS almost full. People were traveling back to Tobago after the holiday weekend. I found a quiet place upstairs where the breeze was blowing and I propped myself up against the side of the boat, looking back through the railings at the island I'd come to know as my home. I watched its lights twinkling, and I watched as Port of Spain got smaller. I hardly knew this place. What had I seen: Port of Spain, Arima, Tamana, Pointe-a-Pierre. What about the wild parts beyond the American camp? And the beautiful North Coast that everybody talked about? I was thinking about this, and then Port of Spain was suddenly gone and there was nothing but blackness.

Inside, I bought a rum and soda and sat on a chair at the bar. Nearly everyone was asleep. There was a row of children lying side by side; they must have been on a school trip of some sort. A couple of older men were talking nearby, they looked drunk and I thought they might try to speak to me, so I went outside again and lay down on the upper deck. I pulled out a blanket from my bag and put it over me. The boat was rolling. I listened to the drumming of the engine. I soon fell asleep.

I dreamt of Aunt Sula; she was young and pregnant. She was sitting in her chair, in her little house at Tamana. I was trying to talk to her, but she couldn't hear me. She kept smiling until I realized she was just a picture on the wall in somebody else's house.

By the time we reached Tobago, the sun was coming up. I could see the familiar coastline and the place I knew to be Scarborough. And as we got closer, and closer, the blur of things started to take shape, the buildings and the trees and the long road along the beach-front, and I could see the hill that led up to the hospital and the row of shops that ran along it. I could see the spire of the church where my mother was buried. I could see Bacolet and the hotel perched there. And to my surprise, at the sight of these things, I did not feel dismayed as I thought I would; I felt something almost like relief. Like when you're tired and you put your head on a pillow. Like that. So that when I saw the Port Authority building and it was time to gather my belongings, I got up and did so more easily than I had expected, and with a slightly lighter heart.

I NEARLY WALKED by the three women waiting on the other side of the ramp, and if Aunt Tassi hadn't called out, I probably would have. Aunt Tassi looked a lot older than when I had last seen her; she had put on weight and her hair was completely gray.

"Oh my good Lord, Celia!"

She put her arms around me and kissed my cheek. Vera and Violet were dressed up in simple cotton dresses; with their hair plaited and pinned up at the back in the same way. I thought how old-fashioned and serious they looked. They were carrying handbags!

"Sula told me how you had grown up but I never thought you'd get so tall!"

I went to Violet and Vera, and I hugged them too. They were staring at me as if I was a movie star, their faces open and admiring. I didn't want them to see me in that way, I didn't want them to feel insecure. "Look at you," I said. "You must have all the boys chasing you." Vera giggled and I could tell that they were both pleased. They were looking at my sandals, my hair, the elegant, shiny belt I had taken from Helen Rodriguez. Violet, without thinking, felt my skirt between her fingers. The floral pattern was unusual, the cotton crisp.

"I like your dress," she said, beaming. "It's very modern."

I said, "Well, Trinidad has a lot of good stores and you don't need so much money to buy nice material."

"Will you help me choose some material? I have a party to go to in two months."

"Yes," I said, "of course."

Suddenly there seemed to be a lot of people wanting to pass and I realized we were blocking the way. Aunt Tassi said, "Let's go get the bus."

"HOW LONG CAN you stay?" Aunt Tassi was settling herself into the seat. "You can stay for a while I hope. There's a lot to catch up on."

I said, "I don't know. A little while."

She touched my arm. "We're so glad to have you home, Celia."

THE ROAD WAS quiet and empty, but for a few cars here and there. Some people were walking on the side of the road with baskets on their heads; I guessed that they were going to market. A herd of goats was coming down the hill with a barefoot man. He looked as if he didn't have a care in the world.

Aunt Tassi said I was lucky because Vera and Violet didn't have work today. They had told their boss they were meeting their cousin from Trinidad, and everybody in Black Rock was talking about it. "Mrs. Maingot is coming over later for a drink. She said you must stop by and see Joan. If you see her tiny baby how sweet."

I put my head back, suddenly feeling exhausted.

"We'll be home just now," Aunt Tassi said.

I closed my eyes.

THE HOUSE FELT bigger without Roman. And yes, it was in need of paint, but it was brighter than I remembered. It might have been the breeze blowing through the shutters that made me feel this way, as if there was more light, somehow. There were new pictures on the walls; it turned out that Violet liked to draw. She had painted the beach with a sailboat on the water, and sketched two parrots sitting in a tree. When I told her she was gifted, she said, "Do you really think so?"

While everyone was in the kitchen, I went down the steps and looked underneath the house. I checked where the Coca-Cola crates used to be kept and they were still there. I looked for my things, wrapped inside the old curtain, and they had gone. There was the place where I liked to sit and watch Antoine and Antoinette. And in that quiet moment, I made myself look out at the yard and the frangipani tree, still white like old bone, and the long grass, and beyond that to where the road began, the road I took to school, the road where I found the dead kitten, and at the side of the road—the huge breadfruit tree.

.   .   .

I ASKED VERA about the goats.

"One of them died, and then the other died too. Probably of a broken heart."

I was sorry to hear this.

"And what happened to the vine, it's gone from the tree?" I said, pulling out a chair.

We were gathered around the table and Aunt Tassi was serving lunch. She had fried bakes and saltfish cakes. There was callaloo, cooked-up rice, and cristophene. There was a jug of ginger beer, and another of sorrel. She had made a special effort.

"Yes, the vine has gone! Violet has a nice boy who comes looking for her, and he knows about trees and plants."

Violet put her hands up to her face. "He's not my boyfriend."

"Oh yes he is," said Vera. "If he isn't, then he's making a very good impression of one."

Vera and Aunt Tassi laughed. Then Aunt Tassi asked if I had a boyfriend.

"No," I said. "If Mrs. Jeremiah's right I won't ever get married."

"Mrs. Jeremiah told you so?"

"She told me other things, too."

"What things?" said Vera.

"This and that," I said. "Things best forgotten."

Aunt Tassi let her eyes settle on mine. "Mrs. Jeremiah died last year; you probably didn't hear."

"No," I said, taken aback.

"She was hunting for crabs in the moonlight, when a branch from a coconut tree fall and hit her on her head." Aunt Tassi thumped the heel of her hand and made a thudding sound. "There was a proper funeral, with a lot of singing. But everybody want to know, if she was so clairvoyant, how come she never saw it coming."

·   ·   ·

AFTER LUNCH, VIOLET and Aunt Tassi were making up the bed
in my room, and Vera and I were putting away the dishes. I was thinking about Mrs. Jeremiah, how strange it was that she had died so suddenly. And I wondered if she had in fact known the end was coming,
but never told anybody. It must have been quick, without too much
suffering or pain. There were worse ways to die. Then I thought of
Roman, and I asked Vera about him. I wanted to know exactly what
had happened. Vera didn't seem surprised; she looked down the corridor to check for Aunt Tassi, and then she sat down at the table and
spoke in a low voice.

"He went to visit Ruth Mackenzie. You know how he liked to do
that." Vera rolled her eyes. "Well, she had to go out to get bread and
he said he would stay and mind Clara."

"How old was Clara then?" I remembered the little girl being
very young.

"She had just turned nine." Vera sighed, and shook her head.
"Next thing, Ruth comes back because her purse was empty. There
was music on so they never heard her. She watch through a gap in the
door; they didn't know she was right there. Daddy had his thing out
and Clara was sitting next to him, and she had no panties on and
from what Ruth say, Daddy was looking to put his thing in her. Ruth
run into the room and start to beat him with her fists. And then she
pick up a vase and break it on his head and he get a big cut. When he
fly out the house, blood running down his face, all in his eye and
everything. Ruth call the police and next thing you know a big police
car come here to the house and they take Daddy away to Scarborough
police station."

"Oh Vera," I said.

"It is one thing for him to do that with a woman, but another
thing when he does it with a little child. Ruth said she never ever in a
million years expected that of him. And after that, everybody say they
don't want him back in Black Rock. So when he get out of jail on bail,

he sit right here and he get very drunk. It got late and Mummy say she want him to go to bed. But he went out. Next thing two little children find him dead on the sand covered in blood. Some say Earl was waiting for him and he come back and kill him that night. Or maybe the men were there and they do something to him. The badjohns. But I don't know."

I thought how hard this must have been for the twins.

I said, "He never did anything like that with you?".

"No, never. He was always good to us. He tried to be a daddy, you know."

Then Vera got up and started to wipe the table. She didn't ask if Roman had ever done anything to me. I was glad. There would be time to tell Aunt Tassi if I wanted to. I wasn't sure what good it would do now. Aunt Tassi was sad enough as things were. I always imagined that I would tell her, just so that she knew why I had left Black Rock. But even that didn't seem to matter anymore. There were other things to think about.

I DIDN'T KNOW that Aunt Tassi had secrets of her own.

"Celia," she called, from her room, around three-thirty. "You want to take a walk with me to the river? It's a long time since I went there."

"Sure," I said, surprised. I put on my slippers and tied up my hair.

"There are some things we need to talk about."

THE SUN WAS starting to go down, and the golden light of late afternoon made everything look kinder and softer; our feet moved together in the same, slow, left-right way. I could hear the swish of my aunt's dress, and I could also hear a corn bird singing somewhere nearby.

Aunt Tassi said, "You know when you were a little girl, you were always asking questions. I used to say, Where did this curious child come from? What was my mother's hair like, what color were her eyes. And when I said black, you'd say, What *kind* of black? Black like wood or black like bees? Just when I thought you were finished, it would start again."

"Maybe I felt like I never got a proper answer."

"That might be true. It wasn't easy answering you."

"I don't see why."

She smiled in a strange way. "Let's sit down here on these stones."

The stones were warm from the sun. There was a dragonfly hovering above the water. I saw another and another. We sat for a few moments in silence. The water was clear and I could see dark rocks gleaming underneath. It was all familiar, as if I had never left.

Then Aunt Tassi said, "I've something to tell you, Celia. It's very hard to say. So please forgive me if I don't say it right."

Something fluttered in my stomach.

"When you said you were coming, I thought it was a sign."

"A sign of what?"

"A sign that you should know."

Aunt Tassi watched me closely.

"How would you feel if I told you that Aunt Sula was your mother?"

"Aunt Sula?"

"Yes," she said.

I half expected her to break into a smile as if she was joking. But she didn't.

"Aunt Sula was my mother?"

Again, she told me, "Yes."

I stared at her. I felt as if I was in a dream.

"Are you telling me the truth?"

"Yes, Celia." Aunt Tassi's eyes were suddenly watery, sad.

"You tell me this now; Aunt Sula was my mother?"

"Aunt Sula was your mother."

Everything was starting to whirr around and I was glad to be sitting down, otherwise I might have fallen into the river just as I did when I was a child.

"Why didn't she tell me?"

"She wanted to tell you when you first start going to Tamana. But then she got so sick. What was the point in telling you when she could die. You were used to living without a mother."

"But I saw her before she was sick."

"Sula was sick for a long time."

I put my hands up to my face.

"Celia, she wanted you to be happy. It would have turned your world upside down."

"What difference would it have made, now or then?"

Tears stung my eyes.

"What about Grace?"

"Yes, she died. She died of TB the day after you were born."

"And so you said she was my mother?"

"For Sula it felt like the right thing to do."

"The right thing or the convenient thing?"

Aunt Tassi shook her head.

"What about you?"

She turned up her hands. "What could I do?" Aunt Tassi looked away at the side of the bank where the grass grew tall. After a few moments, I saw her expression change. I knew there was something else.

"It was more complicated than that. She couldn't keep you with her at Tamana because of your father."

"My father?"

She looked at me steadily. "Joseph Carr Brown."

As if he was right there, I saw Joseph Carr Brown step in front of me. I saw his hat, his long face, his dark blue eyes.

I stared at my aunt as if she was a jumbie.

She nodded.

"Sula was in love with him. They were in love."

I saw them sitting together on Aunt Sula's porch, playing cards, drinking tea.

"I don't know if she ever told him about you. He might have guessed in his own way." Then Aunt Tassi said, "She loved you very much."

I couldn't move. I couldn't speak. There was only the sound of the water, the breeze in the dry leaves.

"I'm sorry, Celia, this isn't easy for you. It was never going to be easy."

"How long?"

Aunt Tassi looked confused. ·

"How long was she with him?"

"More than ten years." This was a shock. I expected her to say a year, maybe less. Ten years was a long, long time.

"It started a few months after she went to work there as a servant. She didn't want to have an affair, but she didn't want to come back here. So she stayed. At that time there weren't so many choices."

"But what about his wife?"

"They say she knew. He'd had affairs before Sula; he always liked women, but he'd never really cared for the others in the same way. Sula was different. As long as he didn't shame his wife with an outside child, Mrs. Carr Brown turned a blind eye. It's not unusual. But then Sula got pregnant. She told him she was coming here for a while to take care of Grace, who was very sick. He never had any reason to think otherwise. She stayed here for six months."

I took a deep breath in. This was all too much. I felt as if I was about to burst.

Aunt Tassi got up and held out her hand. "Come, child."

I could never, ever have imagined this. I let Aunt Tassi put her arms around me. She patted my back.

AT THE HOUSE, Violet and Vera were quiet. They left me alone in my old room. I sat on the bed and stared out the window at the yard. I don't know how long I sat there. Then I lay down and fixed my eyes on the ceiling. It was as if I had been put on a different world, or had my world tipped upside down.

I ran through my days at Tamana, looking for signs I had missed; the afternoon tea, the familiarity, the tenderness between Aunt Sula and Joseph Carr Brown. Did he know? And if he did know, why didn't he say anything? How did Aunt Sula keep it to herself? If I'd known my life would have been completely different. If I'd known I would have left Black Rock and gone to Tamana, I would have felt differently about everything—my home, myself, my life. I thought about Mrs. Carr Brown and how she had taken such a dislike to me.

THAT NIGHT, AUNT Tassi came and sat on the side of my bed. Her shoulders drooped as if the world was on them.

"I always used to say to Sula, Lies make more lies. And it's true. The more you go away from the truth, the harder it is to come back."

I asked if Roman knew and she said no.

"Sula was so proud of you."

"She had no right to be proud," I said, suddenly angry. "It's easy to make a baby."

Aunt Tassi looked at me with a kind of pity; she tucked my hair behind my ear.

I felt tears run down my cheeks.

FOR THE NEXT few days, I stayed around the house. Aunt Tassi was never far away. She would do her best to answer all my questions, she said. She cooked my favorite meals, and I was surprised to find myself eating. She cared for me as she might care for somebody who is unwell. I had never known her quite like this.

She found some old photographs of her with Sula and Grace. I had not seen them before. One of them was taken right there on the beach in Black Rock. I looked hard at Sula and, yes, I thought I saw myself there. I asked if she had any photographs of Joseph Carr Brown. There was one of him standing on the top of the cocoa shed. It was taken from a long way back. It reminded me of when I saw him at the estate the first time I visited Aunt Sula. My mother.

"Why Southampton?" I asked.

"It was just a place I knew about. I had a postcard from someone who went there. Father Carmichael, you remember."

"DID SHE HAVE me in Trinidad?"

"No, she came to Tobago just when the baby started to show, so that no one would know."

I put my hands on my small round belly.

"Were you there when I was born?"

"Oh yes. Sula laughed and cried at the same time; for the first time in her life, she said she was happy. She said, 'What a beautiful child I have.' And she cried the whole way back to Trinidad. It was the biggest mistake she ever made. She told me so when she came to visit.

She said she should have kept you; you were more important than anything. She'd listened to her head instead of her heart."

Aunt Tassi smiled. "Do you remember when she came, and you found the manicou in the road?"

"Yes," I said, "and Roman threw a plate at you."

"Roman threw a plate at me," she said, her voice suddenly flat.

ONE DAY, IN the kitchen, I asked Aunt Tassi, "Why did you go along with it?"

Aunt Tassi put down the yam she was peeling. "By then I'd met my husband, Violet and Vera's father. I wasn't going anywhere. She always sent money to pay for things for you."

I remembered the parcels that arrived every month.

"And you were a beautiful child, how could I have said no. Not always an easy child," she said, and laughed. "But beautiful."

I KEPT THINKING of Joseph Carr Brown and his daughters. I thought how lucky they were to have him as a father; to have known him as a father.

"Maybe I'll go back to Tamana before too long and speak with him."

Aunt Tassi said, "Now Sula's gone, what harm can be done?"

"He might not believe me."

"Why wouldn't he? At times, you remind me so much of Sula." Aunt Tassi's eyes welled with tears. "Lime tree can't bear orange, Celia."

I THOUGHT OF how quickly I'd settled into life in Tamana; the "easy way" I'd had with the horses. Was I like my father in this way? I remembered when my mother told me I was "brave like Joseph Carr Brown."

ONCE THE SHOCK had gone, I started to feel differently about things. When I thought about Aunt Sula, and how she had passed away without telling me, I felt angry and then very sad. I kept thinking of her face, that last day, when we stood at the top of the steps and looked out at her little yard. I tried to imagine them together, my mother and father. And in some strange way that I didn't quite understand, their relationship made perfect sense.

Knowing my father was in Trinidad and I didn't have to go all the way to England to find him was, in some ways, a relief. But how would he feel about me? Would he see me as his daughter? Would I remind him too much of Sula? Would he want to help me? He would expect me to ask him for money. This, I told myself, I would never do.

And in all this, I thought about my own life. I felt differently about the baby I was carrying. It seemed clear to me that I was following my mother's path. If my mother had got rid of me, I would never have known life. I would keep my baby. For now, Dr. Emmanuel Rodriguez did not have to know my decision. Of course, soon I would have to tell Aunt Tassi.

BLACK ROCK VILLAGE had not changed. St. Mary's school was still there, although the outside had been freshly painted a light shade of green. When I passed one afternoon, I glimpsed Miss McCartney through the window standing at the front of the classroom. She looked exactly the same: her red hair pinned up, wearing a long skirt and blouse. I decided that I would visit her after class one day. I would tell her about my life and what had happened since I had seen her last. I hoped she wouldn't be too disappointed. I wanted to ask her: Can you *really* be anything you want to be?

I walked up the main road and looked in at the church. I had always liked the church, the plain white walls, and the wooden altar. I sat for a moment. I closed my eyes. I thought about my mother, and wondered if she could see me. I clearly remembered her face, her round cheeks, her slightly slanted eyes.

At the small post office, I checked to see if there was any mail. I stopped in at Jimmy's bar, and then I went over to Uncle C's. Apart from the old barman, there was no one there. The place smelled of cigarettes and stale beer. The barman asked if I was looking for someone. "Roman Bartholomew's ghost," I said, and half smiled. He looked surprised. But then he waved his hand as if shooing away a fly, "Roman went where he belong—to hell."

For some reason, I started up Stony Hill, and got as far as old Edmond Diaz's house. I could see the dark path that led to Mrs. Jeremiah's; it was thick with mahogany leaves. It was all there, just as I remembered it. I wondered where Mrs. Jeremiah was; I hoped she was at peace.

I walked home along Courland Bay. I couldn't see any fishermen. There were pelicans diving into the sea, rising up, throats like buckets and filled with fish. The waves were bigger at this time of year, sloshing over the black rock. As I walked farther around the other side, the beach became narrow. There were little chunks of broken coral and shell, and pieces of driftwood scattered. The wood was soft to touch. I walked as far as the dark, tangled mangrove, alive with large blue crabs; it no longer frightened me.

JOAN MAINGOT LIVED in a small house on a piece of land behind her mother's.

"Celia?" she said, screwing up her eyes as if she hardly recognized me.

"Yes, Joan," I said, "remember me?"

And I laughed and then she laughed, too, and welcomed me into her home. She handed me her baby. His name was Wilfred, after her father.

"You know how we still miss Daddy? Not a day goes by that I don't think of him."

Little Wilfred smelled of soap and powder; his skin was soft like a new plum. I looked into his dark wet eyes.

"Oh good," she said. "He's been bawling all afternoon; he must like you."

Joan looked a little older, and she had put on weight. She showed me around. I could tell that she was proud, especially when she took me into the bedroom she shared with her husband. On the wall, there was a photograph of their wedding. Joan looked elegant in a long white lacy dress. I knew his face, but I couldn't remember his name. "I don't know how long you're here, but maybe you'll meet him," she said, beaming. "He's away in British Guiana panning for gold."

I carried baby Wilfred across the grass to Mrs. Maingot's house, where Aunt Tassi was waiting. "Look at you," she said, and lifted him into her arms. There was the spiky plant with eggs, and beside it another smaller plant with shorter spikes. "Just now you'll have to watch him with these plants," Aunt Tassi warned, as she made her way up the steps.

WE SAT ON the porch and Mrs. Maingot brought out a tray with tea. There were sweet buns and coconut cake from the bakery in Buccoo.

"Celia looks so glamorous," Joan said, and she leaned in to look

at the earrings Dr. Emmanuel Rodriguez had given me. She asked
about my plans.

"I'm not sure just yet."

"You were always talking about going to England."

"Yes," I said, and looked at Aunt Tassi.

Then Mrs. Maingot said, "Remember how we used to say what a
strange girl Celia was?"

"She turned out fine in the end," Aunt Tassi said. My heart felt
full and warm.

DURING THE DAY, Vera and Violet worked at the Blue Range
Hotel, but they were back in the evenings. They seemed happy
enough: sewing, talking, listening to the radio they had saved up and
bought between them.

One night, by candlelight, I taught them how to play hearts.
They soon caught on. When she saw me expertly shuffling the pack,
Aunt Tassi's eyes opened wide.

"Where you learned to do that?"

I told her, "My father showed me. In Sula's gambling parlor."
And we all looked at one another.

IN ALL THIS time, I knew that my baby was growing. Soon it would
start to show through my dresses; they were already feeling tight. I'd
heard that this is how it happens, one minute you look the same, and
the next you are big as a house and the whole world knows. I wanted
to tell Aunt Tassi. But I also wanted things to settle, at least for a few
more days.

THIRTY-FOUR

THE BANGING CAME AT ABOUT SIX-THIRTY. THE COCK had just started crowing. I heard one of the girls get up, and then I heard her shout, "Who you want? You come to the wrong house." I leapt out of bed, pulled on my dress, and ran to the door. William was on the steps, his face hot, wearing an old shirt and trousers and sandals. I said, "William, why you didn't tell me you were coming?" Aunt Tassi was behind me, "Who it is, Celia? You know this man?" "Yes," I said, "I know him."

After a few minutes of introductions, where I explained that William was my good friend from Port of Spain, and that he had just arrived in Tobago, everybody calmed down. The girls went inside to dress, Aunt Tassi went to the kitchen to make a pot of coffee; I took William onto the veranda.

At first, I didn't know what to say, so I said, "How was the crossing?"

"Okay," he said, but I could see that he was fraught, like somebody who has been without sleep; there was a hint of wildness in his eyes.

"What's going on? There's something."

He glanced toward the kitchen. Then he said, "Are you all right?"

"A lot's happened since I got here. Nothing bad. I'll tell you in a while."

Aunt Tassi brought out hot bakes on a tray and put them on the little round table. "You've been to Tobago before, William?"

"Yes, Mrs. D'Abadie. I was in Scarborough a few years ago."

"Maybe Celia will show you around Black Rock."

"That would be nice," he said, and looked at me. Then Aunt Tassi went to her room, as if she knew we wanted to be left alone; I was relieved.

William hardly ate. Instead he looked out at the yard; he was nervous and distracted. He said he wanted to go somewhere we could talk and be alone. Now I was feeling nervous, too.

I told Aunt Tassi we were going to the beach. Quietly, she asked if everything was okay, and I told her, yes.

WE WALKED IN silence; William looking ahead now and again, but mostly his eyes were low on the ground, as if thinking hard about something. He was carrying a large bag. I had told him he could leave it in the house, that it would be safe, but he had insisted. "This isn't Laventille; people leave their doors and windows open all day."

We turned down the narrow path. The almond trees had thrown their big leaves on the ground; the grass was green-brown, and then it was soft with sand. At the tall trees, we stepped out onto the beach; already the sun was blasting down. "Come," I said, "let's go to where there's shade." We sat near the sea grape trees, and I could see the branches were full of little pinkish green grapes.

"You know they say a witch came here from Africa. Her name was Gang Gang Sara. After a while she wanted to go back home, but she couldn't because she had eaten salt. There's a grave right there in Golden Lane village."

William watched me; his eyes steady for the first time.

"Sometimes I feel like Gang Gang Sara. Like I'll end up here, no matter how hard I try to get out." From my pocket, I took out the piece of black rock that Mrs. Jeremiah had given me. "Did I ever show you this? The soothsayer gave it to me." Then, "She died last year."

William examined it, held it up to the light. "You deserve much more than this place," he said, and looked out at the sea.

"Tell me, William. Tell me what's happened to you. And then I'll tell you my news."

William put his hands up to his face. "I have to move fast, Celia. I shouldn't even be here. Somebody might have seen me getting on the boat."

I felt my mouth go dry. It was worse than I thought.

"Say it, whatever it is."

He looked at me. "Solomon kill a man."

This wasn't such a surprise; I knew he had it in him.

"But what did you have to do with it? Tell me that part."

I kept thinking: If I can keep calm, then he will tell me. If I start to panic, it will take too long. I had never seen William like this.

"Solomon say he going to see Nathaniel and he want me to come with him. He say there's a little job to do up there in the east. I ask him what kind of job and he say he going to collect some cash from somebody. So we drive to Arima and he stop and buy a few beers; he drink them right there, with his friend from the rum shop. I have a drink, too. But only one, because he say I need to have my wits."

William was looking down, trying to remember.

"We carry on to the country and he never say too much. Next thing I know, we reach El Quemado road, and he park up, and tell me to keep watch from the bush. He say when a car come, I have to sound the horn. I tell him yes, but I want to know what going on. He say it's better if I don't know anything. I say better for who, he say better for me.

"I see him talking to someone and it's Nathaniel. Then I can't see them anymore. Ten minutes pass and an old truck drive by. I sound the horn, just like he tell me to. I wait. Nothing happen. Another fifteen minutes pass. This time I see a white car come. I hear the car running and then I hear it stop. Then I hear a dog barking, and there's shouting, a lot of shouting, and a noise like bamboo splitting, and I feel something bad happening. I hear more shouting and more bamboo splitting. Then I knew it wasn't bamboo; it was gunshots."

He was shaking now.

"Carry on," I said.

"I see Solomon running down the road, like somebody chasing him, and he have a gun in his hand. I throw open the door, he jump in and he drive away. We drive past the white car and we almost run over the body lying right there. I tell Solomon to go around. And he did, and then he go fast like the devil behind us. He drive like this all through the country to Arima."

"It sounds to me like you didn't really do anything. It sounds like Solomon's in a lot of trouble."

"When we get to Arima, I ask Solomon what happen. He say it all went wrong; how he'd needed money for the new business. And how Mr. Carr Brown drive from Port of Spain on the last day of the month with plenty money to pay the wages."

I fixed my eyes on William's; there was something else happening here now.

"Nathaniel and Solomon had put a log in the middle of the road. The white car I see was Mr. Carr Brown's."

William looked at me.

I felt my stomach rise. "Go on."

"Mr. Carr Brown drive until he reach the log and he get out to move it. That's when Solomon come at him with a gun, and ask him for money. If he'd given him the money it would have turned out different. But Mr. Carr Brown's dog rush at Solomon. Remember how that dog didn't like him at Tamana? Well it was the same black dog. Solomon shoot it. Mr. Carr Brown so mad he lunge at Solomon and next thing the gun go off. And Mr. Carr Brown fall down in the road. Mr. Carr Brown dead, Celia. Mr. Carr Brown dead."

I looked at William as if he was making this up. He drew his hands up to his face, so that I could only see his eyes, his forehead speckled with sweat. "I so sorry, Celia. I know how much you like Mr. Carr Brown."

I kept looking at him.

"We were supposed to do a job next week, not this one. I didn't know anything about this one. I feel Solomon trick me."

For a few moments, we stayed like that, him looking at me and me staring at him. This could not be true; this could not be possible.

I did not sound like myself when I said, "Are you sure he was dead?"

"Yes. When we pass, I see blood coming from his mouth. He so big, he stretch across the whole road."

Now William did not look like William. He looked like someone I hardly knew.

"The police searching all over Port of Spain for Solomon and probably me, too."

He drew his knees up to his chest. "The law don't make joke when a man like that get killed. They come down hard." Then, "Please say something, Celia."

But I couldn't talk. I looked down at the soft, fine white sand and I wished I was somewhere else, that I was someone else, that I could find myself in a dream and wake up from it.

Eventually, in a voice thin like thread when it is frayed enough to break, I said, "I want you to go," and I pointed to the path that led to the village. "I need you to go."

And then I got up and walked toward the bright sunlight; away from the shade, away from William. The ground was hot, a floor in hell. I stood for a moment in the familiar bright white light. Then I walked until I reached the sea, until the water licked over my feet and my ankles. I waded into the sea, until it was up to my knees, then my waist, then right up to my neck. And I let my head go under and the world became silent.

THIRTY-FIVE

THERE WERE NO ANSWERS. I HAD NOTHING. THERE WAS only heat and the bright light that made that kind of heat. There was no shade, nowhere to rest, nowhere that the sun was not. You follow your life, you don't lead your life. I could sing with pain. Sing so high, high, high. Would my mother hear my singing? Once I had nothing. Now I had less than nothing. My whole life. My whole life I wanted to know my father. I wanted him more than anybody. More than Dr. Emmanuel Rodriguez. I shall never know happiness. The light was on the other side of the world, in Southampton, England. All my life I stepped toward it, little steps. I was halfway there and then I sank. The light pulled me from my darkness. I remembered the light when everything was bad. And now you put out the light. Just like that. I had less than nothing. It couldn't be like this. It couldn't be this way. God is good. They say God is good. How was that so.

WHEN AUNT TASSI came home, she found me in my room, sitting on the floor looking at photographs she had given me. When I told her what had happened, she brought her hands up to her face. "Oh God, Celia, no." Then, "Why this have to happen. Why?" She asked me how I knew. "The boy who came this morning had something to do with it?" I said, "Yes." She looked out the window, as if trying to understand.

"Where is he? Where he went?"

"I don't know." I leaned against the wall and closed my eyes. I was exhausted. I wanted to be alone.

LATER, SHE BROUGHT a newspaper. *The Gazette* had a full front-page report and a photograph of my father. Perhaps when I felt better, Aunt Tassi said, I could read the article and tell her what it said. I had forgotten Aunt Tassi could not read.

THIRTY-SIX

THE HEADLINE OF *THE GAZETTE* READ ESTATE OWNER
ATTACKED IN FOUR ROADS. I studied the photograph next to it, and
tried to see myself in Joseph Carr Brown's face.

YESTERDAY AFTERNOON, FRIDAY, April 7, 1958, Joseph Carr
Brown picked up his brown leather money bag and went to his bank in
Port of Spain where he withdrew three thousand dollars to pay his
workers at the Tamana Estate. After lunching with a friend in Bayshore,
Mr. Carr Brown began his journey home. At approximately four
o'clock he reached Arima, and after a short break started toward Talparo. Half an hour later Mr. Carr Brown's vehicle was at a standstill in
the center of the El Quemado road and he was lying in a pool of blood
next to a log about three feet in front of the car. The planter had been
shot in the chest. Lying beside him was a black dog, also dead.

By the time police arrived, all investigators could confirm was that
the fatal bullet was discharged from a person at close range. There was no
attempt to search the victim's pockets. The door next to the driver's seat
was open and there was no evidence that an attempt was made to force
open the trunk of the car. It is thought that the killer was disturbed. An
eyewitness from Four Roads, who recognized the driver as a "familiar
face," saw the truck traveling at high speed toward the main road.

THIRTY-SEVEN

THAT SAME DAY, I TOLD AUNT TASSI ABOUT THE BABY I was carrying. I told her that the father of my baby was the man I had worked for, a man I had loved and still loved. The master of the house. I told her that I had not wanted to have an affair with him, but I didn't have much choice. He does not love me, I said. But that doesn't matter. I want to be a good mother and I will never give my child away, and one day I will tell my child exactly who her father is. And if my child is a girl, I said, I shall call her Sula, after her grandmother. And if my child is a boy, I shall call him Joseph, after his grandfather. There will be no secrets. There will be no lies.

For some reason, Aunt Tassi was not so surprised. She was sorry for all this pain, she said. Sometimes life is very hard. One soul flies in, another flies out. She put her arms around me. The news of my baby was the best news she could have hoped for. She begged me to stay in Black Rock. "There's so few of us now; we must stick together. We can all help out with the child." She had never understood why I had left in the first place. I knew that one day I would tell her about Roman, but not yet.

WHEN HE WAS arrested, Solomon did not tell the police that William was involved in the robbery. For once he did something

good. They say he is on the island called Carrera, the prison island off the northwest coast of Trinidad. If I close my eyes I can see it sticking out of the sea like the back of an animal. It is old and broken down. I imagine him killing rats—beating them with his hands, putting the meat on the iron bars, and roasting it in the sun. You know how many restaurants cook dog and rat and call it chicken? And then I make myself open my eyes.

I believe that William is in British Guiana. A postcard arrived from that place, with a picture of the Virgin Mary floating above the shining Essequibo River. I recognized his handwriting, although there was no message, just the initials: WDS.

TWO WEEKS AGO, a crate arrived from Trinidad. There were things from Tamana: a painting of a Spanish girl from Venezuela. I had never noticed the colors before—the green of the girl's dress, her copper eyes. Wrapped in sheets of thick cloth was Aunt Sula's beautiful mahogany chest. I ran my fingers over the carved shapes—tall peacocks, long wavy grass, palm trees. Inside the chest, was Aunt Sula's gramophone player. I took it out and opened it there on the ground. There were records, too.

I found a white plate with a gold rim, a shiny vase I remembered filled with ginger lilies; there were many Reader's Digest books. There was also an envelope. I opened it, and counted five hundred dollars. His short note read: "Dear Celia, I hope this will help in some small way. Yours, Joseph Carr Brown." On the day my father was shot he had arranged for these things to be shipped to me in Tobago, care of Aunt Tassi.

NOW I LOOK to the future; perhaps I will make something of it.

Acknowledgments

SPECIAL THANKS TO Ali Smith, Teresa Nicholls, Barrie Fernandez, Michelle Tessler, and Lucy Luck for their great support. Kate Kennedy for her passion and commitment, and all the team at Shaye Areheart Books for their hard work.

My deepest gratitude to Wayne Brown for showing me how.

Thank you to my wonderful mother and grandmother for sharing their stories with me.

And finally, to Lee, for his love and support without which the road would have been so much harder.

About the Author

AMANDA SMYTH is Irish Trinidadian and lives in England. Her short stories have been published in *New Writing 12, London Magazine,* and *Jamaica Observer Arts Magazine.* She completed an MA in creative writing at East Anglia, and some of her short stories from the collection *Look at You* were broadcast on BBC Radio 4 as part of the series, *Love and Loss.* She was awarded an Arts Council grant for *Lime Tree Can't Bear Orange.*

Note on the Type

THIS BOOK WAS set in Mrs. Eaves, a modern revival of Baskerville that retains the openness and lightness of the original. In 1996, when Zuzano Licko, cofounder of Emigre Foundry, designed the typeface, her aim was to explore possible alternatives for Baskerville, which critics claimed was illegible due to the high contrast in its stems and hairlines. Licko reduced the contrast by widening the proportions of the lowercase letters. Mrs. Eaves was one of the first digital typefaces to be designed on Apple's Macintosh computers. The typeface is named after Sarah Eaves, who was the first housekeeper and, later, wife and partner to John Baskerville in his print and type shop.